The Valdeor Chronicles

Book One
Champion of Valdeor

Book Two
Waykeepers of Valdeor

Book Three
Pilgrims of Valdeor (2022)

Waykeepers of Valdeor

Book 2 in the Valdeor Chronicles

Sandralena Hanley

Dedicated to my husband Tom.
Life's adventure wouldn't be fun without you.

Table of Contents

Table of Contents

VALDEOR

VALDEOR
HAMLEOR
Lost Mts.
Loser Harbor
River Ost
Oster
Cleethe
Nyrmidion Isles
Stormy Sea
Everlasting Mts.
Mts. of No Hope
Winterhome
Icemelt River
Lake Beckar
Feornang
Skupe
VALDEOR
Mintara
Fortress
Zendira
Capall
Smoky River
Fister
Eastern Garrison
Briartown
Motari Desert
Blue Range Mts.
Lake Genesay
Laketown
Western Garrison
Windmyr River
Forest of Domadaria
Forestown
Glame River
Samarantha
Southern Garrison
Tulken Harbor
To CANTEOR

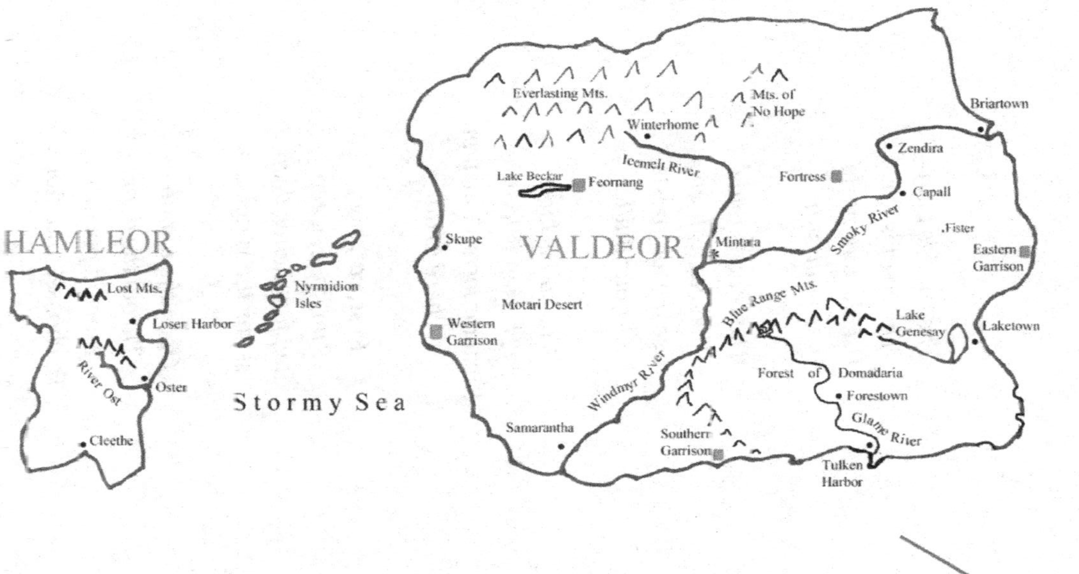

The road is long
The road is far
Use the wayposts
As your star.

The road is wide
The way is high
Use the wayposts
As your guide.

The sun is high
The sun is low
The wayposts show you
Where to go.

Rest, eat, sleep
Run, hide, weep
Beg for shelter deep
Ask for the Waykeep.

Open the window
Throw the door
Myriad portals
To choose, and more.

Chapter 1

An ancient stone waypost sat at a crossroads. It leaned away from the prevailing wind, its rough surface pitted, with a mysterious symbol carved near the top. In the afternoon stillness, a wisp of fog curled around the post, growing and billowing up from the ground on an otherwise clear autumn day.

Under a nearby tree, a rabbit stopped licking its paw when a cloaked figure stepped out of the mist, followed by a big black horse. The odd sight sent the rabbit scurrying into its lair.

A chill wind blew down the road, tossing leaves before it like mice scuttling from a cat's smell. It dissipated the fog and stirred the figure's dark cloak. Wearing a ring with the interlocking ovals design matching the waypost's symbol, the person's hand pulled back the hood, causing dark ringlets to blow across the face of a girl.

Donella stood for a moment, considering each way. Both roads were well worn, rutted by constant travel. She pulled out a small pouch that hung around her neck. She removed a small clay bead, parted the grass at the waypost's base, and added it to a collection of pebbles and shells there. She led the horse to a rock, stepped upon it, and mounted.

"I feel we are close to the one we seek." She nudged the horse to the north. "Let us go and find him, Seeker."

Three hours later, the girl in the cloak returned to the same waypost.

Dismounting, she spoke to the horse. "I fear we took the wrong road. Let us stop and eat before we try the other way. We are two days journey from the northern city of Zendira. That is a lot of territory to cover."

She wanted to find the presence rippling through the portals. Maybe he would be the fabled Gifted One. The one who could answer all her questions about the portals: Who made them, what they were, and why they were built.

Early the next morning, she stopped the stallion before an unprepossessing farmhouse set back from the rutted dirt road. The house reminded her of a once jolly lady gone to seed. The roof sagged, the door frame was crooked, the windows were dirty with torn curtains, and the whole place could use a fresh coat of whitewash. But window boxes held herbs, and the kitchen garden seemed well-tended, or she would have thought the place abandoned.

She dismounted and tied Seeker to a tree where he could browse the long grass beside the broken gate leading to the front door. She stood still, her head tilted to one side, tuned into an unheard sound. The ripples of a strong presence emanated from the farm, although she couldn't see a waypost nearby. Yet, she unmistakably felt a waykeeper very near. Avoiding the farmhouse, she made her way to the outbuildings in back.

She skirted the chickens pecking the sparse yard and headed past the pungent-smelling pigpen to the stable when she heard a voice cheerfully whistling. She stood in the doorway till her eyesight adjusted to the dim light, while smelling the sweet mix of hay and horses.

A teenage boy about her age mucked out a stable as a broken-down nag watched. He had dark blond hair. He was medium height with a wiry build, wearing a dirty brown tunic over his brown leggings.

Could he be the one she searched for?

"Good day." She stepped inside.

The young man swung around, startled, still holding the pitchfork, now pointed at her. She held up her hands as if in surrender, and he lowered the pitchfork, his cheeks blushing.

"Where did you come from?" He leaned against the pitchfork.

Her eye caught the trinity mark on the back of his left hand. Goosebumps tingled along her spine. When he perceived her gaze on it, he pulled down his shirt cuff.

"I'm a wayfarer." A mewling kitten caught her gaze. She reached down and picked it up. "Is it possible for me to get breakfast here? A traveler told me this was once an inn." Actually, no one had told her that, but sensing his presence through the waypost's portal—the door between places—and now seeing the mark on him, she made an educated guess.

"When my father was alive, a long time ago, travelers stopped here. I'm sure I can get an egg, and maybe a hunk of bread, if that will suit you." His gaze traveled over her cloak and dress, which were serviceable, not fancy. He put down the pitchfork and stuck out his unmarked right hand. "My name's Gyfar, but everyone calls me Guy."

She gave his hand a quick shake. "Donella," she replied with a smile, which showed her dimples.

She followed him out of the stable, squinting from the change of light from dim back to bright. They passed the foul-smelling pen with six pigs, as Guy headed for the chicken coop.

As he foraged in the hen house for her egg, he asked, "What brings you here? Are you on the way to, or leaving, Zendira?"

"I bypassed the city." Donella put down the curious kitten from the barn. It sat and began licking itself. "This road is fairly well traveled. Wouldn't an inn bring in more money than raising pigs? Or are the pigs for your own use?" She chattered as they headed to the house. "Anyway, an inn would provide much more excitement with people coming and going and telling stories of their travels. Don't you agree?"

"You do ask a lot of questions, don't you?" Guy wiped his feet as he led her into the farmhouse, not realizing that she hadn't answered his original question of where she came from.

The inside of the house matched the outer dilapidation. The floorboards creaked as they walked across the main room. Piles of dirty crockery overflowed the table. A washtub stood by the fire filled with soiled clothes. An enormous woman poured warm water in the tub. She didn't bother to turn around as she spoke.

"You cannot be done with your chores this soon. No breakfast for you till you muck out those stables and feed the pigs their slops. Then you have them dishes to wash. I have got a week's worth of wash to do, and Mistress Poggins breathing down my back to get them back before her husband and sons come home from market. I will be earning the few coins she gives me for this lot, I can tell you."

Guy's neck turned red as he shuffled his feet. "We have a guest for breakfast," he blurted out.

"What?" The woman finally looked up from her work. Her plastered on smile disappeared and her eyes narrowed as she took in the girl's age. "A paying guest?" she asked.

Before Guy could speak, Donella stepped further in the room. "Aye, I can pay." She held out a coin. The large woman snatched it and pocketed it in one movement.

Guy lifted a teetering stack of crockery and placed it on the floor. He pulled out a chair for Donella. "Have a seat." He reddened as they both spotted the crumbs on it. He pulled out a handkerchief from his back pocket and wiped it.

Grumbling to herself, the woman fried the egg in grease, while Guy cut a thick piece of bread from a loaf. He served her and pushed back his dirty-blond hair. As Donella sat on her chair's edge and ate, she felt his hungry eyes on her food, until the woman shooed him out to finish his chores.

Donella's gaze roamed around the untidy room until it landed on a faint trinity symbol etched over the fireplace. *Safe haven.* This had once been a pilgrim's inn.

When Donella finished, she went looking for Guy in the stable. He wasn't there, but Seeker ate fresh hay in the nearby field. Guy must have untied him. She wandered around the farm seeking Guy. It seemed too big for one woman and one teenage boy to run. She finally tracked him down weeding the garden.

"I haven't seen your waypost anyplace. Where do you keep it?" She faced him with her hands on her hips.

"What is a waypost?"

She blinked at his ignorance, considering he had the interlocking ovals marked on his hand. "Every, um, inn has a stone marker letting travelers know it is a resting stop."

"This is not an inn. Not anymore. Not since my father—" he stopped. Pain crossed his face. When he didn't continue, she sensed that he didn't want to talk about it.

"Well, it has got to be somewhere. Come on. I bet it is near the farmhouse gate. That would be the obvious place." She strode toward the road and didn't look to see if Guy followed, sure that curiosity would make him leave his dull duty.

Guy watched as Donella dug in the long grass near the gate by the road and uncovered a long, thin stone marker lying on its side. Its weathered state bespoke its great age.

"I never beheld that there before!" Guy knelt in the grass beside her. He glanced from her back to the post. "How did you know this was here?"

"Markers are usually placed along the main roads. Help me

unveil the stone," she told him. They pulled the grass and leaves away and uncovered the whole length, which was about half the size of a tall man.

"Do you have a farm tool to dig out the post hole?" She sat back on her heels.

He walked to an outbuilding and retrieved a shovel. When he returned, he noted she had continued to brush away debris, and found the hole where it once stood upright.

"This should do it." He held out the narrow shovel.

It took them an hour, taking turns, to dig out the detritus that had accumulated over a dozen years "Let us put it back where it belongs." Donella told Guy, "Go to the post's head," as she positioned herself at its center.

"Ready? Heave," Guy commanded when they both had a good grip. They struggled against the heavy post but couldn't lift it more than a few feet from the ground. They dropped it back down with a thud. Guy figured it must be a hundredweight.

Wiping the sweat from his face with his hand, he stepped back. He probably put a dirt streak across his cheek, seeing dirt on his hands and knees. He gazed past the stone and started laughing.

"What is so funny?" Donella asked, looking just as grimy as he, as she pushed back her hair from her forehead, unknowingly adding leaf bits to it.

"The answer has been before us all this time," he replied, gesturing behind her with his right hand.

On her knees, she spun her upper body around and espied her horse watching from the field behind them. She rolled her eyes. "Of course." She whistled, and the horse lifted his head. "Seeker! Here boy!" she called.

The horse calmly trotted over to his mistress.

They soon rigged up a rope over a nearby tree branch. At a signal from Guy, Donella urged the horse forward. Seeker easily hoisted up the stone, and, with manhandling, Guy managed to drop it into its original hole. As Donella freed the horse from the harness, Guy ran his left hand over the symbol now exposed. A tingle ran from his hand up his arm. Startled, he snatched his hand away.

"You felt something. I knew you would!" She smiled, showing her dimples, as she glanced at his birthmark.

How did she know that? What is going on here? How did she know this had once been an inn?

Guy didn't like mysteries. Unease sat in the pit of his stomach since this girl showed up with her talk about wayposts.

"Just what is this thing? And why does the mark on the back of my hand match the ovals on the stone?" Guy stood frozen, his thoughts in a whirl, confusion warring with disbelief, and underneath it, a growing fear. He had an odd sensation that this thing was something significant.

He knew that strangers often stared at the symbol on his hand. *And now to find it embedded in this post at his front gate . . .*

Donella walked up to the stone. "Don't be afraid of the portal." She seemed to look fondly at the post. "It is a rare gift to open it." Her tone sounded almost reverent. She glanced at him. "Watch."

She reached out and held her right hand near the waypost. For the first time he noticed she wore a ring with the same symbol. She closed her eyes. Mist swirled up from the ground and hung in a spiral pattern. First, a small opening in its center showed green grass, then the spiral spread out until another place lay exposed before them. A building sat in a field alongside another road.

"You see, I can summon my home on a busy wayfare."

Guy gasped as the portal emerged, and involuntarily took a step back, feeling that he might be sucked in. He could see trees and the birds jumping from branch to branch. Then he heard their song and smelled the new spring grass. "How?—you said I can— No, it's impossible!" Amazement, doubt, and fear all assailed him simultaneously.

"No, it isn't." She withdrew her hand and the image faded, the mist breaking up and dispersing. Putting her hands on her hips, she faced him. "Opening the portal is a learned skill, just like riding a horse. It takes practice, that's all."

"And I have the skill to open this portal? Where does it go? How does it work?"

"You have the portal key on your left hand."

He looked down at his hand, then at hers. A vague memory drifted into his consciousness. "Father used to wear a ring like yours. As a small boy it held my attention. I remember it now."

"Didn't you say your father kept this place as an inn? My mother, an innkeeper's daughter, taught me how to wield the ring since I was very small. It opens the portal, which allows you to travel from place to place, as you just discovered."

"My father died when I was very young." Guy shuffled his feet. "My stepmother won't talk about him."

"I see now why you are ignorant of your heritage. Your stepmother kept it from you." Donella tapped her lips with her finger. "Well, no matter. I can teach you the basics so you, too, can be a waykeeper."

Guy glanced back to the garden full of weeds. The morning was half-spent, and he had so many chores to do. He ruefully hung his head. "I am afraid I don't have time for this."

"But you want to follow in your father's footsteps, don't you?" She seemed to know the only argument that could reach into his heart. In a rare moment of rebellion, he nodded his head 'yes.'

She took a bead from the pouch she carried. "Take this. It is my token. Every waykeeper has their own. If you use this while opening a portal, it will lead you to the one closest to me." She pulled a brown stone with a hole in the middle from the pouch. "See? This is a waykeeper token. My mother's."

"Do I get one for myself?"

"You must choose one yourself and have some on hand. There are only a few keepers now. Mother said there were once fifty or one hundred, one for each stone marker in the land." Donella put the bead in his outstretched hand, and he examined it.

She turned back to the waypost and opened it. When her home appeared again, Guy stared, fascinated by the scene.

"I am going to step into the portal and back to my home. When the portal closes, I want you to hold my clay bead in one hand, and with your hand that has the birthmark I want you to touch the waypost. Think of me and open the way." With that, she stepped through. Guy had no chance to ask any questions as she disappeared in the mist, which closed behind her.

He stood alone near his fence, gazing over the familiar road, unsettled inside. Disbelief warred with an odd longing in his heart. *If Father was a waykeeper, I can be one, too.*

He stared at the little clay bead in his hand. He folded his fingers over it, stepped up to the post, and took a deep breath. He held out his hand and touched the cold stone. A tingle ran up his arm and into his shoulder. He gritted his teeth and let a wave of sensation flow over him like a shock. He closed his eyes and thought of the girl with the black hair and the tree with the birds. The tingling sensation left him, he opened his eyes and viewed her standing before him on the portal's other side.

I did it!

Donella's dimples showed again as she smiled at him and beckoned him through. He couldn't help but grin back.

Guy's heart raced and his palms sweat, but he pushed himself to step through the portal. He heard a sound as of rushing wind. He perceived the place ahead down a long dark tunnel. His head felt detached from his body, then waves of dizziness washed over him. He fought the desire to empty his stomach. His foot found solid ground, and he stumbled beside the girl. He found himself on his hands and knees. He took deep breaths to steady his rolling stomach.

She knelt beside him and put a hand on his shoulder. "The dizziness will pass. It gradually affects you less and less the more you travel through the portals." She stood up and reached a hand down to him. He blinked a few times and the dizziness receded. He grasped her hand, stood up, and absorbed his new surroundings.

He stood by an oval-marked post on a hill overlooking a two-story building. He could see the sign hanging in front, which said the Greensward Inn. A large yard enclosed it, with a stream bounding it at the far end. It had a stable for horses and several well-maintained outbuildings. From its size, and the much wider road it sat near, he figured it was near a large town. The quiet was only disturbed by distant clinking of dishes and cutlery from an open window. Beside them stood the tree he had seen earlier.

Donella turned her back on the building, sorrow etched on her face. "After my mother died, my uncle took our home, with a few spare rooms for travelers, and turned it into a large inn."

"Is he a waykeeper, too?"

"No," her voice grew hard. She walked over to the tree, reached up, and plucked an apple. "Uncle Warun thinks our traveling method is sorcery and helping wayfarers isn't profitable. And he acts as if the portals don't exist. He is always after me to settle down. He wants me to work as a servant, but he doesn't want to pay me. He says I am a poor relation, and providing my room and board is pay enough. So I ran away." She rubbed the fruit on her skirt and bit into it.

"How far away are we from my home?" He reached up and took an apple. His stomach growled, and he remembered he hadn't eaten yet. He bit the ripe apple and juice dribbled down his chin. He wiped his face with his sleeve cuff.

"This is the main road to the city of Zendira. About a week's journey."

"That far!" Guy nearly choked from surprise. "I have never been farther than the local village, except once to a horse fair." He peered around with renewed interest. Fear and delight warred within his breast.

"There is no limit to the places you can see when you learn to use the wayposts." She threw away the apple core and picked another.

"My stepmother will never allow me. In fact, she is probably looking for me right now," he sighed, a hollow spot opening inside him. He longed to stay and learn more about his supposed skill, and unknown power, yet leaving his familiar surroundings filled him with dread. "It is time to go back and give slop to the pigs."

"Is that what you want to do with your life?" She leaned against the apple tree.

"Of course not, but I cannot just leave." He wiped his hands down his trousers. Not just because his stepmother would punish any dereliction of his chores. He also had a sense of duty which Father had instilled in him when small. "If I don't work the farm, we won't eat. So, how would I live?"

"We barter for the goods we need. It's a life of freedom." She spun around with her arms open. "No chores. No one telling you what to do. And, certainly, no pigs!" She laughed.

Her words stung. He stomped over to the waypost. "I have to get back. I have spent too much time away from my chores."

"You had rather spend time with the pigs than me?" She crossed her arms over her chest, pouting.

"I had rather go home to the life I know." He kicked a grassy tuft. "Are you going to help me get back or are you going to gorge on apples?"

He regretted the words as soon as he said them. She was a pretty girl his age. Guy didn't have any friends. She had taken an interest in him and showed him possibilities he had never dreamed existed.

Why did I offend her? What if she leaves me stranded here with no idea how to get home? His throat closed with fear.

"Fine! Go back to your pigs." She didn't walk away, as he feared, but joined him by the stone marker.

He reached out a tentative hand and touched the stone. Fears of getting stuck in the portal's in-between space made the sweat run down his back. He shoved the fear down, trying to relax. Cool mist rose at their feet. His left hand itched, followed by the familiar tingle going up his arm. The fog formed into a whirling spiral. The portal expanded, showing the newly-placed post at his home. Guy sagged with relief. He prepared to step through when the image changed.

Before them stretched a brown desert with towering red stone bluffs.

"What—?"

Then it changed again, showing a path on the edge of steep drop-off and snow-covered mountains as far as he could see. Next, a town appeared before them, people at a market haggling over goods laid out on stalls. Then a sea seethed below as they gazed down from a cliff.

Guy, a ripple of unease quivering through him, yanked his arm back, as the mist dissipated. He turned to demand an explanation, but Donella stared, white-faced, at the closed portal.

She tore her gaze away and met his eyes. "What did you just do?" She seemed as shaken as he felt. "I thought you said you never traveled."

"I haven't. The only place I recognized was the market at our local village, half a day's walk from my farm."

She pushed back a dark strand of her hair from her eyes with a hand that trembled slightly. "I don't understand. I've never had that experience before. Usually, I can see the nearest waypost, or where I've left a bead, or I can summon my home. But never places

I haven't visited."

She stared at him. "You must be the Gifted One."

Chapter 2

"The Gifted One? What does that mean?" Guy feared the answer.

"Mother told me a story about how long ago every waypost had a waykeeper. Once they were waystations for pilgrims, to help them on their journey, which is why many wayposts are still found outside of inns."

"Where did the pilgrims travel?" Guy interrupted.

"Ah, I asked the same question. That is the mystery. No one living knows." Donella threw her hands up in the air. "The waystations that became today's inns are ancient—many are hundreds of years old. But Mother said the Gifted One could master all the portals. Travel anywhere in Valdeor and beyond with a thought, not a token. The Gifted One would even find the original pilgrimage destination." Her eyes sparkled. "Wouldn't finding a lost city or shrine or treasure be an adventure?"

"Count me out." Guy crossed his arms as he contemplated her. "Adventures sound uncomfortable. I heard a storyteller at a fair once. The hero or heroine tangles with bandits and all sorts of unsavory characters and has many misadventures."

"I suppose you see yourself fat and happy living your whole life on the farm. What a waste of talent. You obviously can do more than I can with my ring," she huffed. "Oh, how I wish I had the symbol imprinted on my hand." He heard genuine longing in her voice.

"If I could remove it, I would give it to you." Exasperation bubbled up inside him. He didn't want any part of being gifted. "You have your ring. Maybe you are the Gifted One! You have the desire and the knowledge. You can chase down the myth."

Donella blew out her breath in an annoyed puff and marched toward the apple orchard.

"Hey, wait! Send me home first." Guy hated the pleading tone in his voice.

"Why?" she asked, as she turned around but kept walking backwards. "I told you, you have the ability."

"And I told you, I don't want it. Besides, I can't seem to get my farm's portal to stay open."

She put her hands on her hips. "Put your hand out toward the post. Imagine your home." When he complied, the portal opened. She let out an ear-piercing whistle and her beautiful black horse trotted through it toward them.

Guy jumped back.

"If you don't want to use the portal yourself, Seeker will take you where you want to go. Go ahead, mount on his back." Guy did as she said. As he got on, he spotted a medallion with the three interlocking ovals on the horse's bridle.

"Think about where you want to go, and he will take you there. If you want to send him away, you have to say 'Cereth Bra' which means 'find another'."

"You are giving me your horse?"

"He's not really my horse." She must have seen the puzzled look on his face. "And no, I didn't steal him."

Heat suffused Guy's face. "I didn't say that."

"You didn't have to. Your face said it." She walked up and stroked the horse's nose. "He chooses who he wants to be with. He is a wayfarer—a traveler through the portals. He is the only animal I know that can travel at will, like people." She held her hand palm forward as Guy opened his mouth. "Don't ask me how. Just like a dog seeks out its master by smell, Seeker sometimes finds me. Maybe he will convince you that your gift is worth using." Her eyes seemed to challenge Guy. "That is, if you can leave your pigs."

Stung, Guy replied with the first thing that popped into his head. "Better an honest farmer than an adventurer or beggar." He regretted the harsh words as soon as he said them, as tears sparkled in her eyes. She gave him a hurt look that haunted him for a long time afterward and stormed away down the hill.

"Donella, I didn't mean it!" But she was out of range. He shouldn't have insulted her and called her names. He sat undecided whether to chase her but decided it would only make matters worse. *Why, oh, why did I let her irritate me?* He must curb his temper.

Guy closed his eyes and imagined the farmhouse. He kicked the horse gently and made a clucking noise. The horse leapt into the portal. Guy's stomach rebelled, and he shut his eyes tightly. When he opened them, he was on the road beside his home.

Guy dismounted and let the dizziness pass. He put Seeker in a clean stall in the stable with a pitchfork of fresh hay.

"Where have you been?" his stepmother asked, angrily, when Guy entered the house through the back door. "No matter. You just take the slop out to the pigs." She put down the iron and crossed the room. She handed him a pail of smelly scraps sitting by the wash basin. "Then I want you to finish weeding the garden. Planting season is coming, and the last person I need is a layabout. Not if you want to eat. And don't come back till all your chores are done, including chopping more wood for the kitchen fire. You should have done that this morning." She practically pushed him out the door and turned back to the ironing.

He reached out and grabbed a chunk of bread from the table while her back was turned, as his stomach grumbled. The apple at Donella's old home was the only thing he had eaten all day. He ate the bread as he carried the pail to the farmyard.

He wanted to ask his stepmother about Father, but now didn't seem the time. He sighed as he walked to the pigpen. If only he could follow Donella and her free lifestyle. But Father had raised him with a strict code of duty. *You do the task the One Who Fashioned All put you here to do.* He could hear his father saying his favorite idiom.

As he poured the slop out, he watched the pigs as they stuck their noses in the trough. Guy tried to recall any memories of his father. Guy had been very young when Father died. He hadn't thought about him for years.

He did remember a jolly man, who gave Guy a ride on his shoulders as he walked to the fields. More memories flashed through his mind as he walked from the pigsty to the vegetable garden. He used to help Father pick carrots, turnips, and potatoes and put them in the basket. Afterward, Father would sit him on his knee at the evening fire and tell tales. The big man embellished his stories with hand gestures, and suddenly, in his mind's eye, his father's ring caught the firelight.

Guy knelt in the garden and resumed weeding. As a child, his job had always been to weed after Father hoed the land. Working here brought him a sense of peace today. A connection to the past.

Now Guy knew Father had been a waykeeper, he remembered many strangers sitting down to eat a meal with them. Father made friends with everyone he met. Their home hadn't been an inn, exactly—more like his father always had an open door, welcoming people. Father always had his stepmother set an extra place at the table for "possible friends," as his father called them. As a child, he had assumed these were Father's friends, but now he realized different people visited from one night to the next.

He thought he could smell his stepmother's baking. The smell of bread brought back the memory of how she had been kinder in those days. Not so worried about the roof over their heads. Odd, now they didn't feed any extra mouths, how they had less than before.

He sighed and walked over to the chopping block. The smooth motion of whacking one log at a time soothed his restlessness. He emptied his mind and concentrated on the rhythm of task.

When Guy finished up his chores, he washed up at the pump outside, then went in for dinner. Normally, he had no time to dwell on the happy times, long past. But with all that had happened today, it had caused the floodgates of memory to open.

"Did you chop that wood like I asked you?"

Guy sat at the rough-hewn bench by the table. "Yes, ma'am." His heart beat faster at the thought of the coming interrogation. He drew strength from thoughts of his father, and, though he didn't like to admit it, the courage of a certain black-haired girl.

"I went out to look for you this morning, when the firewood became low, but you hadn't stacked any wood by the door. And what did I find except you had wasted your time putting that stone marker back up." She plopped a bowl of broth with a few vegetables floating in it in front of him. "Planting time is around the corner, and you cannot find anything more useful to do around here?"

"I wanted to ask you about that," he said, ignoring the second half of her tirade. "What happened to the waypost?"

"After your father died, I knocked it over." She grunted. "Huh. It was harder to do than I thought it would be." She sat down across from him at the table with a bowl of soup and waved her spoon at him. "Last thing I needed was strangers come looking for a handout. We could barely survive, as it was, without sharing what we had with them." She stressed the word "them" as if they were something she found crawling in her soup.

Guy knew he should let the conversation drop there, but the desire to defend his father's actions was stronger than discretion. "But Father was a waykeeper. It was what he did."

"Waykeeper? Who has been talking to you?" She peered at the hand that held his spoon. "That girl spotted the crazy mark on your hand, did she now? If I could remove it, I would."

He had a sudden flashback of his stepmother doing just that, with a rag and some liquid that burned. He had howled with the pain. He switched the spoon from his left to his right hand and clenched his left fist under the table. He gathered his feet under him, ready to bolt if she showed signs of doing it again.

"It doesn't mean you are going to pick up where your father left off. Not if I have anything to say about it." She waved her spoon at him again, spraying him with droplets of soup.

Chapter 3

After leaving Guy, Donella walked off her anger. She was disappointed in Guy's reaction. She had expected him to show more enthusiasm for his gift.

She passed by her uncle's inn, heading for her hideaway half a day's walk down the road.

It was a beautiful crisp autumn day. Lazy clouds drifted through the sky. The sweet smell from the haystacks in nearby fields mingled with the smell of the apple orchard.

Her thoughts drifted to Guy. She had let him think she traveled all the time across Valdeor. But really, she had regularly visited four wayposts, not including his. They were all located close to her home. Mother had taught her the longer the distance, the more disorienting traveling through the portal became.

Had Guy tried to access the portal since she left? She feared she hadn't given him enough instructions. He could find himself in danger if he didn't focus on where he headed before stepping through. But she knew the perfect guide for Guy. She would travel to his house and enlist his help.

Meeting Usher, another waykeeper, had been the biggest blessing of her life in the months following Mother's death.

He would be most interested to learn about Guy and his

powers to open the portal without a ring. She knew Usher would be perfect as Guy's teacher, as he learned to navigate his way.

Donella sighed. If, of course, the stubborn boy wanted to learn to travel through the portals. She hoped Usher could convince him.

But she had better tell Usher soon, before Guy got in trouble.

When Mother lay sick, near the end of her life, she told Donella. "My daughter, I have nothing to give you except this ring I wear. It is your heritage. You are descended from a line of waykeepers. Few are left, but I hope you can pass on our traditions as I have taught you. Our house will pass to your father's brother. Warun will not support you, but someday, find a way to offer hospitality to those who cross your path."

When Mother died, Donella wanted to support herself and have provisions to share with the wayfarers she met. But she was only sixteen. She decidedly didn't want to be a servant in her Uncle Warun's inn, but what else could she do to earn a living?

That's when she met Usher, the first waykeeper, other than her mother, that she knew.

Donella's thoughts went back to how it all began with an accidental meeting. She remembered the day well, but it had started out disastrously.

The sound of breaking crockery disturbed the kitchen routine. Donella stared in resignation at the soapy dish at her feet.

"Wretched girl! Can't you pay attention? That is five dishes you have broken this month!" Aunt Sinlindra's hand smacked Donella's cheek.

Tears welled in her eyes and a lump formed in her throat as she fought the wave of grief for Mother. It had only been months since her death.

Donella ducked from further blows. She ran around the

hostler, smelling like the stable, coming in for his lunch, and dashed out the door.

Donella blindly stretched forth her hand and reached for the waypost at the side of the inn. She wanted to escape to a grassy knoll beside a bubbling stream where she had left one of her clay beads.

She heard a step behind her, and a touch brushed her shoulder, so she leapt into the portal before the image fully coalesced. The spiraling mist enveloped her, with no up or down. Her stomach started doing flips, far worse than any she had experienced before. It seemed an eternity before the spinning stopped, the light brightened, and she crashed on the ground. She lost her meager breakfast on the grass.

When the nausea passed, she lifted her head and studied her surroundings. She knelt on a gently, rolling hill, but not the one for which she aimed. She didn't see a stream, and the brown mountains across the wide, grassy valley and road were unfamiliar. A feeling of panic rose in her throat, but she pushed it back down. She spun in place until she discovered the waypost on the hill above her. The sight calmed her. She was never lost as long as she could find a stone marker. Home was always a thought away.

She climbed the hill and beheld a small hut of large leaning stones on the other side. Each stone composed an entire wall of the dwelling. Amazement and wonder filled her at the sight of the unusual dwelling. She had never seen anything like it. Moss covered the stone rooftop, making it appear ancient, as if the structure grew there from the earth.

A fat man carrying a bucket stepped out of a grove of trees on the left and followed a path toward the structure. He wore a simple gray robe, tied with a cord. His balding crown gleamed in the warm sunshine. She heard him humming a tune as he drew closer. Unsure whether to make her presence known, she stood, undecided, a moment too long. He glanced up and stopped.

"Welcome, friend. I have a pot of tea on the boil for any travelers that happen along." He put the pail down, pulled out a handkerchief, and wiped the sweat from his head. A waykeeper's ring glinted on the hand holding the handkerchief. The tension in her shoulders loosened.

She advanced down the hill and met him at the door. The house looked even more impressive up close. The stones dwarfed the old man, who must be close to six feet tall. She rubbed her hand along the smooth surface of the door lintel.

"Ah, I see you are admiring my dwelling." He motioned her to enter. "I wish I could claim that I built it by my own hands, but alas, that would be beyond my abilities. In fact, I know no one that could attempt it." He entered behind her. "I am quite fond of it, though it can be drafty in the winter—so hard to get the fire to draw properly, too—but I wouldn't change it for a castle. Not that anyone ever offered me one. A castle, that is."

Donella stifled laughter at his humorous speech.

While he prattled, he pulled two mugs from a shelf and busied himself making the promised tea. Donella took the opportunity to look around. A kettle bubbled over a small, cheerful fire. A chair stood near it, with a table and benches in the center. A bed was tucked along one wall.

He put a pot of jam on the table. "The elderberries were quite prolific this year." Then he offered her a plate of biscuits, which she reached for with her right hand.

"A little snack to go with our tea is most welcome—" He stuttered to a halt, and Donella glanced up to see him staring at her ring.

"I don't often meet other waykeepers." Donella took a biscuit. "In fact, you are the first." She put down her plate with the biscuit, stood and curtsied. "I am Donella, a traveling waykeeper."

"Where are my manners? I should have introduced myself before." He set the teapot on the table and pulled out a chair for her. "Usher, at your service, milady." And he bowed with a flourish and winked at her.

She couldn't but help the giggle that escaped as she sat down. The contrast was too great between the way Usher acted toward her, compared to the treatment she received at the inn. She wouldn't call it "home" anymore, not since Mother died and her uncle took over. She could never do anything right as far as her uncle and aunt were concerned. Her fear of being unable to please them made her stiff and clumsy. So from being a wretched oaf to being treated as "milady" all in the space of an hour was too much. The slap, the cruelty toward her and now his kindness overwhelmed her.

But she would forget her problems and enjoy the light meal set before her and the company of the jolly man. She bit into a flaky biscuit, which she followed with another one. Breakfast had been a long time ago, in the early morning hours before the guests awoke.

"Enough about me. Tell me of yourself. Where do you come from?"

"My mother owned Greensward Inn. Now it belongs to my uncle." She frowned and used her spoon to stir up the crumbs left from her second biscuit.

"You aren't happy. I can see it in your eyes." He poured more tea in their mugs. "Let me guess. No longer are you the dear daughter, but a servant in what was once your home."

Her eyes widened in surprise. She could only nod, miserably.

"Did you run away?"

"How did you guess?"

"You may not know it, but you have a hand mark on your cheek." His eyes dwelt on her, sympathetically.

She put a hand up to her face, where she felt a blush heat her face.

"Yours is a common story." Usher shook his head, sadly. "Many orphans find themselves hard used by their relations." He leaned back in his chair and stroked his chin. "What you need is an occupation to provide you with enough money to support yourself."

"Oh, yes! That is what I want above all things." Donella dropped her barriers, as his sympathetic eyes shared her hurt, and she blurted her dreams out loud. "You see, I would love to follow my vocation and be a real waykeeper, as my mother before me. I have seen a snug little place like this—the previous waykeeper long gone. It's near a well-traveled road, with fresh water nearby. I could move in tomorrow," her shoulders sagged, "but I have so little money saved up."

"It will be a lonely life for a girl alone. We must sleep upon it." He smiled kindly, stood up and searched in a box under his bed. He came forth with a small leather bag, which he held out to her.

"Oh, no. I cannot except a gift." She almost added, "we just met," but swallowed the words. *I could tell him anything without fear, as if we had been friends for a long time. He's the grandfather I never knew. So, she took the offered coins he poured from his pouch and put them in her pocket.*

"Must I go back?" She gazed at Usher with her best sad-eyes look.

"You may stay here for now."

She sighed and relaxed. All her worries could be put off until tomorrow.

Early in the morning the day after finding Guy, Donella stood by her waypost. She pulled a clump of moss, which Usher had given her as his token, from her pouch. Holding it in the same hand wearing the ring, she reached toward the waypost.

Shortly, she sat in Usher's stone dwelling, eating a biscuit with jam and drinking hot tea.

Once they finished, Usher pushed his plate away and sat back. "So what about this mysterious presence we've felt through the portal these last few weeks? Did you find him or her?"

"I did as you instructed and jumped through the portal where I felt the strongest pull." She brushed the crumbs from her fingers. "I rode Seeker for several days until I found a new waypost. I rode a day in each direction until I found a farmhouse on the road to Fister. I didn't see a waypost, so I almost went past."

"No waypost? That's odd. Then how did you know someone was there?" Usher's brow creased.

"My ring buzzed with such a vibration that I stopped and decided to check it out." She crumpled her linen napkin.

"Did you approach him? Is he another waykeeper?"

Donella nodded. "He had no idea of his power." Donella twirled a strand of hair as she recounted her meeting. "Guy's father was a waykeeper, but he died years ago. Guy's stepmother is totally against the idea. I cannot imagine why she married his father in the first place. She must have known what he did." She brushed her hair back from her eyes letting her impatience show in her voice.

Usher sat back with his hands folded over his rotund stomach. "And what did Guy think when you told him of his power?"

"He resisted the thought of becoming one of us, which is a shame, because I never imagined the gift so strong in anyone." She sat up and gestured with her hands. "I showed him how to use the waypost. Of course, he was shocked at first, but he seemed interested. Then his sense of duty overcame him, and he wanted to get back to his chores. But as he tried to go home, he opened portal after portal of places he never visited." She couldn't keep the envy out of her voice.

"Is that so?" Usher sat up. "Hmm, I must not leave him on his own. You have done very well finding him, my dear, but I will take over." Usher put his hand flat on the table and leaned toward her. "Don't be so hard on him. Imagine how unsettling it must be for him, to say the least, to suddenly find out he had the power to travel anywhere at a whim. In time, Donella, I am sure he will be eager—"

"No!" Donella shook her head. "He wants nothing to do with our way of life. Adventures scare him. He pretty much said he would rather tend his pigs." She snorted in disgust.

Usher chuckled. "Give him time. You have done this since a toddler. Curiosity is a powerful motivator. You might say he is afraid to try, but human nature will get the better of him. Why, he's probably on an adventure right now."

"Since Guy was so adamant he didn't want his gift, he didn't give me a token, although I gave him mine." She clasped her hands together, vaguely worried about leaving Guy to his own devices. "But I left Seeker with him."

"Very good, my dear. A farmhouse on the road to Fister. His presence combined with Seeker should be easy to find. I'll keep an eye on him."

Donella gave the old man a hug. "I knew I could count on you. Thanks for breakfast."

Chapter 4

*D*onella's arrival had stirred up Guy's past. As the weeks went by, more memories surfaced of his father.

One night, soon after their meeting, sleep eluded him. He crept out of bed, and drawing back the curtain, he looked from his window. He could see the waypost in the moonlight.

Had I ever seen the spiraling mist as a young lad? A memory tickled the back of his mind. *Snow lay on the ground and his breath fogged the window where he could just reach the sill. Father carried a lantern, his shadow stretched out behind him all the way back to the porch. The mist enveloped his father when he put out his hand and touched the post near the farm gate. The lantern light glowed eerily as the fog swallowed it and Father.*

A branch crackled against the window and the memory faded. How could have he forgotten?

Maybe the fact that his stepmother never spoke of his father hadn't helped. Other than tonight, he couldn't remember the last time she mentioned him.

One day Father had been teasing them in his jovial way— "Hearty stew for a hearty man, mind you. None of that gruel when the lad and I finish our chores," he winked at his wife—then clutching at his chest at the end of that day, when they stopped for the evening meal. Guy clearly saw, in his mind, Father's face turn gray and his breath become labored. The image still caused Guy to choke up as the feeling of helplessness washed over him anew.

Guy threw on his clothes and crept downstairs to pace freely outside.

What could a lad of eight have done? He knew now there was nothing. But, at the time, he blamed himself. He had felt as if he was encased in stone, with slow movements and slower thoughts.

He had thought his stepmother felt that way, too. But with the eyes of a sixteen-year-old, he now wondered if it had been grief, or perhaps anger. She'd found herself left alone to raise a son. Not even her own son. Her resentment made sense to him now.

He stood beside the slightly leaning post, not remembering how he got there. It beckoned to him of freedom. Kinship. Escape.

He stood, tempted, for a long while, the previous day's events playing across his mind.

But then the sun broke over the hills, and his stepmother called him from the doorway. "There you are. Quit your dallying. I need water to heat for the washtub. Mistress Poggins's sheets need washing." She watched his lagging steps with her lips pursed. "You cannot eat daydreams," she repeated her favorite idiom when he stood before her.

Sighing, he picked up the water bucket and headed to the well. The unknown scared him more than the life he knew, no matter how dreary it was.

Harvest came and went, then the winter snows before Guy changed his mind.

One early spring evening, after his stepmother settled down after dinner in a snug chair, she called out, "This lamp won't light. Find me a wick. Look in the stuff I bought from the peddler."

Guy hunted for a wick among the odds and ends near the fireplace. Not finding one, he thought of the supply chest at the foot of her bed. Rummaging through it, he found a batch of wicks tied with string near the bottom. As he pulled on it, he dislodged a scroll which bounced onto the floor. Guy picked it up to put back, but he paused when he remembered his stepmother couldn't read.

Why would she keep a scroll? Maybe it belonged to Father.

Curious, Guy unrolled it. His father had taught him rudimentary reading, but Guy didn't know these fancy words. He labored over it, running his finger along, sounding out the difficult words.

He didn't understand what he found. He read it, then read it again, the words not penetrating. Then, Guy heard his stepmother's footsteps.

"What is taking you so long?"

He hurriedly stuffed the scroll back in the chest.

"Do we have any wicks?" She appeared in the doorway. Her eyes landed on the bundle of wicks in his hand. "Thank goodness. I have mending to do. Don't just stand there. Give them to me."

As he turned it over and over in his mind throughout the evening, he realized that the scroll was Father's will. And his father had left everything to him, not to Guy's stepmother.

Guy owned the farm and the house. He could do with it what he wanted. But what did he want?

Outwardly, things went on the same as they had before for the next few days. But something had changed inside of him. Mucking the stables, feeding the pigs, cleaning up the dishes and pots and pans irked him like it never had before. Even his stepmother's sharp tongue lashings, which he normally ignored, nearly caused him to speak out.

His left hand tingled every time he passed close to the newly installed waypost. He recalled the excitement at seeing those unknown places materialize before his eyes. He longed to explore them. He had never seen the ocean waves or felt the cold mountain air on his skin.

He blamed the girl who had briefly stormed into his placid routine and, as quick as a sudden squall, left it. "If only she hadn't come into my life," he told the big, black horse as he groomed him. "If only she hadn't shown me my gift. If only the growing desire to escape didn't haunt me every moment of the day."

He had tossed and turned last night, as he had often done since Donella visited. He often got up in the wee hours to look out the window at the waypost calling to him, a deep hum emanating from it.

I need to fight this obsession if I am ever going to be myself again. But will I ever be the same again? He wasn't sure he would. *Blast that girl for upsetting my life and showing me crazy possibilities!*

A rhythmic knocking sounded outside the stable. He put down the comb and walked to the open door. Something moved near the old tree by the farm gate. He strolled toward the sound and froze when he beheld his stepmother. With her considerable weight behind it, she swung a sledgehammer at the waypost.

My way out of here!

"Stop it! Stop this minute!" He raced the distance from the stable yard to the roadside.

She ignored him and went on pounding. The post tipped. The ground he and Donella had tapped around its base wasn't hardened enough to withstand the blows.

When he reached her, he grabbed her arm on the upswing. "No! You cannot do this to me!" Breathing hard, Guy fought her for control of the hammer.

Her shocked look soon turned into anger. Short and stocky, her arms were brawny, used to dealing with heavy, wet clothes and sheets as a laundress. He was taller by six inches, with wiry muscles honed by constant physical labor. For the first time, he not only defied her, but he bested her. Through her anger, he saw a flash of fear in her eyes, as he wrested the hammer from her grip.

"And what do you think you are doing? Give me back my hammer, this instant." Her words lacked force, to his ears, coming out more as a whine.

Guy no longer feared her anymore. In an instant, they had changed roles. He was now the stronger, and it gave him a sense of power. Knowing he had the upper hand, for the first time in his life, he spoke harshly to her. "This is my house and my post, by rights."

Surprise and fear chased across her features.

It made him bolder. "You will not touch this post again. Do you hear me? I will go to the magistrate, and he will throw you out on your ear."

"You will do no such thing!" Her fear gave over to familiar anger. She put her hands on her hips. "You ungrateful lout. After all I did to raise you and put a roof over your head."

"No. It is the other way around." A slow anger started burning in him. "A week ago, I rummaged for a lantern wick in the supply chest. And what did I find at the bottom of it?" Her eyes widened, and he was certain she knew what he had found. "Father's will."

Her face blanched.

He continued, her fear giving him courage. "I see you knew of it. I am Father's heir, and he asked me to give you a home in my house for the rest of your life." He hefted the sledgehammer over his right shoulder. "So you see, it is my post. And you are going to leave it standing here."

Bold words, but he wasn't sure if he could keep the upper hand. Habit is a master hard to defeat.

She seemed to see the determination in the jut of his jaw and fire in his eyes and held her tongue.

He had been touched to know his father had taken such good care of him. Now he resented the woman standing before him more than ever.

"You deliberately kept my inheritance from me!"

"You are a child. You think you can run this farm? Make the hard decisions? If not for the coins I get from Mrs. Poggins and her friends, we would have starved long since."

"I'm sixteen. A man, capable of my own decisions. You treat me as a poor relation, even as an unpaid servant. But you depend on me and my good will to live here."

"Your father should have left the farm to me. I was his wife. He promised to take care of me." Her face puckered as if she were about to cry. Pity stirred in Guy's gut.

She gulped. Her expression hardened as she stared at Guy. "But no. You were his favorite. Because he saw *her* every time he looked at you. I couldn't compete with the ghost of his first wife. If I had been able to give him a son, he might have loved me more. So I took what was rightfully mine. I would have destroyed that will if I knew what it was."

Guy lost the respect he had for her in raising him alone. *Had she no compassion for an orphan?*

As he strode back to the barn, her voice followed him, complaining. "Don't expect me to feed the hungry hordes that'll come knocking on your door."

He had no illusions that life with her would be suddenly easy, now that he had stood up to her. Looking back at the scene later, he should have known what would happen.

As he entered the house for his evening meal, his stepmother busily poked at the fire. He wouldn't have thought anything of it, except she hurriedly hid the poker behind her ample skirt. She was unusually silent, too. She customarily berated him when he walked in the door. Guy craned his neck to see what she might be hiding and spotted paper curling up in the fireplace.

Guy's eyes snapped to hers as he froze, his hand reaching for the plates. She blushed and gave him a defiant stare.

Foreboding fluttered in his stomach. "What have you done?"

He raced over and pushed her out of the way. Heavy parchment scraps were scattered among the ashes.

"Something I should have done a long time ago."

Guy gazed at her from where he knelt at her feet. Anguish and anger stirred in his heart.

"This farm ought to have been mine by rights. I was a good wife. Now get up and serve me supper."

On the spot he decided he would leave his home, leave his chores, and face his future.

The road beckoned him more than ever.

The universe spun around him. He only knew up and down by the feel of the horse between his legs. He closed his eyes, thankful that he hadn't eaten a big breakfast, because he feared he would lose it if he had. *What if I am stuck in this in-between place forever?* His breathing became more labored as panic took hold.

After a slight jolt, Seeker snorted, and Guy cautiously opened his eyes. An unfamiliar landscape met his eyes. He was no longer on the road outside his front door. Two tracks went across a flat prairie of deep, green grass. No trees were visible, just endless grass waving with a shushing sound.

A warm spring breeze lifted his hair, the chill morning of his home behind him, and his shoulders relaxed. He made sure he still had his saddlebag. While turning behind him to check, he gazed with wonder at the road stretching endlessly behind him, instead of the farm that had been there moments ago.

He blinked, disoriented. *Getting used to this new mode of traveling will take time.*

Assured that his saddlebag of food, warm blanket, tinder, and his waterskin were all attached to Seeker's saddle, he turned toward the open road before him.

"Let's go, boy." Guy gently kicked the horse, grazing on the sweet grass while waiting for his master's instructions. The trip seemed to have no effect on the horse.

Over the next week, the horse and wheeling birds were Guy's only companions. An amazing number of stars hung over him while he slept outdoors by a campfire, Seeker's saddle as his pillow. The world seemed to be his for the taking. He found the silence restful after the constant complaints and reprimands of his stepmother. He finally understood the appeal of this life.

Maybe Donella had been right after all. Joy is the freedom to choose your own way and live as you please. No one to tell you what to do. No chores. No pigs to feed. This is the only way to live!

Especially no chores. He laughed out loud as he imagined his stepmother mucking out the stalls. Served her right for driving him to leave his home.

His supplies, though, were running low. He hunted rabbits, but he hoped to eat a hearty meal and buy supplies. He kept coins in a pouch tied around his neck. Counting them out from the tin in the kitchen, he'd felt like a thief. But they were his coins. Even if Father hadn't left them to him—which he had—Guy had more than earned them in the years of labor to his stepmother.

As he sat near the evening campfire, he pulled the pouch from under his shirt and opened it. At the bottom of the pouch lay a little clay bead. He reached in and took it out. He replaced the pouch, then he gazed at the bead, turning it over in his fingers.

In the flickering firelight, he thought of Donella. He didn't know if he would ever meet her again. They hadn't parted on the best of terms. Maybe he would keep it as a memento, strung on a strip of leather. He stuffed it in his trouser pocket. Donella had, after all, made this journey possible. Maybe he would use it to find her someday.

The next day he could see a very large town in the distance, the first one he had come across since leaving home.

He got off the horse when Seeker came to a stream across the trail. He filled up his waterskin, while Seeker drank his fill. He would spend some money on new clothes, he decided. His sleeves no longer came down to his wrists, and his trousers had many patches. He wasn't vain, but he didn't want to look like a raw country lad.

Seeker nickered, and Guy stood up. The horse moved restlessly. Then Guy heard hooves pounding, so he looked back the way he had come. Three riders crested the hill. Guy's pulse quickened when they spurred their horses forward upon sighting him. Not wanting to be at a disadvantage on the ground, he remounted as they circled around him.

They had greasy hair, two sported mustaches. Their clothes were made of rough homespun. Knife hilts showed in their belts. Their mounts were smaller than farm horses, yet not as noble and powerful as Seeker.

"He looks to be traveling alone, Jed. 'Tis a dangerous thing to do in these hills."

"Mayhap you can use a guide." The second rider grinned at him, showing rotting teeth.

"I don't need an escort." Attaching his full waterskin to the saddle, Guy whirled Seeker around, looking to escape.

The third man said nothing, but stared, seeming to weigh Guy up. He had a scar along his cheek, while a leather thong kept his long hair out of his face. He pulled his horse closer to Seeker, who sidestepped. The brown gelding Scarface rode snapped his teeth at the black stallion.

"Take him, boys." Scarface backed his horse away.

One of the bandits grabbed Guy and pulled him out of his saddle as he struggled. Guy managed to jab him hard in the jaw with his elbow. The other put Guy in a headlock while Guy kicked out, hoping to connect with something vital. They wrestled Guy to the ground and tied his hands behind his back. The one whom he had jabbed kicked him several times in the ribs. Guy gritted his teeth with the pain.

"What do we do with him, Jed?" The first man spoke to the man with a scar, who seemed to be the leader.

"Throw him on the horse."

The two men hauled Guy up and tossed him back on Seeker. Sitting upright, Guy scanned the area, hoping for a waypost.

Guy could do nothing but watch in anger as they went through his saddlebag and divvied up his belongings. The leader, Jed, nudged his brown gelding closer, reached over and yanked the pouch's string from around Guy's neck. The string cut into him, but Guy refused to cry out. He had suffered worse at the hands of his stepmother.

Anger coursed through him. "That's mine." He kicked Seeker and tried to move closer but subsided when Jed removed a knife from his belt and threatened Guy with it.

"Not anymore. If you cooperate, you can live."

Jed waited for his men to mount, then led Seeker by the reins attached to his pommel, in the direction Guy had originally been going.

Guy hoped to meet another traveler on the road or attract attention of the nearby town's inhabitants. They hadn't gagged Guy, so he planned to yell if they came across a passerby. But his hopes were dashed when they left the main path before entering the town and headed up a track into the woods.

Guy mentally kicked himself for thinking he was anything but a raw country boy.

Chapter 5

An overgrown path led to Donella's favorite place—a snug shelter dug out of the hillside. A little fresh spring a short walk away served her needs. She loved the out-of-the-way dwelling, with the road which it had serviced long overgrown and mostly forgotten. Only local shepherds used the footpath to take their sheep to winter pasture. But most of all she loved the peacefulness.

She had shown it to Usher in the weeks after he spoke of earning her own living.

Glancing around, she remembered his reaction.

The afternoon light showed all the flaws of her first waystation. In front of her, Usher stuck his head through the door frame. "Snug. Almost too tight for me to squeeze through. You need not fear entertaining any fat merchants here. Or giants," he added when he nearly hit his head on the low ceiling.

She giggled at his absurd comments. She welcomed Usher's sense of humor. He was so different from her staid uncle, who was always grumbling about something. "The bed isn't made properly!" "Beat the rugs harder! They are still dirty!" "Wash the dishes faster, but for goodness' sake, try not to break them!"

Donella entered behind her new-found friend and tried to

see the room from his perspective. She kept the area neat and clean, if not well furnished with a few things of her own, or Mother's. She had secretly brought a chair from her own bedroom, and a small table and rug from Mother's bedroom. The quilt on the bed shelf against the wall was Mother's last gift to her. A chipped plate, a dented mug, and a pitcher with a broken handle sat on the table. Pots of herbs sat in the windowsill. She had bargained with a tinker for the pot and kettle hanging over the unlit fire, trading Mother's hand mirror for them. She hated to part with anything that belonged to Mother, but she had no need for a mirror for herself. Who was there to impress?

"Very snug, indeed. You have done well, my child. But it is a lonely place, with few who travel this way."

"I know, but it is my retreat, my secret place. I will show you where I do most of my work as a waykeeper."

They returned to the wood's edge. In two hours, they stood on the hill overlooking the crossroad to Zendira. This waypost had no dwelling, only a cluster of trees for shelter. The dust down the road obscured several wagons on their way to the city.

Usher pulled open a satchel of food he brought from his house and spread their meal on the blanket Donella provided. She filled the bucket at the well and had it ready as the wagons rolled up. They would likely appreciate the cool water after riding on the dusty road. She and Usher invited the travelers to rest and join them at their meal.

Road dust covered the men. They washed their faces and hands before sitting around the brown wool cloth which Donella arranged with loaves of bread, a hunk of cheese, and a little bowl of freshly picked elderberries. They grumbled about the condition of the roads, the length of their journey, and the bad weather they encountered which ripped the wagon top's canvas.

The three children squabbled over the cheese until their mother slapped them.

A woman among the group had a baby which she tried unsuccessfully to quiet. Donella asked, "May I try?" The mother gave her permission. Donella took the little one in her lap and sang a song she remembered her own mother singing to put her to sleep. When the lullaby came to a close, the baby yawned. Donella followed the first song with a sweet ballad. Soon the baby dozed in her arms.

As her songs progressed, the other children settled, the youngest sucking his fingers. The men quit their grumbling, and the women's chatter petered away.

When the travelers left, the two of them were several coins richer.

As they sat that afternoon in her secret place, Usher smiled at her over his mug of beer. He had bargained with one of the merchants for a keg destined for market. "Why don't you make a living in the market with your talents?"

She stared at him over the rim of her mug of tea. "What talent is that?"

"Why, your singing, of course! Didn't you see how the sweet refrain you sang captivated that surly lot?"

"I know the baby liked it." She blew on the tea before taking a sip.

"Baby? They all liked it or they wouldn't have given us so many coins." Usher waved his hand in dismissal. "The food wasn't spectacular." He gestured at her. "They appreciated your beautiful voice."

Donella shook her head modestly, but the idea stayed with her as the evening waned. She loved to sing. There would be no harm in trying. Hope surged in her chest. After all, the worst she faced was a few rotten fruits lobbed her way.

Spring air drifted through her window, filling Donella with the desire for adventure. As soon as she finished making her bed, she collected some dried cheese and bread for a meal.

From a shelf she took down her most prized possession, a zythrin. The small instrument was shaped in a half-circle with two arms jutting out. Between the arms were five strings attached to a crossbar. She put the zythrin in a leather satchel.

She set out for Zendira. She walked for two hours before a city lay spread out in a valley before her.

She left the road and entered the woods. She pulled clothes from her satchel. She dressed as a beggar in an old gown with frayed edges and many patches. She put a thin shawl around her shoulders.

She rejoined the throngs traveling to the city, as she had done weekly for most of the time since Usher's suggestion.

They entered the city of Zendira through the western gate. Clad in cast-off clothes—rags, really—most everyone ignored Donella in her disguise as she wove through the masses of people and animals heading for the weekly market. Donella dodged around the horses and carts pulled up at the entrance.

She loved the market: the sounds of the hawkers calling out their wares, the smell of fresh bread displayed by the baker with his apron covered in flour, the herbs hanging from a stall managed by a wizened old woman smiling a toothless grin. Gaudy fabrics hung by pegs strung across a wooden stall fluttered in the breeze.

Two small girls wearing pinafores, braids flying, chased one another around the finely dressed women in silk gowns and lace caps. They nearly tripped a priest headed for the cathedral. He admonished them as they sprinted past a turbaned merchant in a striped robe. Their nursemaid held up her long skirt as she trailed behind them apologizing.

Donella took it all in as she went to her favorite spot by the rug merchant, Rongel.

At the end of the day, she would pay the rug merchant for the use of his rug, but really, she paid him for his protection. No one, if he had all his wits, would take on the burly merchant. With a body like a barrel, his upper arms were twice the size of any man. Rongel had been a wrestler in his youth, who had taken over his father-in-law's business when the old man died.

Rongel barely gave her a glance as she took a small rug remnant and sat on it. From her satchel, Donella first pulled out a woven straw bowl and set it in front of her, and then her zythrin, which she tuned up.

At a lull in the crowd around the rug stall, Donella started playing her zythrin, soft at first, until she settled into the song. Her rich voice rang out in a popular ballad. She scanned the faces around her, until she caught an old man's eye. She turned on her shiest smile and beguiled him as she seemed to sing just for him. Her technique worked. He came forward and dropped sixteen coppers in her bowl.

"Blessings upon you, kind sir." She smiled up from under her lashes, and he nodded and moved away. A few others tossed her coppers, which she scooped up and put into the bowl.

Ladies shopped at the fabric stall across the way, bargaining for silk. Donella admired their brightly colored cotton gowns with lace trimmings around the cuffs and neckline, and the broad-rim, straw hats decorated with ribbons matching the gowns they wore. Their servants trailed behind them holding baskets of their purchases. Donella chose to sing a lovely, old, romantic ballad that might appeal to them.

As one lady finished her purchase, she peered around. She moved a few steps closer to Donella, who put her head down, concentrating on her instrument. A bold, direct approach wouldn't work here. Instead, she kept a dreamy look on her face. The other ladies clustered around as Donella's voice rose at the tragic conclusion of her song. When she finished, she left a haunting note hanging in the air before she glanced up. The women had tears in their eyes, and so Donella earned three gold crowns. She smelled their floral perfume as they stepped near to drop the coins in her basket.

As soon as they left, she pocketed the coins, put her zythrin in her satchel with her bowl, and paid the rug merchant one fourth of a crown.

Rongel nodded at her, his black ponytail bouncing as he took it. "You have done well today."

"See you next week." She snatched an apple from his lunch, and automatically ducked his half-hearted swipe at her. He pretended to be annoyed with her, but Donella knew he liked their weekly rituals as much as she did.

Donella didn't play after her windfall. In fact, staying around would only encourage the thieves and pickpockets to shake her down. Right now, they were busy working the crowds, but as the afternoon wore on, they would target the beggars. She knew this from experience, hence the business deal with the rug merchant.

She used one crown to buy provisions from a reputable grocer whom she knew well, and a hot bun to eat on the way home. Donella secreted the other crowns in a hidden pocket in her rag outfit. She left the small coins in her money purse.

Donella hummed a cheerful tune as she walked down the road away from the market town. A carriage passed her heading the other way. Other foot travelers turned off the busy road as they reached their houses on the outskirts of the town. Eventually she took a narrow path into the woods and came to her odd little home.

She wondered how Guy fared.

Chapter 6

The bandits propped Guy against a tree, tied him to it with a rope, and left him, taking Seeker with them. He didn't know if they planned to return or if they intended to let him starve. No matter their intention, he didn't let any time pass waiting to find out. He worked the knots that bound his hands. They chafed his wrists raw.

Every moment, Guy expected the bandits to come back. Heart pumping, he stretched his hands behind him searching for something to break his bonds. His shoulders ached as he pushed them to their limit. Finally, he found a sharp rock. He rubbed it against the rope. Sweat poured down his face and trickled down his back as he worked to loosen the bonds before the thieves returned. It took a very long time. Sure that Jed and his cohorts would find him and tie him back up, Guy's heart jumped whenever he heard a rustling in the woods. Untying the knot at shoulder height that held him to the tree was time consuming.

Finally, he freed himself. He ran deeper into the woods. Crouched behind a fallen tree, he listened for any sound of their return. When his heart stopped pumping in his ears, he heard water flowing nearby.

Tired and discouraged, Guy followed the sound of gurgling

water. After drinking his fill at a spring with his cupped hands, he sat down to think what to do next. He figured they had taken Seeker to sell at the town. It had looked large enough to have a horse market. A stallion like Seeker would bring a good price. His heart sank at the thought.

He had to do something to prevent that from happening.

Guy trudged back near the road, careful to stay in the woods parallel to it. Only when a group of several wagons and men walking came along, did he slip into their midst and join them the rest of the way to the town. He kept an eye out for the bandits.

Donella will kill me when she learns I lost her horse.

He recognized the town of Capall where Father had taken him to buy their workhorse.

Soon he stood in front of an inn. The bustle and noise informed him it must be market day. He jumped back as a team of horses nearly ran him down.

He joined the crowds heading to the trading area, seeking for the three men who had held him up, as well as the lost stallion. Near the corral, he ducked through the milling crowd, getting as close as he could to see the horses for sale. The sweetish smell of horses, straw, and dung filled his senses.

He heard snippets of conversation as he moved through the press of sellers and buyers.

"Limped as soon as I led him away—"

"Look at that nag. Why, Lem, do they allow—"

"Good farrier, none better—"

"— hope that foreign trader don't scoop up the best of the lot like the last few times."

"I heard him say he bought a ranch near the coast. What can a foreigner want with so many horses?"

Guy circled the whole area before spotting Seeker. He sought the thieves in the crowd. Soon he focused in on the scar-faced man named Jed talking with a richly-clothed man. This man had a pointed beard and wore an embroidered vest. In deep conversation, they didn't observe him as he got close enough to overhear them.

"Finest horse in all of Valdeor. Just take a look at those shoulders, Lord Tastaver."

"I have seen some very fine horses in my weeks since arriving in Valdeor. What makes this stallion so pricey?"

Guy studied the stranger. He must have come from across the seas. No wonder he dressed outlandishly.

Why didn't the buyer see the kind of man he dealt with? Jed looks like a brigand, not a horse breeder. Yet, if Lord Tastaver was the foreigner buying all the best horses, maybe he didn't care where they came from.

Guy knew he had to get Seeker away. But would it be best before the sale or after? Lord Tastaver sported a fancy scabbard. Did he wear it for show, or would he use it?

Guy needed a plan, fast. A diversion?

Someone behind him grabbed his elbow. Guy swung around to face one of Jed's cohorts.

"Look who we have here. Escaped, did ya? Ain't you got enough sense to go home, boy?" Guy fought against the man who dragged him over to Jed and the buyer as they inspected Seeker. The horse neighed upon seeing Guy.

"Caught this little sneak, boss. What do you want me to do with him?"

Seeing his chance, Guy spoke up. "This is my horse!" Guy faced the man with the beard and gestured to the thieves. "These men stole him from me on the way to the horse fair."

Lord Tastaver looked him over. A flush rose up Guy's neck as the man took in his disheveled appearance. At least Guy had washed his face and brushed the leaves out of his hair before coming to town.

"A boy like you with a horse like that? How can you prove it?"

Lord Tastaver touched a giant pearl in his left ear.

The other three horse-thieves grinned at Guy. He had no papers, like most owners would. He had been foolish to hope he could rescue Seeker.

Donella would never forgive me if foreigners shipped her horse to a distant land. I'll never forgive myself, either.

Thinking of her gave Guy an idea. Guy held up his left hand with the birthmark clearly visible. "My horse wears my mark on his bridle." He smirked at the astonished looks on their faces.

The lord inspected the bridle. "I find no such thing."

Jed crossed his arms and gave a cocky grin back at Guy.

"What! Let me see." Seeker's bridle no longer contained a metal disk with my mark stamped on it. Guy glared at Jed, and the thief lifted his shoulder in a slight shrug, a smug look on his face.

One of the men went in search of the town marshal. When he returned, the town marshal listened to the tale. He took Guy's arm to lead him away. "Now, young fella, let the men conduct their business."

Before they went three steps, a mark on Seeker's flank as they passed behind the horse caught Guy's attention. "Wait!" Guy resisted the marshal's pull. "Look for yourself. My mark is branded on his flank, matching the one on my hand."

Usually Guy's birthmark embarrassed him, but he forgot that in his desire to regain the horse. Guy waved his left hand in the marshal's face.

The marshal stopped to examine the horse, as did many spectators who had watched the proceedings with interest, smug or sympathetic, depending on their point of view.

"It's his, alright," an old farmer in the crowd piped up.

"Let the lad go. He's telling the truth," another trader chimed in.

"Outrageous!" Lord Tastaver pushed his way forward. "The boy is likely a thief. How could a lad like this afford a nobleman's horse?"

"Yes, just look at the lines of the stallion. He's worth a small fortune," Jed added.

"Hey!" A fat man stepped up. "Didn't you try to sell me my own horse, after you stole it?" He shook his fist in Jed's face. "Marshal, this man is a thief!"

As the bystanders argued, the marshal gave the reins of Seeker to Guy. "You'd better get along before a fight breaks out."

Relief flooded through Guy. He didn't waste any time but led the horse out of the corral and mounted away from the crowd. Afraid that the rich buyer's gold coins might change the marshal's mind, Guy rode as fast as he could through the traders as they gave way before him.

He headed for the inn. But when he reached it, he pulled Seeker up short. He couldn't use the portal as a quick escape route, because the inn yard bustled with carriages and wagons. People streamed into the taproom for their afternoon meal. The inn must have good food. Guy's stomach rumbled at the thought. He ignored it and contemplated his options.

He sat undecided. He could wait around the corner for things to quiet down, but that could be a while. Meantime, many of the traders still gave Seeker a second look. Most everyone came to the monthly market in Capall to buy or trade horses. One man, who had been staring at Seeker while Guy decided what to do, approached him now.

That decided Guy. He turned Seeker's head down the road leading toward his house. As little as he wanted to return, knowing the reception he would no doubt receive from his stepmother, he had nowhere else to go.

Better the evil he knew . . .

As he rode out of town, he thought of one place he could try.

He still had Donella's token, the clay bead, in an inner pocket of his trousers. Maybe he would find her. The thought barely crossed his mind, when he pushed it away. *I cannot show up and beg for her help, not after I insulted her the last time we met.* He groaned. *I must reign in my temper, even if she provokes me.*

He rode the rest of the afternoon. Tired, he stopped beside a stream and drank fresh water and picked some berries. More reasons against adventuring—no food and no money to buy any. He suddenly remembered the saddlebag still on the horse. He rooted through it and found a bit of dried jerky. He ate it with relish. Reaching in farther, he pulled out some coins scattered at the bottom. He smiled, glad the thieves overlooked them. They didn't amount to much, but it might buy him some bread at a cottage along the way tomorrow.

The only part of this journey he did enjoy, curled up next to Seeker for warmth, was gazing at the blanket of stars that night.

As he rode, the next morning, Guy contemplated his future. He didn't want to go back home. Nor was he ready for another disastrous adventure.

If he had been in a better mood, he might have appreciated the vista around him—the lonely beauty, the soft rolling hills, the early spring flowers and droning bees. But he hardly noticed them as he wrestled with his so-called gift and what he should do about it. If he did anything at all.

There are so few waykeepers, their purpose obsolete, so why bother learning the trade? And as for using the portals for sheer adventure, as Donella seemed to do—well, he was a farmer at heart. Or so he had always thought.

He was used to hard work. His stepmother made sure of that. But the more he thought about it, he didn't have a love of the land, or a connection to it. He didn't farm because he wanted to, but because it was the only life he knew. The only way he could feed and clothe himself.

If I could be anything I wanted, do anything I wanted, what would it be? He recalled happy days of his childhood. A time when he was satisfied with all life had offered.

I would be an innkeeper like Father.

Inn-keeping was more interesting than feeding pigs or weeding. Aloud, he spoke to Seeker, "I could hire someone to do those menial jobs. I could be the congenial host who greets the guests and serves them meals and drinks in the barroom."

The stallion made a huffing noise and pranced sideways. Encouraged, even though he knew the horse couldn't understand him, Guy continued. "That way I could hear all about their journeying and not have to leave my own hearth."

The more Guy thought about it, the more the life of an innkeeper, not a waykeeper, appealed to him.

Seeker whinnied, reminding Guy to feed him. He dismounted and let the horse eat grass in the meadow. As Guy dug in his pack for dried nuts and fruit, he addressed Seeker, "Of course, even though I owned a former inn, my stepmother would fight me all the way to reopen it." The horse's ears twitched as Seeker responded to Guy's voice.

Guy continued, "I don't know if there'd be enough money to pay others to do my old chores."

Guy picked at blades of grass. "Worst of all, I'm only sixteen. I cannot run an inn at my age." He groaned as his frustration mounted. "If only I were a few years older!"

But what could he do in the meantime? He wished he knew the answer.

Chapter 7

Becoming tired of her own company, Donella longed to hear from Usher about Guy.

Glancing around her snug little home, she decided what to bring. She gathered her zythrin and put together a bundle of provisions for her mid-day meal. She put them in her leather satchel. She rummaged through her healing potions, choosing a few to take. Then she picked up a vial of sleeping potion. It could come in handy. She tucked it in the pouch around her neck.

She left her hideaway and traveled to the crossroad's post, a walk of two hours without Seeker.

When she arrived, she unclasped her cloak and laid in on the grass. She opened the bundle which contained a crusty bread loaf and a large chunk of hard cheese.

A dusty cloud in the distance grew nearer. Soon came the sound of wagon wheels and harnesses jingling. The cloud revealed itself as a wagon with a family aboard.

Giving food and rest to weary travelers was what a waykeeper did. Charity—or hospitality, Mother had called it—did not wait for visitors to show up. Hospitality meant going out to find others in need.

Donella stood and waited to meet the travelers.

The wagon driver pulled up his horses even with her. Sand rolled over them.

"Are you looking to join us on our journey into town? Pretty lonesome for a maid alone on the road." He glanced her over.

She unconsciously smoothed down her wool dress with its hidden patches.

"No, thank you." She broke eye contact and motioned behind her with her hand. "But I did stop for a mid-day meal. There's a well. The dust made me think you would appreciate a cool drink of water." She smiled a welcome. "My name is Donella."

One of the boys jumped off the back. He was about five or six, the smallest of five boys crammed in the wagon. "Water? Where?" Donella showed him the well near a cluster of trees. He hauled up the wooden bucket suspended on a rusty chain, gulped its pure freshness unabashedly, and let the water run down his chin onto his dusty overalls. His family soon followed.

The boy watched with hungry eyes as Donella picked up a loaf of bread and tore off a piece. She put it on a clean, linen napkin.

"Would you like some?" She cut a portion of cheese and put it beside the bread. The boy stared at them greedily, then looked to his father for permission.

"I will trade you some vegetables for your food." The farmer gestured at his load.

Looking over the wagon's side, Donella saw it full of turnips for market.

"It's a deal." She smiled at the boy as he took the food from the linen square. The man and woman and the other four boys sat down in the grass and ate till they had their fill. When they ate the last morsel, the farmer again asked if she needed a ride into town, but she declined.

After the farmer's wagon disappeared over the distant hill, Donella pulled Usher's clump of moss from her pouch. A tendril of fog swirled around her legs and she imagined Usher's stone house. In the spiraling mist, she couldn't bring her destination into focus. The distance was too far for her to travel with one step. She couldn't have put into words how she knew that. She just did.

And she had never traveled to Usher's house from this portal.

So Donella waited for another image to coalesce—the nearest waypost between this waypost and Usher's. From this place she would again open a portal. She would do it as many times as needed to get to her destination. She wished for Guy. From what she could tell, he had opened portals all around Valdeor, from the forbidding Everlasting Winter Mountains to the seacoast.

Only that one time, in panic, had she stepped into the portal without seeing where it led. Fortunately, it turned out to be Usher's dwelling. But it had been a dangerous thing to do. Mother had warned her that she could stumble out, disoriented, and trip in front of a horse's hooves, or fall off the edge of a cliff, or some other disaster, depending upon where she landed.

"Never take risks, my daughter. It is better to make many steps than go blindly into danger," Mother's advice rang in her ears.

Donella, seeing a clearing among trees through the portal, stepped through the mist and found herself on springy moss in a damp forest. She looked around at the unfamiliar place in wonder. Lichen covered the trees. Humid air enveloped her. A stagnant pond produced an earthy smell alongside the path she walked. She assumed it was a path, though it seemed more like a deer trail. It disappeared through the trees. Wherever she was, it wasn't well-trodden. It must be one of the forgotten wayposts.

Donella shivered in the cool air and drew her cloak tighter around her. The dense forest blocked out the warm mid-day sun.

She didn't see any obvious dwelling. Intrigued, she strode in a circle around the whole clearing. As she did, she had an odd feeling that she wasn't alone. She darted a glance over her shoulder. It dawned on her how still the glade had become. No wind sighed through the leaves of the trees. A bird that had fluttered from branch to branch when she arrived disappeared, his cry stilled. She listened intently for any sound but heard only a rustle in the bushes.

Heart pounding, she spun in place, peering at every dark shadow in the trees surrounding her. She hugged herself as goosebumps coursed over her body. When nothing else happened, after a seeming eternity, but probably ten minutes, Donella tried to shrug off the feeling. She wasn't usually over-imaginative.

I am seeing shapes where there are none. This place is spooky. No leaving my clay bead here after all. I never want to visit this forest glade again.

As she headed back to the lichen-covered waypost, her wary glance darting around, she spotted a cave opening hidden behind a clump of bushes. As she stepped around a fallen log, it disappeared in the foliage.

No wonder I couldn't find it.

She stepped back to where she could see it again. Curious, she picked her way through the thick underbrush, as thorn bushes scratched her arms. She stood before the cave's opening, slightly taller than she. Hairs rose on her arms. *Not a very welcoming place for visitors.* Even in the midday, she couldn't see more than a foot into the opening. The gloom of the woods let little light through, turning the area into twilight.

She retreated and sought out a stick to use as a torch. She used her flint stone to light some dried grass, then lit the torch. She headed back to the cave. She didn't want to disturb a big animal in its den. She flattened herself against the side of the opening and threw a big rock inside to bring any animals out. Several bats burst into flight. She shuddered and pulled up her hood in case any remained.

Undeterred, she stepped into the dark and moved her torch around in the circular room. She gave a sigh of relief when she found nothing bigger than a spider, although several animal bones lay scattered on the floor. Either a bear or a big cat used this as a lair. But since the bones looked old and brittle, she didn't fear the immediate return of a predator.

She explored farther and confirmed that this had once been a waystation. A leg of what she assumed to have been a table or chair rested in the corner, and a broken piece of crockery still lay on a natural stone shelf along the wall. A steady drip set her teeth on edge. Someone abandoned this place a very long time ago. The overgrown path should have warned her of that.

But, once again, she had let her curiosity get the better of her. She regretted the time she spent exploring this waystation. She should have left the gloomy forest as soon as she realized it was uninhabited.

Just then she heard a noise close behind her. Her scalp prickled as her heart raced with fear. She whirled around to find a cloaked figure blocking the cave's entrance.

She couldn't see the face of the figure in the shadows of the hood it wore. Nor could Donella tell, at first, whether a man or woman stood there, but something about the figure exuded evil. Maybe the unsheathed knife glinting in the figure's hand had something to do with that.

Donella pushed herself up against the cave wall, while she looked around for a weapon greater than a rock. The brittle bones wouldn't do her any good. And the old chair leg lay too far away. She gripped her torch so tight splinters dug into her palm.

The silence stretched between them and she grew more tense, ready to spring or fight. She wished the animal of this den would suddenly appear.

A male voice broke the silence. "What are you doing in my cave, girl?"

"I sought a place to rest." Surprising how calm she sounded when her knees shook under her dress.

"How did you come here? The old trail is so overgrown that it would take a dozen men with axes to hack through the woods to this hidden place." Something about his accent sounded foreign to her ears.

He stood in the doorway, threateningly. She wondered if he waited for something. Or someone. *The path might be impassible, but he was here, wasn't he? And this cave would be a perfect meeting place for people with something to hide.*

Her heartbeat ratcheted up and her palms began to sweat. The man blocked the door, trapping her in the cave. How could she save herself if a second person came? Outside she had a better chance at escape.

She thought she heard a noise beyond him, and when he shifted to cock an ear behind him, she decided to act. She threw the torch where the water collected from the drip, and in the sudden darkness, she bolted to his right. The air whooshed as he passed by her, headed where she had been. She ran blinking in the change from torchlight to dim sunlight. She blundered toward a cluster of trees on her left. She considered climbing one, but she would be trapped just like she had in the cave. She crawled under deep brush and crouched low to the ground. She pulled her brown cloak around her. She tried to control her breathing.

Donella peered between the branches of her hiding place and watched as the man stepped from the cave. The hooded figure held his knife menacingly, searching the area for her. The waypost stood across the clearing. So close to safety—one step through it— and yet he would see her if she exposed herself and ran for it.

Hands shaking, she searched her memory for anything among her mother's teaching to help her. A phrase popped into her head. Donella did something she had never attempted before. She clutched the pouch with the other waykeepers' tokens in one hand while she stretched her ringed hand forth. She closed her eyes. "Dulee firth!" she intoned, meaning "come to me. "

The intruder stopped his search as the mist begin to roil around the post. He seemed to stand undecided. Then he stepped into the shadows, his dark cloak making him disappear.

Donella left her hiding place and ran for the portal.

As she approached it, four figures stepped through, one after another, three men and a woman. They ranged in age from teen to eighty. All held weapons, of a sort—a club, a rolling pin, a staff, and a sword.

"My child, are you hurt?" Usher asked her. She hardly recognized this stern figure with flashing eyes as her friend. He looked formidable with his staff at the ready.

"Where is the danger?" A brown-haired woman with flour on her cheek brandished her stout rolling pin. That and the apron she wore over her plain dress made her look more like a middle-aged cook than a rescuer. A giggle welled up in Donella's throat, but she felt gratitude foremost that the woman answered her call.

The four spread out and created a circle around Donella. Their gazes darted around, hunting for the threat.

"Thank you for coming to my rescue!" She pushed back her hood and let the dark ringlets fall around her face. "I'm Donella." She told them what happened, her words tumbling out in quick succession.

The rescuers spread out and searched the area. Donella joined them, her courage restored. Thick brambles blocked their way and the carpet of old leaves didn't show any prints. They found no signs of horse hooves, so the man must have come on foot. They soon gave up the fruitless search. Presumably, the hooded figure had slipped away.

"My lodging isn't too far from here. I will keep an eye on this place." The lean, wiry man re-sheathed his sword. He was clean-cut with short, dark hair. The insignia on the clasp of his short red cloak declared him a commander. "My name is Odem." And he shook hands all around.

"Odd that someone would choose this out of the way place—unless they were up to no good. I agree with you there. Name is Evodia." The cook gave each of the waykeepers a feather. "If you have no need of me, I have a pot on the boil." As she passed by, she whispered an invitation to Donella, "Come to my inn anytime. The Forest Deer." Then she stepped back through the portal.

The youngest rescuer, a boy of about eighteen stepped forward. He was tall and lank with hair like straw atop his head. "Brodyn," he squeaked, staring at Donella, his Adam's apple bobbing as he cleared his throat. "Um, I hope you call on me. If you need me again, that is." His faced flushed as he stumbled through his greeting. He held her hand longer than necessary, then, as if he realized that, he let it go abruptly. "I hope to see you again," he mumbled, never giving Donella a chance to respond before he stepped through the portal.

They had passed out their tokens—clay bead, feather, shell, pebble, and moss—as they introduced themselves.

Only Usher remained. "I don't like this. I think I, too, will keep an eye on this place. You wouldn't think an old man like me could remain hidden, but I can make this fat body very still."

Donella knew Usher tried to lighten the mood, so she gave him a weak smile in return. The thought of the knife in the hand of the assassin, as she now thought of him, still haunted her.

"Let us discuss this over a nice hot drink, my dear. You still look shaken. A cup of tea will bring the apples back to your cheeks."

She nodded, secretly relieved to leave this place, though she would never admit it out loud. But Donella found that, with Usher, one didn't have to say anything.

Chapter 8

$\mathcal{D}$onella seemed relaxed in Usher's snug home. She ate the last bite of the little cake and brushed away the crumbs. They had kept a companionable silence while they ate, neither one speaking about Donella's brush with danger.

Once she finished, Usher asked the question on his mind. "What brought you to the forest waypost?" He leaned forward slightly.

"I was on my way to see you when I landed in those woods." Donella's shoulders hunched. "I hoped to hear news of Guy from you."

"Ah, yes. I found his farm. I kept an eye on him this past winter. He only recently used the portal. In fact, I was preparing to search for him when I received your distress call." Usher rubbed his bald head.

"I best hurry and extricate him before he gets in any real trouble." Usher pushed back his chair, and hurriedly threw a few things in a brown cloth sack.

"That's one of the things I like about you. You seem to have a sense when someone is in trouble. Whenever I'm lonely, you appear at my door with a homemade cake and a bit of gossip. It's as if you *knew*. Once you showed up when the big beggar boys in the market square surrounded me. Just when I thought they would steal my coins, you appeared and scattered the boys with your staff."

"That's my sense of charity working overtime. It's because I care."

Usher finished his packing, took up his staff, and crammed a low, round-brimmed hat on his head. "I don't mean to be rude, but I feel I must find him. Stay here, where it is safe, until I send for you." He turned around at the door with a last, hurried instruction. "And keep the stewpot ready. You never know, we might have company." He winked and departed.

From his dwelling in the valley, Usher stepped through the swirling mist portal. When he didn't find Guy at the farm or surrounding areas around the village of Fister, he traveled to the inn-yard of the horse market at Capall where he felt an echo of Guy's presence. He wandered through the town, no longer busy on the day after the market. He went to each road leading from the town, spinning his ring around his finger. He waited for a vibrating tingle detecting Guy. He perceived a strong vibration at the western route.

As the sun beat down mercilessly throughout the day, Usher was glad he crammed the hat on his head before leaving home. He trod the wide road, humming a jaunty tune. He joined other travelers leaving the horse fair. But as he traveled farther, their numbers became a few stragglers as people took byways and lanes off of the main road toward their homes. As the afternoon wore on, he became the only wayfarer.

Hungry and thirsty, he stopped by a stream to fill his flask and pulled an apple from his pack. After a short rest, he turned to leave when he observed an unusual horseshoe print. Seeker's left front shoe was wider than his others. He scanned the area closer and found signs of a camp the night before. Surely the boy had been here.

With renewed purpose, Usher strode forth.

He put in another hour of walking before halting for the night.

Mid-morning the next day found Usher standing on a hill looking across vast farmland. A distant rider on a jet-black horse approached a lone tree in a farmer's field. Usher recognized Seeker from afar. He knew if he didn't act soon, he'd never catch up to Guy. If the untrained boy lost focus next time the horse went through a portal, he could appear anywhere on Valdeor, making Usher's job that much more difficult to find him again.

Usher cupped his hands around his mouth and gave out a loud whistle three times.

The horse came to a halt and the rider struggled with him. Seeker turned about and came racing back toward the hill. Usher put down his pack, rested on his staff, and waited to meet the boy Donella claimed was the Gifted One.

In a short while, the horse changed his gallop to a trot and then a walk, neighing as he came abreast of Usher.

"Good boy, Seeker." Usher gave the horse his favorite treat, a sugar cube.

The boy's face went from angry to astonished. "How do you know my horse's name?"

Usher smiled up at the lad. "Don't be angry at Seeker. He and I are old friends. I've known him since a colt. He is as beautiful and brave as his sire was. Aren't you, boy?" He rubbed the horse's nose and it snuffled his robe, looking for another treat.

Guy stared at the old man's ring. "You're a waykeeper, too. Is Seeker yours then?"

"Once upon a time. But he is his own master now. No other animal can find its way through the portals. He is very, very special." Usher transferred his gaze back to the horse for a moment.

"I thought so. Thank goodness I got him back—" Guy caught

his breath, blushing. Usher raised his eyebrows and Guy reddened even more.

"You must be Guy." Usher smiled up at him. "I am Usher, a friend of Donella's, and I hope to be yours, too." Usher cocked his head. "I have sought you out to mentor you in our ways. The portals can be dangerous if you don't focus on what you are doing. In fact," he rubbed his chin, "that is how I came to meet Donella, a few years back. She ran away and flew through the portal before she settled on where she wished to go. Fortunately for her, she landed in my backyard, so to speak. That is another story, though.

"Anyway, I am getting a crick in my neck looking up at you, so maybe you would be so kind as to help me up on Seeker behind you and we can ride to my house."

Guy gave him a hand mounting the horse and Usher directed him to the nearest waypost.

"Donella should have a pot of stew on at my place. You are welcome to join us. Unless you have a pressing need to be home?"

Guy imagined how his Stepmother would react to his appearance after more than a week away. She wouldn't be happy. Especially with another waykeeper and a horse in tow. Guy wasn't ready to face her wrath. Not now. Maybe never again.

"I would be honored. I haven't eaten a proper meal in days." Guy's stomach rumbled at the thought of hot food.

"Good, good." The old man grabbed him about the waist. "I only hope Donella remembered to add onions. They add such a rich, savory flavor to the dish."

But when Guy, with Usher clinging to him, trotted up on Seeker to the stone dwelling, no one met them at the door. Inside, they found no sign of Donella. But she had cut up vegetables for the stew and left them in the pot, ready to be heated.

Guy couldn't decide whether he was relieved or irritated that she hadn't stayed when she knew he was coming. She had that effect on him. He wanted to tell her of his adventures. Although ashamed of losing Seeker, he had outwitted the thieves to regain him. Thinking on the last time they met, though, he could understand how she might not want to meet him after he had insulted her.

"Ah, I see you admiring my humble dwelling." Usher must have mistakenly thought Guy stared at his odd house. So Guy pulled his thoughts back and took stock of his surroundings. He blinked at the strange structure.

"I wonder how much each of the massive stones making up the walls weighs? Only a giant could have lifted them in place." His mind boggled at the sheer difficulty in making such a dwelling.

"It is quite ancient. In fact, I don't think anyone could build it today." Usher made small talk while he got the stew going. Usher didn't seem to expect Guy to answer the ramblings. Guy's shoulders relaxed, his nervousness eased, which was probably Usher's intent.

Over their meal the old man related how he had come to meet Donella. Then, as they sat over their drinks—ale for Usher and honey beer for Guy—Usher told Guy of Donella's recent encounter with the hooded figure in the cave.

A shiver went over Guy. "What was he doing there?"

"Ah, that is the question. But I fear we will not soon know the answer." Usher pushed away his empty mug of ale. "I hope that headstrong girl didn't go chasing after answers. But I am pretty sure she took up Evodia's invitation to visit. Donella is ever curious.

"But enough of this. I am going to tell you the history of the waykeepers, and tomorrow we will work on your focus."

Usher got up and poured himself another mug of ale. "Storytelling is a dry business," he said with a wink.

Guy couldn't help liking this man. He got caught up listening to the tale.

"My grandfather told me this story," Usher began. "It is the little-known history of the Waykeepers. Actually, our true name is the Waystation (or Wayhouse) Keepers. The wayposts marked the route to the Isle of Origin."

"I thought the Isle of Origin was a myth." Guy sat up straight with surprise. "A story to explain the creation of the world to children."

"Alas, no. It's a real place." Usher crossed his hands over his ample stomach. "The first king of Valdeor was Gildran."

Guy nodded. Every child learned that.

"Well, King Gildran made a point to send his knights on a mission to find the Isle of Origin, for the location became lost in the memory of mankind." Usher took a drink of his ale and wiped his mouth with the back of his hand.

"But . . . that was a thousand years ago."

"Aye. Now are you going to let me tell this story, or are you going to keep interrupting?"

Guy ducked his head with a sheepish look.

Usher took a sip. "Let's see. Where was I? Oh, yes. Gildran the Virtuous. The first king who won the heartstones of virtue—which is a story for another day. He sent his knights to all corners of the globe, looking for the isle or any clues of its whereabouts. But many of the men were lost or never heard from again. The world had lost belief in the One Who Fashioned All. Unfortunately, non-believers killed many of the Valdeorans who entered their lands."

Usher absently scratched behind his ear. "Years passed, then decades. Gildran feared he would die before seeing the quest fulfilled. His son, Gilbreth, begged his father for a ship to sail the seas and find the isle. Gildran was loathe to send his youngest son on such a dangerous mission. But in the end, he relented and gave him his fastest ship and most experienced captain and crew. For two years they sailed the seas, following clues found in the old tales and gleaned by the knights on their travels.

"But one day, while following a promising lead, a great storm blew up and stranded the ship on a reef. Only Gilbreth survived. He spent a week aboard a raft he made of the shipwreck's lumber. His provisions grew low, and fearing to die forsaken, he pleaded to the Guardian of Valdeor, the spirit of light, to save him for his father's sake. He promised to build a shrine to the One Who Fashioned All in whatever place he landed.

"His prayer was answered. On the horizon, a mountain rose out of the sea. He paddled all the rest of that day for the shore. Trees came right down to the shore, loaded with fruit. Lush vegetation abounded. Animals he had never seen before grazed placidly. Not only had the Guardian heard his prayer and saved the prince, but Gilbreth had found the mythical Isle of Origin. Gilbreth got down on his knees when he reached the shore and thanked the Guardian and his Maker for saving his life. He later went back to the isle and built a grand shrine to the One Who Fashioned All."

Usher paused, filled his mug, and drank deep. He added another log to the fire, which had died down.

"Have you ever visited the shrine?" Guy stretched his legs toward the fire.

"No, for its location was again forgotten in the passage of time. Pilgrims flocked to the shrine in the first centuries after Gilbreth found it. The keepers built a great number of waystations to offer the pilgrims hospitality. But as people stopped worshiping the One Who Fashioned All, fewer and fewer men made pilgrimages to worship at the shrine. The Isle of Origin again disappeared from memory." Usher sighed. "My grandfather told me that his grandfather claimed it was the most magnificent building in the world. Greater than Reina Lauressa's palace in

Mintala."

"But the wayposts to it still exist." Guy leaned forward. "Surely they can be used to find it again."

"Yes, but there are only five of us now. You've met Donella and me, and there are three more waykeepers. But only someone who can travel the long distances over the seas will find the lost island. One with great control over the portals." He paused and stared at Guy. "Someone we refer to as the Gifted One."

Guy leaned back from the table and shook his head, no, when words wouldn't come.

"The Gifted One? I'm nobody but a farm boy, fit for nothing but cleaning out stables."

Usher continued, "Yes, it could be you. Do not underestimate yourself, Guy. If what Donella said is true, you have greater power than she or I to work the portals. You can open any portal at will. And I can train you to do more. I can help you focus your abilities."

"You are mistaken. I hate to disappoint you, but I'm not the one you are looking for." Guy rubbed his hand over his face and blurted out, "What I did was an accident! You must understand. I couldn't open all those pathways to different locations again, if I tried. Please, believe me!"

Usher smiled. "My boy, how do you think Donella and I found you? We can feel your power pulling on us like a vibrating hum from the wayposts. You are very strong. You might even be powerful enough to reach the Isle of Origin. Won't you give it a chance?" Usher spread out his hands, as if in supplication. "If you could find the way, maybe pilgrims would once again worship at the shrine. They could reestablish belief in the Maker throughout the known lands."

Usher shook his head at Guy. "It is my belief you are called to do this."

In the end, Guy couldn't resist his plea, so he reluctantly agreed to study under Usher. "Just don't get your hopes up. I will try to learn to be a waykeeper like my father before me. But quests are for champions, not me."

In the following weeks, Usher would set Guy a task, and then try to distract him.

After that, Usher taught him to juggle. Guy was a natural. Then Usher would spray him with water, pelt him with rotten fruit, sing off-key, or whatever he could devise to make Guy lose his concentration. Guy found it amusing, but Usher didn't.

"Your very life may depend upon your ability to focus." Usher's face took on a somber expression. "Let us try something more serious."

Usher sent Guy outside in a storm with a candle. Guy's task was to keep it lit using his hands to block the weather. Guy no longer grinned. He ignored the water cascading down his back. As the hours passed, his hands went numb with cold, and he couldn't feel his nose, yet he kept the little spark alive as long as there was wax left in the stub of the candle.

Usher put him to bed in the morning with a cup of tea to warm him up first. But Guy had remained focused, earning his mentor's praise.

Late the next afternoon, Guy sat before the fire, a bowl of steaming stew in his hand. "What connects the portals?"

Usher put down the book he was reading to answer. "That is a very good question. Unfortunately, I have no answer. Some say it is magic. Yet my wise grandfather described it as a tunnel from one place to another. Something about a fold in the air. The rings, which are somehow intrinsic to its working, activate the portal, as we call it now." He scratched his chin. "Someday I would like to visit the Reina's archives and see if I can find any references to them in the ancient scrolls."

"Can anyone use it? Even if they aren't trained?" Guy wanted to know.

"Yes. Of course, they might end up anywhere if they just open the portal and walk through. And they can only get back if they find the same portal that they took. That is why we leave a token at every waypost. Also, they must still possess the ring." Usher tapped on the book cover. "I heard a story about a boy who stole a ring after seeing his neighbor use it. He lost the ring to bandits, and it took him a year to return home. He didn't thieve anymore."

Guy thought about it. Finishing his stew, he put his bowl on the table. "I have been wondering, if so many wayposts are scattered around Valdeor for the pilgrims, then they must each have a ring associated with them." He sneezed and pulled the blanket closer around his shoulders. "But if there are only a few waykeepers left, where are all the rings? And if anyone can use them, even if they aren't trained, why don't they? Isn't there danger of misuse?"

Usher sat up straight in his chair and stared at Guy as if he saw him for the first time. He snapped his fingers. "The mystery man in the cave. We couldn't find his trail into the woods. Why did we never suspect he used a ring?" He stood up, walked to the fireplace, and picked up a small box on the mantle. "If that is so, then Donella may be in more danger than she realizes. She cannot escape him through a portal, if she encounters him again.

"I must warn her. I have to go to Evodia's inn." He carried the box over to Guy. Opening it, he pulled out a green clump. "Listen carefully. I want you to wait one hour, then try to come to me using this chunk of moss. Since you cannot feel my presence yet, use my token. Bring Seeker with you. He isn't safe while these conspirators are loose in the countryside."

Usher grabbed a pack and threw a few things in it. He headed for the door. "Remember, give me an hour to find Donella." He crammed his hat on his head and picked up his wooden staff leaning against the doorframe.

Stunned by Usher's sudden departure, Guy sat still with an effort.

He had so many more questions to ask.

He sighed. He wasn't going to get the answers today.

Chapter 9

onella didn't like sitting around. And she certainly didn't like waiting so that Guy could insult her when Usher brought him home.

It had only been a day since Usher left. She busied herself sweeping the old man's place, as well as harvesting and chopping leeks, rutabaga, and potatoes for his ever-present stew. But after the second day, restlessness seized her.

I'm wasting my time here.

Mother had scolded her many times for her lack of patience.

A gust of wind slammed the door and she jumped. *Now I am afraid of shadows and noises.* She hadn't fully recovered from her run-in with the man in the cave. From there her thoughts went to her rescue and meeting the last of the waykeepers.

She snapped her fingers. *I'll visit Evodia.* Not only was it a chance to meet with another waykeeper, but she could find out what the woman knew. For, as Evodia had slipped her a feather token, she had said, so only Donella could hear, "Come to me soon."

Maybe Evodia knew something. Who was that man? An assassin? A conspirator? What was he doing there? And a tiny voice whispered, *and you'd rather not be alone.*

Donella left Usher a note: *Gone to meet with Evodia.* Usher had her clay bead and could find her when he wanted.

Donella grabbed her pack, stuffing her few belongings inside. She walked up the hill to the waypost, the strong breeze whipping her hair. She held the feather in her ring hand and activated the portal. A building appeared in the mist, the sign showing a painting of a deer beside a pine tree: Forest Deer Inn. Seeing no one about, she stepped through.

The moment of disorientation, floating with no up or down, was familiar enough that she didn't stumble upon leaving the portal.

Donella blinked away the dizziness, then took in her new surroundings. Chickens flapped their wings at her sudden entrance, then settled back to pecking in the yard. Laundry flapped in the breeze. A delicious smell of meat and onions wafted through the air. Following her nose, she went around to the back door. Evodia worked in the kitchen, rolling out dough.

Evodia glanced up and spotted Donella. Her face split into a grin.

"Come in, child. I hoped you would come soon." She dusted off her floury fingers on her apron. She walked over to the oven, pulled a hot, small pastry out, put it on a plate, and motioned Donella to sit at the table. "Eat it while it is hot."

Donella put her bag under a stool and sat at the table. While she waited for the pastry to cool, she glanced around the tidy kitchen while Evodia shaped the dough. Herbs hung from the ceiling, their aromatic smell mingling with the pies. Polished copper pots and pans neatly lined the shelves, alongside tins of ingredients, and jars of distilled herbs in liquid.

Evodia put her finishing touches on the batch of pies she worked on. She removed the rest of the cooked meat pies in the oven in the wall of the fireplace and replaced them with the uncooked ones, before pouring herself some tea and joining

Donella at the table.

When Evodia sat across from her, Donella took the pastry and bit into the baked ham and potato pie. She smiled with pure contentment and greedily ate it. "This is the best meat pastry I have ever eaten!" She licked her fingers delicately when she finished.

"I am glad you came. I feared the encounter in the forest would leave you too shaken to seek me out." Evodia cocked her head at Donella.

"It would take more than that assassin to stop me using the portals." Donella thrust her chin out.

Evodia sipped her tea, holding the mug with both hands. "I've been thinking about your encounter with the stranger ever since I got home. The man you described brought to mind a couple of fellows that meet occasionally in my husband's bar. I've observed them a few times. They have a foreign look about them, with pointed beards, shifty eyes, and they speak with accents. I asked my husband Burl to listen when he serves them, but they always stop speaking when he is near."

Evodia put down her tea and seemed to be considering Donella. "Have you ever served in a tavern?"

The abrupt change in subject surprised Donella. "Yes. My uncle owns my family's inn." She twirled her hair around her finger as she answered.

"These men are due to show up sometime this week. I wonder—maybe if you saw them, you could spot your man."

"But surely he would recognize me," Donella protested. She shivered at the thought of encountering the assassin again.

Evodia snorted. "How good a look did he get in that dark cave? He shows up at his rendezvous and there is a girl instead of a conspirator which he is expecting. He reacts without thinking. You wore a hood, and you said you threw the torch almost as soon as he entered." She drummed her fingers on the tabletop. "He won't have any recollection of your features. Imagine a girl serving him in a tavern many days journey from the cave. He won't connect the two, as long as you remove your ring."

So Donella found herself working at the Forest Deer Inn, not unlike her job back home. She scrubbed pots, swept floors, and dusted the bedrooms. Donella realized she didn't dislike it so much. *Here I play a role in order to fulfill a secret mission.* It somehow made the work lighter and not so much a chore.

"I haven't seen you before," Evodia's husband, Burl, commented that night in the barroom. He was a short man with a bulging belly. Whiskers sprouted under his chin, but the rest of his face was shaven. He reminded Donella of a gnome.

"Donella is a temporary hire." Evodia laid her hand on Burl's arm. She leaned in close, but Donella heard Evodia say, "She really needs the work after losing both her parents."

Evodia pointed out the regulars, whose faces became familiar to Donella as she worked in the smoky atmosphere filled with the smell of beer and pipe tobacco.

Night after night Donella searched the faces of those who came to eat and drink. She listened for foreign accents among the strangers.

On the fourth night, wind and rain whipped around the inn, like an animal seeking entrance. Few ventured out, so when the door flew open and four men entered, bringing gusts of rain with them, everyone looked up. The newcomers' faces were hidden beneath their hoods. The group chose to sit in the farthest corner from the lamps and firelight. The regulars stopped speaking and stared for a moment, then went back to their usual gossip and dart game.

After Burl took their orders, he came back to the bar. He muttered to Evodia and Donella, "It's those foreigners again. I don't like the look of them."

"Let me take them their ale," Donella offered so she could get close enough to hear them. Burl agreed. Her heart pounding in her ears, she carefully balanced the tray and walked over to the table. *Would they see her nervousness and look closely at her?* She was careful not to look at any of the men directly but surveyed them under her lashes. Evodia was right. No one paid any mind to a serving girl.

The men wore embroidered vests under their cloaks, an unusual sight outside a city. Definitely not farmers.

Her natural courage soon returned, and stepping back, she put her hands under her apron in an attitude of subservience but watched and listened closely. Surely the man across the table from her was the man she met in the cave. She recognized his voice when he spoke. He had a narrow face, long brown ponytail and a pearl earring in his left ear. He caught her eye on him and frowned. Her hands trembled, afraid he had recognized her and would denounce her to his companions.

"Be gone, girl. We will let the bartender know when we require ought else." As he leaned forward, an amulet slipped from under his shirt. She glimpsed the pagan goat-headed god before he stuffed it back out of sight.

She managed a curtsy on shaky legs and withdrew. But she had hung around long enough to hear his name, Harban. They discussed buying horses from a man named Tastaver, and they referred to ships from across the sea. It sounded innocent enough, but the furtive way they spoke told a different story. Something didn't feel right.

She didn't know what it all meant, but she had a bad feeling. Somehow, she had stumbled into the middle of a conspirator's plot.

When the foreign men finally went upstairs to their room, Donella told her new friend she meant to follow them when they left the next morning. Evodia forbid her in strong terms. "A young girl following those foreign plotters? Never! 'Tis foolishness, child." She must have seen the stubborn jut of Donella's jaw. "I'm not questioning your courage, but there are four of them, with weapons no less."

Donella's stomach fluttered as she remembered Harban threatening her with a knife in the cave. She secretly quaked at the thought of four men with weapons pulled on her.

As they finished clearing the barroom tables, Donella told Evodia what she managed to overhear.

Evodia nodded. "Lord Tastaver frequently leads a string of horses through here after the horse fair in Capall. He flashed his money around and told my husband he started a horse ranch." She snorted. "I don't care how rich he is, that is a lot of horseflesh to feed and care for. And if he is a horse trader, then why not say so. Something odd is going on."

Donella longed to do something productive.

As if she read her mind, Evodia suggested, "Tomorrow, go see Odem. He hears lots of things at his waystation, the eastern garrison. And he will keep you safe."

"The soldier? I met him when you all rescued me. He gave me his shell."

Evodia helped Donella prepare for her journey. As they hugged, Evodia whispered, "Come back soon, child."

The portal transported Donella to the rocky eastern coast. She held Odem's shell and searched for a dwelling nearby.

The sound of rumbling waves was a distant backdrop to the seagulls crying overhead. Donella smelled the salty water though she couldn't yet see it. She strode along the path which led uphill. From the hill's crest, a garrison spread out below her. She asked for Odem at the gates. She learned that he was the commander of the garrison.

A soldier escorted Donella to the central building, past the practice field, a forge, and barracks. He led her to a side room and knocked on the door. He gave her name. A voice inside answered, the soldier nodded at her and departed.

Odem stood up from the desk where he sat reading. He was in his mid-thirties, tall, with a square jaw. Donella thought he seemed familiar somehow, though they only met once.

He relaxed his stern countenance with a smile when they were alone. "You look like your mother," he motioned her to a seat.

"You knew my mother?" She froze halfway to the chair. She stared at him closely, and a vague memory stirred. "You brought me a seashell once, and I fancied I heard the sea in it." She recalled playing with the shell, and Mother hugging Odem when he left. "I remember you now."

She took the seat he pointed at. "Evodia calls you a wayfarer."

"Yes. I'm one who travels through the portals but doesn't tend them."

He got a faraway look in his eyes. "I used to visit your mother frequently when I was young. I am your mother's cousin. But I didn't think you remembered me when we met in the woods. The last time I came to your house, you were very small." He leaned against the desk with his muscled arms crossed over his chest armor. "Janyssa was my favorite cousin. Beautiful, but headstrong."

He sighed, and she wondered if he had been in love with her mother.

Even after the father she never knew died, Mother had plenty of chances to marry. Donella watched the many men who beat a path to her door, but although she charmed them, she seemed content as she was, and never remarried. Donella had been secretly happy, because she didn't want a man to break the close bond she had with Mother.

Odem brought her back to the present when he asked, "What can I do for you? No more encounters with the hooded man, I hope?"

She told him of how she next met Harban and his co-conspirators at the Forest Deer Inn, and the conversation she had managed to overhear. Odem frowned, uncrossed his arms, and paced around the room.

"I tend to agree with Evodia. What can one man want with so many horses? We keep many at the garrison, but there is something odd about that many on a private ranch." He stopped in front of her. "What did Harban say again about the ships? Try to recall the exact words."

She curled a strand of her hair around her index finger, concentrating. "'Meet at the dock at midnight the twelfth of Luneta. The merchandise will sail homeward.' Then I heard something odd, which is why I remember it. One of them said, 'Free the birds—'" She put her finger along her lips. "Wait. No! Loose the hawks.'" She looked up at Odem and smiled. "I thought it unusual and pondered what that meant."

Odem sucked in his breath, a hard look on his face. "This is more serious than I thought." The soldier replaced the friendly man of a moment ago. "It is a military phrase. In some cultures, a hawk is used to hunt, or sometimes scout enemy territory. It translates as 'set in motion the machines of war.'" He stood frowning in the middle of the room. "But who is thinking of going to war with us?" He rubbed his chin and let out a frustrated sigh. "We need more information."

Odem gazed intensely at her, similar to the way Evodia had before asking Donella to spy as a barmaid.

"What is it? Why are you looking at me like that?"

"I am trying to gauge your abilities."

She looked him in the eye and said, "If you are wondering, I am as brave as my mother before me."

"Aye. I can see you have her look of determination, which I know so well." He shook his head slightly. "But are you foolhardy, or will you follow my commands? If I give you a mission, will you follow orders?"

"Yes, sir." She stood before him and hoped he could see beyond her youth to her soul of iron.

"Very well. I want you to go back to the Forest Deer Inn and wait for the foreigners to return, or at least watch for this Lord Tastaver to come through with more horses."

She gave a weak smile, as if she weren't disappointed. She thought he would give her a real assignment. But she perked back up when he went on.

"Today is only the sixth of Venusia. So, let us say, we give them two weeks. If they don't show within that time, I want you to go to Tulken Harbor to a tavern called Bottom's Up. Apply as a barmaid, and I will come to you there. Watch for plotters. If they do come back to the Forest Deer Inn, listen at keyholes." He pointed a finger at her. "But don't get caught. Do whatever it takes to find out what their plans are. Then report back to me here. Do not—I repeat—do *not* follow them. They could be very dangerous. This is not a game. Keep your wits about you, Jan—Donella."

She agreed, a wide grin on her face.

She went back the way she came, satisfied that adventure still awaited her. But also determined to live up to the trust Odem put in her.

Donella's first week back at the Forest Deer Inn was uneventful. She awoke early to sweep the floors, make the beds, light the patron's bedroom fires, and carry chamber pots. She thought she had left behind these tasks at Uncle Warun's inn.

But now the everyday tasks gave her time to think and kept her busy during the weeks while she waited for some sign of the conspirators. She knew the satisfaction of a job well-done, which she hadn't appreciated before.

She was grateful to Evodia, of course. Evodia sort of reminded her of her own mother, or how she imagined a grand-dame, if she had one. Aunt Sinlindra had a temper and a backhand when you crossed her. Evodia could make Donella feel guilty with a disappointed look, so she took care to never give her new friend any grief.

"I know you are impatient for something to happen, but you really are a help to me," Evodia told her several times. "Doing our duties well please the One Who Fashioned All. Even if they don't seem important in our eyes."

A smile accompanying a tiny, sweet cake or scrumptious meat pie went a long way each day to making Donella's duties light. If Donella ever had her own inn, she would treat her employees with kindness and friendliness, the way Evodia treated her.

Early in the morning, soon after the monthly horse fair in Capall, she filled up buckets of water at the yard pump. A cloud of dust billowed on the road. She continued working while keeping an eye on it. The inn had a few unoccupied rooms. That much turbulence probably meant several horses, therefore several clients. She sighed at the thought of work it would involve.

Emerging from the dust cloud, Donella discerned a horseman at the front of a long string of riderless horses tied to one another. She stood straight to count them. Seventeen in all. Odem told her to watch for a foreign horse trader. Could he be the one? If so, she would soon be able to hurry to the garrison to inform Odem.

The sound of the horses' hooves, snorts, and neighs broke the silence. Dirt swirled around them, lodging in Donella's throat. She coughed, tasting the acrid sand.

As she stood there, waiting for them to pass, she heard a hiss. She ignored it. Evodia had two cats to keep down the mice population. She heard it again, and turned around to see not a cat, but Usher beckoning to her from a doorway. He stepped out of her view.

Just as she stepped toward him the richly-dressed horseman stopped at the pump and called out, "Ho, there, girl. Give me a drink."

She didn't like his tone, but she gave him a bland look, as any servant would, and fetched him a dipper of water. She dropped her eyes before his haughty look but studied him under her lashes.

He had a pointed beard, a curled mustache, and a pearl earring. She had seen him before. He was one of the plotters! He wore a linen shirt and fine breeches, with an embroidered vest under his cloak. *Arrogant dandy*. Even his short, blade hilt and scabbard looked more decorative than harmful.

When he thrust the dipper back at her, she wiped all expression from her face. She meant to curtsy, when her eyes landed on the ring he wore. She froze.

"What is it, girl? Are you a simpleton? Take the dipper and step away. I am Lord Tastaver and I do not have all day to wait on your pleasure."

She snatched the dipper from his hand and stepped back, thankful that he didn't realize what had startled her. The hostler appeared at the horse's head and took care of watering the horses.

Donella backed up near the wall where Usher hid. When the hostler finished, the stranger kicked his horse, who still had his head in the trough, and led the procession of horses away.

Usher joined her as the last horses passed. "Unfriendly sort. Evodia should be glad he doesn't stop, though he did look like he could pay well."

When she didn't respond, he said, "What is it, child? You look troubled."

She turned away from watching the line of horses depart. "He wore one of our rings. Surely he couldn't be one of us?" She put her hands on her hips. "He has no manners. I cannot see him helping anyone if his life depended on it."

Usher frowned. "What do you know about him? Does he stop here?"

"Yes. In fact, the last time I saw him, he sat with that assassin I met in the woods." Donella's gaze narrowed as she watched the retreating horse train. "He called himself Lord Tastaver. Something doesn't sit right about him." Her gaze returned to Usher's concerned face. "Odem told me to keep an eye out and let him know if the horse trader came through here."

"That is also why I came."

Thinking about it, she realized how odd it was that Usher was here. And without Guy, as far as she could see.

Usher lacked his normally smiling expression and jolly attitude. "Lead me to Evodia and I will explain."

When the three of them were seated at the kitchen table, mugs of aromatic tea in their hands, Usher spoke first. "I found Guy and have been training him. He's a natural."

"I knew it," Donella piped up.

"But we have bigger concerns. Yonder horse trader wears a waykeeper ring."

"One of the foreign plotters?" Evodia asked Donella, gripping her mug with both hands.

"The same." Donella nodded. "But how can that be?" She looked from Evodia to Usher.

Usher cleared his throat. "Wouldn't it be reasonable to suppose that every waystation once had a waykeeper?" When they nodded, Usher went on, "As Guy asked me—where, then, are all the rings?"

They looked at him and each other. "Oh!" Donella gasped in unison with Evodia.

A feeling of foreboding settled over Donella.

"There are but a few of us left. You, Donella, wear your mother's ring. I inherited mine from my grandfather." He leaned forward. "Evodia?"

"From my aunt, who called herself a wayfarer." She set her mug down, carefully. "I see what you are getting at. If the ring didn't get passed down from one generation to the next, nor buried with the waykeeper, they could be anywhere." Her frown grew. "Anyone could have one. Good or bad."

Usher turned his gaze on Donella. "As I surmise, the plotter, or assassin in the wood, as you call him, may have had one as well." He rubbed his hand over his balding head. "We never found traces of his coming or leaving the forest glen. You say he showed up after you used the portal?"

"Yes, but I would have seen him come through." Donella furrowed her brow. "I was always in view of the waypost. Although . . ."

She spoke slowly, as she worked it out for herself, "If he followed immediately, before the mist dissipated, I wouldn't have detected him. I was too busy exploring my surroundings. Whereas he might have been startled to see me, and hid, until he was sure I was alone, and no one else followed me."

She clenched the mug's handle, apprehension rising. "I did wander around a bit. He might have thought I waited for someone. In his mind, what other reason would I have to linger in such a lonely spot?" She shivered when she thought of the danger she had been in at the time. "He was here recently. His name is Harban. He spoke of Lord Tastaver."

"How many rings would you say exist?" Evodia asked the old man, following her own train of thought.

"Hard to estimate." Usher squinted his eyes, gazing into space. "Not every waypost has a dwelling associated with it today. But is that because there was none? Or because the lodgings fell into disrepair and have disappeared over time as the pilgrimages to the holy shrine ceased? I don't know about you, Evodia, but Donella and I watch more than one place. Maybe that is how it has always been done. Who knows?" He squeezed his lip with his thumb and index finger. "A rough estimate—maybe fifty. My grandfather visited at least thirty in his lifetime. I have his map. I myself have been to a couple dozen."

"But that doesn't mean all the rings are in circulation," Evodia reasoned, pouring herself another mug of tea from the pot between them, and staring into it. "Some might have been buried with their owners, as knowledge of the rings' ability to open portals was lost. As travelers stopped coming, waykeepers could have left the hospitality trade." She looked up and met Usher's eyes. "In fact, my aunt didn't use her gift more than a few times in her lifetime, certainly not in her later years. She gave me the ring as more of a curiosity. I read about how to use it in an old family history account and convinced my husband to buy this inn because it came with a waypost out front."

"Nevertheless, in the wrong hands, the waykeeper ring can be a dangerous tool," Usher warned them.

Chapter 10

Seated on Seeker, the warm sunshine on his back, Guy held the moss chunk that Usher had given him before chasing after Donella. Doubt, like a dark cloud, washed over Guy.

Guy glanced from the moss to the interlocking oval design on the back of his left hand, to the ovals carved into the waypost.

I can do this. I must believe in myself.

Just before Guy urged Seeker to enter the mist, he remembered to focus, as Usher had taught him. As the vapor's tendrils closed around him, he put all his concentration on Usher's image—fat, kindly, and balding—and wished with all his heart to see his mentor. Suspended in the between place, he feared he hadn't done it right, until the horse emerged on solid land.

Guy gritted his teeth and fought down the nausea that threatened to overwhelm him. After several gut-wrenching minutes, he could concentrate on his surroundings. He had landed in front of the Forest Deer Inn, as the sign above the door attested.

The sky here was overcast, and oppressive humidity hung in the air.

He sighed with relief. He feared he would emerge in a desolate place and be unable to use his gift to leave it.

I'll never get used to traveling between places.

Guy dismounted by a watering trough.

The inn before him was larger than his home. The two-story building, made of wood, stood above a large grassy yard. Flower boxes in the windows and a bright red stable added cheerful color to the well-maintained buildings.

He looked down at the symbol on the back of his left hand. Unbidden, came a memory of Father, holding him on his knee. "You will grow up to be just like your old man someday." Father traced the birthmark with his finger, grinning with pride. Guy held onto that memory.

Seeker's neigh pulled him out of his reverie. He gave the horse to the hostler who strolled over and went into the inn's barroom. Even empty, it held the smell of beer and sawdust. The waypost design carved in the wood panel behind the bar caught his eye.

Safe haven.

Now, where did that thought come from? He didn't know, but peace and calm settled inside him.

Hearing voices, he followed them until he arrived in the kitchen doorway. The aroma of baking bread permeated the air. Usher and Donella sat at a table with a stranger. She wore an apron over a maroon cotton dress. Her sleeves were rolled up and she had a light dusting of flour on her arms and cheek.

"Nevertheless, in the wrong hands, the waykeeper's ring can be a dangerous tool," Usher was saying.

"Like Lord Tastaver, the horse buyer," Donella added. "He is definitely not one of us. I wouldn't be surprised if Harban, the plotter in the cave, used a ring as well," her voice trembled, slightly.

Guy stepped up to the table. His friends and the woman's head swiveled toward him with startled expressions.

Guy's eyes met Donella's.

"Guy! You gave me a start!" Donella squeaked.

"Sorry. I overheard what you said. That is probably why horse thieves tried to steal Seeker. I met a foreign trader at the Capall horse fair. He wore a pearl earring. And he showed great interest in Seeker's brand, now that I think about it." Guy rubbed a hand over his face. "His name was Tastaver. Can you imagine how much he would desire a horse that could take a man anywhere in the realm in a matter of moments? No ring needed. Only a token held by a rider."

"I see you had no trouble following me. Did anyone see you arrive?" Setting down his mug, Usher moved to the window overlooking the yard and the road.

"I assume you must be Guy." The woman stood and brushed her hands down her apron. She was shorter than Guy by several inches, her tidy hair pulled into a bun on top of her head only reaching his chin. "I am Evodia, and this is my inn. Welcome." She gave him a friendly smile and went to pour him a hot drink. Then she pulled out another chair and pushed over a plate of small cakes. The warm cinnamon scent made Guy's mouth water.

"Why did you take Seeker to the horse fair?" Donella frowned at him.

Trust her to get straight to the crux of the matter. How would he explain losing her horse as soon as she entrusted it to him? She was sure to like him even less, just when he wanted to apologize for the way he behaved when they parted.

"It's not what you think!" A blush crept up his face.

Usher came back from the window. "Guy, make sure the hostler takes special care of Seeker and stashes him in the barn, away from prying eyes. Even though Lord Tastaver already passed through today, he could easily have spies. And Seeker isn't safe yet."

Guy jumped up to do his bidding, avoiding Donella's question.

"I'll catch up with you later." Guy had a lot of events to tell her.

Not the least was his change of heart. He wanted her to know his commitment to his gift.

Usher laid a hand on Donella's shoulder when she stood up to follow Guy. "Leave it for now. We have more important business. I think you need to take this new information to Odem. He isn't only a soldier, but a great strategist. If anyone can put all the pieces together and come up with an overall picture and plan, Odem can."

Evodia agreed with him. "And serving the Reina she will listen to him."

Donella glanced to one, then the other. "Very well."

"I knew I could count on you." Nodding, Usher stepped back. "Get ready to leave. I am sure Evodia will give you food for your journey."

Usher hoped Donella could follow directions. She was such a headstrong teenager. But she had a very brave heart, loyal to the core. He would leave her in the hands of the One Who Fashioned All.

Usher would leave the whole enterprise in the Creator's hands. Usher knew he only played a minor role in the larger tapestry.

Knowing Donella treated everything as a lark, Usher warned her of the danger. "Beware! War and lost rings bode no good for Valdeor. And if you are caught, the consequences will be serious.

"In my youth, I would have been the one to volunteer for dangerous work, but now I must leave it to the younger generation." And he trusted Donella. But he also liked what he observed of Guy so far. Usher had a feeling Guy's gifts were greater than they had yet seen. The young man just needed to commit to using the gift the Creator gave him.

"I'm going to send Guy with you to find and report to Odem whether he's at the garrison or Tulken Harbor," Usher told

Donella.

When Guy returned from the stables, Usher filled the boy in on their conversation. "I know you said you aren't ready nor skilled to take on this burden, but there is no one else. Donella shouldn't travel alone, and you have the power to help her."

Guy hesitated for a moment. "I'll do my best."

Usher let out a breath. "I knew we could count on you!"

Evodia and Donella both looked relieved.

Evodia had been busy packing food for the trip. When Donella and Guy were ready to leave, Evodia produced a gift for Guy. "Here is a short sword, should you have need of it. Nothing fancy about it, unlike the fabled Crestin Sword carried by Prince Alloryn." Evodia winked at him.

Guy strapped the serviceable sword on. "Wow! Thank you!"

Donella and Guy took their leave of Usher and Evodia. Usher heard them squabbling as soon as they stepped outside.

"I didn't mean to lose Seeker. I met thieves when I left home—"

"Start at the beginning. So what made you leave home? When we parted, you seemed insistent that caring for pigs was what you wanted from life."

"I never said that! I have a sense of responsibility—"

Usher and Evodia shared a smile. *Ah, to be young again.*

"I beg of you a room for the night. These old bones need a rest before the journey to Mintala."

"Of course, friend." Evodia led the way.

Usher picked up his staff and pack and followed Evodia from the kitchen to the stairwell leading up to the rooms for rent.

Usher woke before the sun. Anxious for answers he left the Forest Deer Inn without rousing Evodia. They had said their goodbyes the evening before. He had told her he would pursue his own mission: searching the palace archives for answers.

Carrying his pack over his shoulder and his walking staff in his left hand, he used the portal outside the inn.

He stepped from the disorienting mist a day's journey from Mintala, Valdeor's capital city. Just before dawn the road was empty. He knew it wouldn't stay that way for long. Ever since Princess Lauressa had won the heartstones, gems of virtue, and was crowned Reina, traffic to the largest city on the continent had picked up. Trade boomed now, unlike during the time of her predecessor, Warlord Feornson the tyrant.

Wagons and riders soon joined Usher on the road, as well as those traveling on foot. They headed for the glorious capital. Some to trade, some to buy, and some to seek audience with the Reina. Usher's purpose was the latter. Only she could grant his request. He wished to hear from Odem before he told their suspicions of impending war to her, though. They needed proof, or they would lose all credibility. The waykeepers had been under royal protection since time immemorial. He didn't want to risk that privilege for the few of them left.

By mid-morning the city of Mintala could be seen in the distance on a slight rise above the plain. The palace tower soared above all, like a crown set with jewels. Several heartstones twinkled in the sunlight, even at a distance. He found his pulse elevated at the thought of seeing the palace again. Five years ago, at Lauressa's coronation, he, Odem, and Evodia had gone to the festivities and had an audience with her. They returned later for her marriage to her champion, Alloryn.

Travelers of all sorts headed toward the capital city: farmers sitting in loaded wagons, merchants in caravans, noblemen on fine steeds, ladies in carriages, priests who served the One Who Fashioned All walking in twos and threes, and ordinary folk plodding along.

Usher munched on the food Evodia packed for the trip, and, in true waykeeper fashion, shared it with those he struck up a conversation with on the road. He listened intently for any gossip about conspiracies, war, or rings.

As the afternoon grew to a close, the city gates loomed. Weariness settled upon him. He knew a waypost existed within Mintala somewhere—he could feel it—yet walking allowed him to gather the latest gossip and rumors.

Sifting through the information, he heard no news of a foreigner delegation visiting, or of any foreigners in the interior. Arranging an audience would take days, if not a week or more, and he would continue to listen for anything odd as he mingled with the visiting crowds and city inhabitants.

His journey served a double purpose.

Odem was no longer at the garrison, a league behind Guy and Donella, as they found when they asked at the gate.

"Tomorrow morning, we'll head for Tulken Harbor and the tavern where Odem told me to meet him."

"I don't think this is a good idea." Guy confronted Donella, stepping in front of her on the route they followed along a cliff above the sea.

"We have to find Odem. He told me to meet him at Bottom's Up Tavern." She stood in the middle of the path and put her hands on her hips. "Remember, Usher put me in charge."

"No, he told me to look after you when he sent me with you." Guy crossed his arms, blocking her way when she tried to go around him.

She scooted past him and marched on along the sea path, head held high. "Odem entrusted me with this mission before you were on the scene. So we do it my way." She whipped her head around to add, "You are too cautious!"

"And you are too impetuous!" Guy clenched his teeth. He wished Donella wasn't so prickly. He sighed and followed her.

The waves crashed below them on the shore, and normally Guy would have been entranced at his first glimpse of the sea, as he strode after Donella. He almost told her how stubborn and unreasonable she could be, for the umpteenth time. But saying it did no good. It only raised her hackles. And so he would continue to do the only thing he could—tag along. Usher expected him to keep her safe.

Guy hoped he wouldn't have to fight. He could handle a scrappy fistfight. But against conspirators with knives? He swallowed convulsively at the thought. He touched the short blade Evodia had given him strapped snugly against his side.

Guy feared the plotters could possibly recognize Donella, so he thought it imprudent for her to work in a seaport tavern. Odem didn't know the danger to her when he conceived the plan.

They walked in silence back to the waypost, neither willing to concede the other's point of view.

As they found a place to camp for the night and ate the food Evodia provided, Guy finally brought himself to ask the question that he wondered about most of the afternoon. "Why don't we jump through the waypost now and just materialize in the town?"

She looked up from chewing her cold meat pie. "You still have a lot to learn. Didn't Usher teach you anything?"

Stung, he replied without considering his words. "He didn't have the time, considering how he had to rush off and rescue you!"

She stopped chewing and stared at him. He braced himself for her onslaught, but it never came.

"Fair enough." Instead, she answered his question. "You know traveling through the portal makes you feel nauseous and tired, as if you have gone a long way. Which, in reality, you have. You get used to it after a while. But the more times you step through in one day, the more intense the nausea and tiredness become." She finished her pie and wiped her hands. "Also, there is the danger of being seen. Once, I am sure, waykeepers were a common sight, but now instant traveling from place to place is regarded as sorcery. Imagine if someone observed you suddenly appear. Not many notice the ring—not knowing its power—but if someone did—" she looked at his hand.

He finished her thought, "—they could compel me to open a portal. So the danger is too great to risk using a waypost and showing up in a town in the middle of the day."

Donella nodded. "Especially if whoever is behind the conspirators finds out the power you wield to go anywhere. Any town, any castle, the palace at Mintala—in the blink of a moment. All they might do to me is take my ring and leave me behind."

But not in your case, the unspoken words hung in the air between them.

He remembered Jed trying to steal Seeker, now safe in Evodia's stable. Jed had seen his birthmark at the horse fair. Guy shuddered. He was probably a target already.

As he followed the porter to the throne room, Usher's footsteps echoed in the palace with its marble floors and soaring ceilings. The hall was replete with rich tapestries and statuary in every corner. Usher was impressed, even though he had visited once before, at the time of the coronation.

Guards in royal blue livery, embroidered with a golden, seven-pointed star, stood on either side of the carved door open to citizens for the weekly judgment session.

In the throne room, ruby, emerald, citrine, azure, amethyst, and topaz gems twinkled high above their heads. Reina Lauressa sat on her throne in the center. Usher found it impossible to decide the color of her dress because the stones of virtue set in embrasures around the room made a sparkling rainbow in the chamber.

Petitioners from every class waited quietly around the room. The well-to-do in satins and perfumes separated themselves from gaunt beggars with missing limbs. Merchants in gaudily striped tunics rubbed elbows with plain robed, tonsured priests with the scent of incense clinging to them.

Usher stood apart from them and readjusted the pack on his back to a more comfortable position.

As he waited his turn, Usher thought how the interim days had proved fruitful. He learned men from the enemy land of Canteor recently appeared in great number in the eastern seacoast towns, some of them even coming as far inland as Mintala. He discovered the tavern which they preferred and sat in a supposed stupor over his drink every night, listening to their murmurings. Unfortunately, he wasn't fluent in their language. Occasionally they spoke in the common tongue as they tried to blend in. The spies in the capital seemed to be assessing the size and readiness of Valdeor's standing army.

The master of ceremony interrupted Usher's thoughts. "Name, please."

"Usher, from the eastern province."

The master of ceremony announced him as he gestured Usher forward into the royal presence.

The princess sat ramrod straight on the throne. Around her neck she wore a medallion set with the many colored heartstones of virtue. Usher revised his first impression that Lauressa was a little older than a teenager when he glanced into her eyes. They had the look of someone who had seen many experiences in a long life. Her eyes were old for her youthful appearance and hard to look away from, once you saw into their depth.

Usher bowed formally.

Reina Lauressa nodded in greeting. Her expression was serious, but not unfriendly. "What is your petition?" Then her brow furrowed. "Surely we've met before?"

Usher rose from his bowed knee. "Aye, Your Majesty. I am the eldest waykeeper."

"I remember." Her face brightened. "You and two others

came to offer me your allegiance."

Amazement rippled through him that she remembered him out of the thousands she must have interacted with since her coronation.

She must have seen the shock on his face. She gave him a warm smile. "I thought your life work intriguing. During a snowstorm on our travels, Prince Alloryn and I took refuge in a mountain pass waystation. The dry wood stored there saved our lives. That was my only experience of wayposts."

"I am profoundly thankful a fellow waykeeper's forethought spared your majesties' lives."

She gazed upon him, benevolently. "In what way may I help you?"

"I wish a private audience with you about a grave matter." Usher clasped his hands around his waist. "Prince Alloryn would be interested as well, I think." Her husband, Prince Alloryn, headed her personal security and that of the realm. Usher lowered his voice so only she could hear. "I have knowledge of spies from across the sea assessing Valdeor's strength."

Reina Lauressa narrowed her eyes at him for a second. She motioned with the lift of a finger, and her attendant stepped forward. She told him to put Usher's name down for a private audience after dinner, the soonest she was able, as it was already mid-afternoon.

"Is there anything else?" Her face troubled, she clenched her hands on her armrests.

"May I have your leave to research a connected matter in the archives?" He hoped that he would find answers to his many questions there. The archives contained all the knowledge gathered over the ages. If any place carried documented lists of rings and wayposts, the archives would.

Lauressa raised her brow a fraction. "Of course." Then she motioned a steward, who stepped forward at her request. "Take this man to the archives."

"Yes, Your Majesty." He motioned Usher to follow him.

Usher bowed again in reverence. "Until tonight, Your Majesty."

She nodded and turned to the next subject waiting for her attention.

The steward led Usher out of the throne room. After several hallways, he took a torch from the wall and lit it. Opening a door, he led the way down a dank, stone stairwell into the bowels of the palace. The air was chill, smelling of dust and mold.

After passing several landings with narrow halls that led off the main staircase, they reached a door and entered. A large room was filled with rows upon rows of shelving, which held parchments, scrolls, and large tomes crammed in every space. A few large tables sat in the room's center for reading, ceiling lamps hung above them. The tables were well-lit islands in the gloom.

The steward rang a bell, then left when a tall man dressed in black robes, nearly old enough to be Usher's father, slowly shuffled over. He had a long, narrow face and beard. His bushy eyebrows raised in inquiry. "May I be of assistance? I am the head archivist, Libran."

"I am pleased to meet you. If I may introduce myself, I am Usher Warbleton, 12th of my line to serve the High Kings and Reinas as Lord of the Way, and by right of my inheritance to serve as the elder of the Waystation Keepers." He hoped to impress the man with his formal title and get his full cooperation.

Libran put his hand up to his chest emitting a gasp. "My, my! I have, of course, read of your kind, but I thought waykeepers had died out a century ago."

Libran turned toward the back of the room and called out, "Come, come, Edo, and meet a live waykeeper!" Usher just glimpsed another ancient behind a of row of shelving.

Edo looked a little younger than Libran, but still had more

wrinkles and gray hair than Usher. He was shorter, rotund, and clean shaven. Bobbing his head forward, he reminded Usher of a sparrow.

Edo smiled shyly. "I've heard of waykeepers, but I'm curious to know what you do."

"We help travelers. We feed them and let them sleep in our dwellings, the original inns. And we can send them through the waypost portals to their next destination."

"Then you practice magic?" Edo took a step back.

"No, no. We don't use spells. Think of our rings as keys. Touch the waypost with the ring, and poof, we open the door." He held up his hand and they both admired his ring.

"I hope you could help me." Usher smiled at them. "You see, I need any documentation of the trinity rings. Not so much what they do, but where they may be found today.

"Also, any figures on how many waystations exist. I brought a copy of a map with all the locations I and my fellow waykeepers have managed to find over the years. I will give it to you for your records." Usher rummaged through his sack of belongings and held out a small, tightly rolled parchment.

Edo took it with a look of gratitude. "Oh my, my! Something new for our archives. We have the greatest collection of maps in the land."

"If you could show me maps of the wayposts' locations, that would greatly help my quest." Usher gazed from one to the other.

"Let me think, let me think." Libran stroked his beard and looked up to the left.

Usher waited patiently.

Edo rolled out Usher's map. "Wonderful, wonderful!"

He looked up from studying it. "The Reina had the archives moved here from the castle in the Domadarian Forest. Feornson banished all books and scrolls. Evil man! Imagine banishing learning!" He shook his head in disbelief. "Libran and I secretly carted them to Forestown many years ago. Quite, quite the endeavor to keep them safe. So much nicer to be back home."

Meanwhile Libran muttered under his breath and went to the far end of the room, pulling out one scroll at a time, glancing at each, and replacing it.

Usher walked over to the tables and looked eagerly at the maps of the realm rolled out. He wished he had time to spend weeks reading all the material they had on the portals and their history. Who knew what secrets may be hidden in the archives? But he had an impending feeling in his bones that time wasn't on their side. Something menaced them from beyond Valdeor's borders. Why did foreigners have a sudden interest in the portals?

After half an hour, Libran brought three scrolls, four parchments, and two books to the main table. Edo hurriedly cleared off a space, heaping all the maps on another work area. Dust rose in the air, causing the three men to cough.

When the dust settled, Libran put down his cache. Usher thanked them, sat down, and eagerly started to read.

Somewhere he hoped to find the number of rings unaccounted for, which might give him an idea of how many enemies they faced.

Chapter 11

Where the Glame River met the sea, Tulken Harbor's whitewashed houses shone with their green roofs. On the headland jutting into the sea, the great cathedral with its emerald green dome seemed to watch over the town.

The Bottom's Up Tavern was a bustling place in the center of the busy harbor town, not as rough as some of the taverns closer to the wharf. The location meant travelers and locals patronized it. It boasted food and song along with drinks. Upon arriving in town, Donella easily got a job as a barmaid since another girl had recently left to tend her sick father. Donella was one of three barmaids in such a popular place and shared a room in the attic with the girls.

At the same time, Guy found a job as a dishwasher at the Black Sails Tavern, on the wharf, in the seedy part of Tulken Harbor. Donella knew he was unhappy with the situation. "How am I to keep an eye on you if we only meet once a day? What if one of the conspirators recognizes you?"

"I can take care of myself, Guy. But it's sweet of you to worry." Donella crossed her arms. "It's better if we keep our ears open at multiple spots."

He reluctantly agreed, after much persuasion, and a promise

they would meet every morning before beginning the day's work.

On her third night, the Bottom's Up bar did a brisk business and Donella could hardly keep up.

Tolly owned the tavern and worked as barman. Shirt straining over rolls of fat, he wore a perpetually harried expression. He wiped his brow as he passed Donella humming in the storeroom. He stopped, frowning. "My singer has laryngitis. I don't suppose you can sing?"

She smiled and sang the refrain of a popular song.

"Here, Cassie!" He grabbed one of the other barmaids as she passed by with empty tankards. "You and Bess will have to hustle tonight. This girl is going to sing, so you will do her work this evening."

"Me sister lost her job last week." Cassie's apron covered her buxom figure. She pursed her lips together. "Can I send the errand boy for her to join us?"

"Very well but tell him to be quick. We have a ship's worth of customers tonight."

Tolly whipped off Donella's apron and motioned for her to release her hair from its ribbon. "You keep them drinking to yer songs tonight and you'll earn a gold crown."

"I'll accompany myself on the zythrin."

Donella raced upstairs. She retrieved the instrument tucked away with her belongings. Coming back down, Donella's palms began to sweat as Tolly cleared a place and introduced her.

Fishermen, merchants, and sailors turned to look at her. Their clothes ranged from rough homespun to fine linen. They smelled of fish, tobacco, and exotic cologne.

Every eye seemed upon her as her feet refused to move. Her throat suddenly dried up, so she took a sip of ale from Cassie's newly filled tankard.

She pushed down her unaccustomed nerves and forced herself to walk out from behind the bar. Her voice warbled as she started. Silence met her for a brief moment as the patrons seemed to decide if she was worth listening to. Many turned away taking up their conversations.

Tolly frowned at her, wiping his hands down his apron.

Donella relaxed her shoulders, focusing on her zythrin, not the audience, and began plucking a tune. She drew a deep breath and sang out the first notes of a sea shanty. Soon most of the patrons ceased their conversations. She knew success when the sailors raised their mugs and belted out the chorus with her.

Tolly beamed at the end of the shanty and made hand motions for her to keep singing.

Donella sang another popular tune with a lively melody. A sailor pulled out a mouth harp and joined her. Soon, she had patrons tapping their feet in time. Several offers of ale followed, so with a flirty smile she took a pull of the handsomest man's offering. That got rounds of catcalls and laughter.

By the evening's end she earned a gold crown from Tolly and coins from the sailors who flipped them at her feet in the time-honored custom of showing approval.

"Barmaids are aplenty. Singers not so much." Tolly winked as he gave her the shiny coin. "You can earn a gold piece every night if you perform like that."

She grinned at him and tucked the gold away in a pocket. The money would be handy while she waited for Odem to contact her.

She shared a room in the tavern's attic with Cassie and Bess. It had one big bed that the two girls shared and a trundle bed that Donella pulled out from under it at night. In the corner stood a tiny washstand with a streaked mirror precariously perched on it, leaning against the wall. A few hooks in the wall held their dresses and cloaks. The tiny fireplace would compete with the ill-fitting window in the cold weather. Fortunately, the weather was warm.

She decided to enlist the girls' help as they readied for bed.

"Do either of you own a shawl I could borrow? Or feathers for my hair? I want to look the part of a singer." Donella placed some her small coins on the bed. "You both do the evening's hard work, so I'll share my tips with you."

That loosened their tongues, so she asked them how they served patrons who didn't speak the Valdeoran language.

"Most sailors know the word for ale or drink," Cassie giggled. "Though you can tell them foreigners by their pointed beards."

"Or their pearl earrings," Bess sighed, her brush stilled in her red hair. "I'd like to get me one."

"Do they come in often?" Donella sat on her bed and hugged her knees.

"Not so much in the past. Although there have been more in the last few weeks." Cassie put a feather in Donella's riotous black curls and contemplated the effect. "You could put a pretty ribbon in your hair. The market is open in the morning. I'll take you with me. Then we can find my brother-in-law and ask him if my sister can work here every night. They could use the coins."

Cassie's long blond hair hid her face as she tucked her earnings in a cotton pouch and placed it under her straw mattress. She pushed her hair back from her face, glancing at Donella. "Tolly runs a decent establishment. No letting the sailors harass the girls in his employment. Not like other places." Cassie shuddered. "There be some awful tales. You be careful in a city like this," she warned Donella.

"We girls stick together when we go out after hours." Bess wrapped her arms around her thin frame.

"Oh, I came to town with my brother. You will see me with him sometimes." Donella glanced at each girl and leaned closer to them. She lowered her voice for dramatic effect. "But maybe you can keep an eye open for me. You see, my brother and I ran away. If you ever see a man wearing a ring like mine, will you let me know? I don't want him to catch me."

Both girls nodded, eyes wide.

Now Donella had two extra pairs of eyes looking for the Forest Deer Inn plotters.

But she worried. Odem was late. She and Guy had been in town for several days. Surely Odem should have been here before them. *I hope something bad hasn't befallen him. Maybe Guy has some news.*

But when she met Guy the next day before dawn, he looked grim. "No sign of Odem," he answered to her question.

They stood behind the bakery in the town's center. The baker reprimanding her hapless apprentice disturbed the quiet. Scents of yeast and baking bread drifted in the air, making Donella's mouth water.

The townspeople were stirring. A man drove pigs past their alleyway. Sounds of merchants calling out to one another came faintly from the marketplace around the corner as the stalls began to open.

"A shipload of sailors showed up at my place last night. I didn't like the look of them." Guy's face hardened.

Guy shifted his weight from one foot to the other. "I have never seen pirates, but I imagine they would look like this lot. Be careful! Don't go around by yourself." He rubbed his hand down his face. " I stood in the back of the tavern and heard you sing last night. You're very talented. But I wish we were out of this. A seedy tavern is no place for a nice girl."

"You better watch *your* step. You are an easy mark, not being from the city," she retorted. His dismissal of her ability to take care of herself stung. Although she was secretly pleased at his compliment.

How is it I can feel both irritated and pleased with him at the same time?

He grimaced at her tone, but said no more as they parted to

go to work after buying fresh buns to break their fast.

Two days later, at the same alleyway corner, Donella tapped her foot. Guy usually met her here, near the market, where they both shopped for supplies, but this was the second day he hadn't shown up.

She feared something had happened to him and it was her fault for not listening. A heavy mantle of foreboding descended on her. It was unlike him not to contact her, knowing she'd worry. Should she search for him?

Maybe Guy was right. He could be in danger.

She hung around the market as long as she could, then returned to the tavern with her purchase of a red hair ribbon. She couldn't come back empty-handed after being gone so long.

As she strolled, her glance darted around, keeping an eye out for Guy. But he was nowhere in sight.

Donella was tempted to use the nearest waypost and go directly to Odem, using his shell token. But he'd directed her to stay put and wait, learning as much as she could using whatever means necessary. For that reason, she faked a cough the evening before so she could work as a barmaid and listen to the loud crew members who entered, two of them spouting off in a foreign tongue until others of their group silenced them.

And it had paid off.

She had more news for Odem. Last night she learned about the ship that Guy spoke of last time they met. It was set to sail this morning for Laketown, on Valdeor's southeast shore, with a cargo of horses. A hundred horses.

Donella thought that odd.

So tonight, Donella planned to give the same excuse. The foreign crew might be gone, but she'd keep a lookout for Odem. The two weeks he had dictated had passed. Where was he? She itched to share the information with him. If she really was in danger, she had to make sure someone knew her information.

That evening, as she passed out mugs of ale, she longed for Odem or Usher to walk through the door so she could pour out her fears.

Halfway through the evening, someone bumped Donella's elbow. With a muttered "sorry" came the feeling of something dropped in her pocket. She finished her order, then scurried back to the bar. Pretending she dropped a coin, she bent under the bar to read the note she found in her apron.

It read: *11 o'clock, corner of the alleyway.* She tucked it back in her pocket, stood up, and glanced at the clock. Two more hours.

The time seemed to drag.

Donella quickly threw off her apron a few minutes before 11 o'clock. She grabbed her old shawl and left from the back door. She crept to the corner and peered around. A drunken sailor weaved his way to the wharf. She hung back to let him pass.

As he came even with her, he hissed, "Follow me to the wharf. Keep your distance till then."

Donella flinched, then relaxed at the familiar voice. She let a moment elapse, then drawing her shawl around her head, and her courage with it, she turned the corner and followed him, keeping a distance between them.

The dark made everything look different. Donella nearly stumbled several times on the uneven pavement. Only a few bar patrons shuffled toward their ship or home. Something darted out of the alley ahead, making Donella's heart leap. A cat yowled and raced away.

When they neared the water, the smell of rotten fish and salt water assailed her. The moored ships creaked eerily in the quiet night. The only other sound was the steady lapping of water.

The man she followed lost his drunken gait. He strode to a dingy tied to the dock. He steadied it while she got in, then stepped aboard. Taking the oars, he rowed in silence until they were out of hearing of anyone on the wharf.

The night was cool, a crescent moon and stars twinkling in the deep black sky. Donella could taste the salt as she licked her lips. The slap of the water decreased as they pulled farther from shore, while the splashing of the oars drowned out all other sounds.

Finally, the man locked the oars and let the dingy drift. He straightened up and Odem's face peeked from under his cap. The shadows made his expression sterner than she remembered. "What news do you have for me?"

Donella hardly knew where to begin, even though she anticipated this question for weeks. Lowering her shawl from her head, she wrapped it tightly around her shoulders against the chill breeze drifting over the open water. She organized her thoughts.

"A foreign ship docked here recently. Guy thought them suspicious. And I haven't heard from him in two days! That is so unlike him." Worry bubbled up inside her again at the thought. "Last night, I learned that the ship planned to sail for Laketown at first tide in the morning." Donella bit her lip. "And do you know what cargo they carried? Horses. One hundred of them."

In the moonlight, Donella could see Odem frown more deeply. "Just what an invading army would need," his voice sounded grim.

"There's more." Donella clasped her hands in her lap. "Soon after returning to the Forest Deer Inn, the horse trader, Lord Tastaver, rode up, leading a long string of horses. He asked me for water. I was stunned to see he wore a waykeeper's ring."

Odem sucked in his breath.

"Not only that," Donella leaned closer, keeping her voice low, "but Usher came to warn me the same day. Then Guy told Usher, Evodia, and me that thieves waylaid him. He caught up to them at the horse fair in Capall when they tried to sell Seeker. To prove the horse was his, he pointed out the mark on Seeker's withers. And because of that, the symbol was exposed to many bystanders."

"He didn't lose the horse!" Odem broke in.

"No. Guy managed to ride away. Like I was saying, Usher is very worried that the plotters have gained access to our rings."

"You said the horse trader wore one. Do the others? Have you seen any?"

"No. But we think the conspirator in the woods probably had one as well. How else did he disappear so completely? You were there." Donella nibbled her fingertip. "But Usher estimates at least fifty waystations once existed. And where are all those rings now?"

"Great stars above!" Odem clenched the oars, his knuckles turning white. "If an enemy kingdom possessed a fraction of those rings, we would never be able to stop them. They could send spies or mounted soldiers through the portals, unmolested, anywhere in the realm! This could spell disaster!"

They were silent, wrapped in their own thoughts, as Odem rowed them back to shore.

Chapter 12

*D*ishes clattered and soap flew as Guy tried to keep up with the tankards and greasy plates that continually needed washing. He didn't like the Black Sails Tavern with its cheap beer, which appealed to the lowest customers. Nor did he like its owner, a short-tempered man. But this was the only job Guy found when they arrived in Tulken Harbor a week ago.

Only this morning Donella had told him to watch himself.

What danger am I in? How can I learn anything if I cannot even hear the patrons in the barroom?

"You, there. Wipe up the spills on the tables. Then finish those mugs," the taverner barked as the evening wore on. Lean and brawny with bulging muscles, he boasted to his customers of his wrestling prowess when a young man. "And no sneaking off before it is done. I fired the last boy for that." He stomped off.

Few sailors remained, and most of those were passed out. Guy gingerly stepped around the ones sleeping it off on the floor. The room reeked of stale brew and unwashed bodies, mixed with tobacco smoke.

He wiped his brow with the back of his hand. Anyone here could be a conspirator. Even in the hot room, a cold shiver ran up his spine at the thought.

Guy wished Donella would listen to reason and leave this town, letting those with more experience catch the plotters. *Who knew what the spies would do with Donella and me if they caught us!*

After washing the tables, he stepped outside to empty the trash in the alley.

A partial moon made the shadows stark. A rat squeaked nearby. The stink of rotting garbage mingled with the tang of seawater.

Hearing a soft step behind him, Guy started to turn. Someone threw a bag over Guy's head and clasped his flailing arms in an iron grip.

Guy jabbed with his elbows and heard a muffled oompf as he hit his target. But his assailant didn't let go.

"Hold him!" a voice hissed in front of Guy.

Guy continued to struggle and kick while his captors bound Guy until he was tightly trussed.

An explosion of pain in the back of his head made Guy cry out.

Blackness smothered him.

Guy woke up with a crashing headache. That, and a swaying motion, made his stomach heave. He couldn't see anything, and panic rose in his breast. The men had tied his hands and feet. But as he gasped for breath, he realized the bag was no longer over his head. Darkness surrounded him. He forced himself to take deep breaths.

But the motion wasn't consistent with a wagon. Something was missing—no feel of wheels turning.

The sounds of creaking penetrated the fog of his brain. A smell of tar and salty air filled his nose. His stomach threatened to empty again when he tried to sit up. He moaned and lay back down. Even though he had never been on one, his senses told him he was aboard a ship.

Time had no meaning in the dark, swaying hold. Once his stomach emptied its contents, he drifted off to sleep.

Guy had no idea how much time passed before a square of light blinded him, stabbing his eyes and causing his head to throb. Footsteps descended the ladder, and then an outline of a man leaned over him. The captor's rough hand yanked Guy to his feet and untied him.

He spoke a foreign language. When Guy didn't respond, the man prodded him, "Up on the deck, boy."

The blurry figure half pushed, half dragged Guy up the ladder.

Guy found himself on the deck of a dirty ship, recognizing some of the sailors from the tavern. He took big gulps of the fresh, salty air. He fought to control his queasy stomach.

He took in his surroundings.

Men with rings in their ears or noses wore filthy shirts, more like rags than clothes, and tattered trousers tied at the calf. Some had bandanas around their greasy locks, dark with sweat. Most went barefoot. A variety of tattoos marked their bodies. Many wore amulets around their neck engraved with a goat. It represented a religion that rejected the idea of the One Who Fashioned All. Guy was truly among enemies.

His captor shoved him toward a one-eyed man, while other men working on the deck watched, surreptitiously, from under their hooded eyelids.

"Here's one fer ye, Drake."

"This is the new boy?" The sailor towered over Guy. "Not much to look at, is he?"

A snicker came from somewhere nearby.

Drake glanced around, and all grew silent. He turned his gaze back to Guy. "I'm the deck master and you'll do as I say, boy." He motioned to Guy's detainer. "Put him to work swabbing the deck. Doesn't look like he's capable of much else." He swaggered off, yelling at anyone not doing his job to his satisfaction.

A sailor gave Guy a mop and a bucket of filthy water and put him to work. At least he knew how to do this. He kept his head down and tried not to draw any attention.

After a few hours, Guy realized that the hard work gave him an appetite, while the earlier nausea had completely vanished. Just when he feared that he was forgotten and wouldn't eat, Drake, the deck master, dismissed him to receive his ration of food from the cook. "And eat it below deck."

Descending into the hold with his bowl and bread chunk, he found one boy shared the cramped space.

"I'm Hiram."

"Guy."

Over their scant meal of watery stew, they struck up a conversion.

"How long have you been aboard?" Guy dipped his bread in the broth.

"About a month. They pressed me into service, too. I never thought to be captured by Canteor pirates when I wandered along the coast, digging for clams."

Suddenly, pounding and a horse's scream sounded through the bulkhead in the ship's main steerage. Neighing and stomping followed.

"What on earth?" Guy could barely hear himself over the noise.

Men yelled and eventually the sounds died down.

"They brought horses aboard with you," Hiram spoke over the racket. "That's our cargo."

That night, Guy fell exhausted into his hammock. He thought he would lie awake, after all that happened to him, but he fell into a dreamless slumber.

The first time Guy climbed the main mast, it was as if the world spun out of control when he looked down. He leaned his head against the cool, damp wood. Closing his eyes, he took some deep breaths. His limbs tingled and he broke out in a sweat.

"Don't worry. It is natural to feel dizzy the first time you come up." Hiram clasped the rigging near him, showing Guy the ropes. "Open your eyes and look straight ahead. Focus on the horizon."

Guy did.

A vast blue sea stretched far ahead. On his left he could see a distant coastline. Sea gulls flew below him. He could make out clouds on the horizon. He felt like a fly in a giant's world, and, as long as he didn't look down, the view filled him with awe.

Guy grinned in spite of himself as he wrapped his hands tight around the ropes.

"You'll get used to it. Just like you got your sea legs." Hiram grinned. Hiram seemed about Guy's age, slightly shorter, lanky, with a shock of black hair.

Over the next week Hiram showed him how to tell north from south, which clouds meant storms, and how to gauge distances to land.

As long as Guy did not dwell on the height, he found he didn't mind it.

Both boys could nimbly climb the mast, so the ship's master made them take turns going aloft. Once Guy got the hang of it, he found he actually enjoyed working above the rough sailors, perched with the occasional bird, feeling as if he could touch the sky. The solitary job suited him.

But Guy still had other chores. Menial ones, like emptying slop pails. "No worse than mucking out stables on the farm," Guy confided to Hiram as he threw a pail of offal over the side.

Hiram wiped his brow. "I'm a town boy, meself. Grew up on the fishing boats. But these pirates never let me on the dingy to help drag the fishing nets. Afraid I might go over the edge and escape." Hiram gave a lopsided grin. "And they'd be right."

"Here, you, boys. Clean the fish. Mend the nets." The one-eyed deck master motioned sailors to dump the day's catch and fish nets beside the boys. "Less talk. More work!"

The fishy smell, which had seemed overwhelming in the first days aboard ship, had become commonplace.

"Follow what I do." Hiram picked up a fish in one hand and a knife in the other. In one quick motion, he gutted it.

Guy, used to cleaning chickens, soon got the hang of it. In no time they had a pile of fish for the mess cook. After carting the load down to the hold and throwing salt over it, they came back to the upper deck and to the pile of the frayed nets.

"Watch and I will teach you to mend the nets." Hiram wiped the salt off his hands and picked up one corner of the nearest one.

Guy's left hand stung from the salt penetrating the many scratches he had from the rough, wet work. He rubbed it on his trousers.

Hiram glanced over at him. "What is your tattoo? Most sailors have one, but yours is unusual."

"Um, it's a family symbol. My father gave it to me." It was partially true.

Guy changed the subject. "This isn't a much different life for you, is it, Hiram?"

"Nah, I worked on the fishing boats since I could walk. Got my first gut knife at the age of six. But I miss my Da and me three brothers. I'm the eldest. I wonder how they are getting along without me."

"I never had brothers or sisters. My pa died when I was young." Guy tried to imitate Hiram's work with the net.

"Then your ma must be real lonesome without you." Hiram sat cross-legged, hunched over his work, dexterously weaving the rope.

"Stepmother," Guy corrected, "and she doesn't care about me

at all. Only that I'm not there to do all the chores."

"Well, then, when we get off this tub, you can join me father and me, and me brothers. You'll know the ropes by then. Get it?" Hiram held up the net to illustrate his joke.

Guy couldn't help but grin back. His new friend considerably lightened his plight.

Does my stepmother worry about me? Does Donella wonder what happened to me? Did either one search for me? Have they given up by now?

That night, Guy lay awake thinking about his future, if he had one, other than this captivity.

"If I have to be on a ship other than my Da's, I wish it were Valdeoran," Hiram's voice broke into Guy's thoughts. "Although not an easy life, they treat men better than slaves." Guy heard Hiram sigh in the darkened hold. "Which is what we really are on this pirate ship, named *Indomitable*. At least Valdeoran captains pay the sailors. And they sign a contract for a set length of time. Only the Creator knows how long we'll be prisoners on this tub."

"You seem to know their language. Can you teach it to me?"

"Sure. I knew some Canteoran before they captured me."

Although Guy didn't hate this way of life, he was not drawn to it either, even if he could be paid. Just like farming. Even free of his stepmother, he didn't think farm life would ever bring him joy or fulfillment. He didn't know what would.

But the birthmark on his hand might define his fate. If the raiders ever realized it wasn't a tattoo, but a portal key, he would be in serious trouble. With his power they could go anywhere in Valdeor. Towns—even well-guarded cities like Mintala—would be vulnerable to a surprise attack.

Sweat broke out at the thought. For that reason, more than slavery, he wished he could just scrape an image of the interlocking ovals in the woodwork above his hammock and step off this ship.

Not that he thought it would work, but his hand itched to try.

He could secrete the fish knife—but no, someone would discover it. Drake would question him, and his secret would be out.

Better to wait.

They had to pull into port somewhere for supplies. He'd find a way to escape and swim for shore.

After two weeks at sea, Guy still hoped for a chance to sneak away.

Gulls with shrill cries swooped the early morning catch on the deck below him.

A small fishing village appeared where the coast jutted into the sea.

Half an hour into his shift on the mast, Guy called out, "Land!" As they drew closer, he counted only a dozen cottages dotting the headland. His shoulders drooped. He could disappear much easier into a big, bustling seaport.

The captain would never choose him to row the dingy ashore for supplies. Although no weakling—farm work had made him strong for his age—the captain had many burly men to choose from.

Even as he climbed down while the sailors adjusted the sails, he decided to slip over the side in the commotion. But a heavy hand descended on his shoulder as he approached the landward side. Drake glared at him through his one eye.

"Below decks with the likes of you." He pushed Guy toward the steerage opening. Guy defied him for an instant, then gave over. The six-foot-tall burly mate holding open the hatch was more than a match for him.

As Guy stumbled down the dark steps, he heard Hiram's voice above him. "But I only want to watch. I won't be any trouble."

"Your middle name is trouble. Stay below until we are underway again." The deck master's voice moved away as he closed the hatch.

"Hiram?" Guy stretched forth a hand.

"I nearly made it to the side!" Hiram's voice was charged with emotion. "I planned to swim for shore." Hiram's shoulder touched Guy's.

"Me, too." Guy's voice shook as frustration coursed through him. *The first opportunity to escape and we're stuck in the ship's belly.*

In the dim light afforded by the gaps in the weathered hatch, they sat down on the floor.

"We need to make a plan. Maybe we can jump from the mast into the sea. Drake wouldn't be able to stop us." Hiram's words lifted Guy's glum mood, but only for a moment.

"Nah. We'd never clear the ship's side. We'd land dead on the deck." Guy placed his chin in his hand. "If another ship attacked us, then we could escape overboard." Guy drew the waypost symbol in the floor's dust with his finger. "But if we haven't been attacked by Valdeoran ships by now, I doubt we will be." Guy rubbed out the mark.

The ship swung gently after a prolonged clanking sound. "They've dropped anchor," Hiram informed him.

Clomping and stomping sounds mixed with curses and neighs. "Whoa, stupid beast!" a voice rang out on the other side of the bulkhead.

"They must be unloading the horses." Guy clenched his fists. If only he could sneak off, hidden among the horses.

An hour passed, by Guy's reckoning. As the day progressed, the heat in the hold became unbearable. Sweat trickled down his back. He wiped his forehead. The gentle rocking at anchor, combined with the heat, made his stomach queasy.

Hiram sat with his knees pulled up and his hands hung between them. "I watched the crew load them at the dock where you joined us. There must be over a hundred."

Guy wondered what the raiders planned to do with them.

They could carry an army.

If only I could get word to Odem!

Each was silently lost in his own thoughts, as they listened to the endless disembarkation of horses.

The close air below decks suffocating him, Guy longed for the tangy air above deck.

Hiram slapped his leg. "I have an idea." He laughed out loud, then lowered his voice. "We make them stop in a bigger port."

Guy stared at Hiram's backlit image. "How do you propose we do that?"

"What if we run low on food?" Hiram rubbed his hands together. "Or even better, fresh water?"

"Why, we stop again, of course." Guy pulled up one knee and encircled it with his hands, staring at his friend's outline.

"You and I are the ones who sight the land, right? What if the next time we see a coastal town, the one on the mast alerts the other. Then a twist of the knife in a water barrel, or a net accidentally lost while fishing, and suddenly the ship needs to make an unexpected port call!" Hiram's voice danced with excitement. "You must admit, it's brilliant!"

Between sighting land and pulling into port, would enough time lapse to deplete the supplies? Enough to warrant a landing party?

And if they were caught? Or even suspected?

Dubious about Hiram's plan, Guy shuddered to think of the consequences. *But what choice do I have?*

"Alright. I'm in." Guy punched Hiram in the shoulder. "But this better work. I do not want to be thrown overboard for a sea monster's meal." He had heard the tales of monsters of the deep with sharp teeth in double rows and seen their fins cut through the waves. He had no desire to see one up close.

Chapter 13

Usher lost track of time in the archives, only remembering his appointment when his stomach protested. He panted when he arrived in the antechamber of the dining hall for his evening meal with the royals. His calves ached from climbing the stairs. He straightened his robe as the Master of Ceremonies opened the chamber door and beckoned him inside.

Light flowed through the ceiling-to-floor windows. A citrus smell tickled his nose, refreshing his senses, as a light breeze moved the curtains. A small grove of orange trees stood in the garden beyond the window.

The table was intimately laid for three with two lit candelabra and a bowl of roses in the center. Servants in royal blue livery waited behind each chair to serve the meal. They had placed a setting for Usher on Reina Lauressa's left, while Prince Alloryn sat on her right.

The royal couple waited with a giant wolfhound at their feet.

Usher bowed. "Your Majesty. Your Highness. I am your obedient servant." The dog walked over and sniffed Usher's shoes.

"Please forgive Trekker's curiosity." Alloryn snapped his fingers and the dog returned to him. "He is ever our faithful guardian."

"Is he the same one who accompanied you on your quest?"

Alloryn smiled. "Yes. Old now, though he continues to sire new generations."

Lauressa motioned for Usher to take his seat and turned to her husband. "This is the elder waykeeper I mentioned to you."

"I am most pleased to meet you. In all my travels, training for six years throughout Valdeor, I never met with a waykeeper. My mentor Justinian did point out the waystations and sat they were connected to legendary hospitality. But even he thought you were just that—a legend."

"Ah, I heard of the great warrior, Justinian, who trained you. I believe my grandfather met him." Usher waggled his eyebrows. "My grandfather was a waykeeper himself, but I doubt he advertised the fact. In those days, the populace began to label them sorcerers and shun them. But when just a lad, Grandfather witnessed the duel between Justinian and Myrkr, the murderer of the Reina's father."

Alloryn begged Usher for details and a pleasant half hour passed while servants brought the first course of beef in mushroom gravy. The Reina did not indulge in rich, exotic foods for her table. She was an example of moderation to her subjects.

Her intelligent eyes darted between them as she listened to Usher's tale and Alloryn's questions, until a lull occurred in the conversation.

"Ever since we took refuge in a waystation in the mountains during a snowstorm, I have been intrigued to learn about your order." Her eyes lit up eagerly.

"The lost history of the Waystation (or Wayhouse) Keepers. Well, well!" Usher sat back in his chair, careful not to let a burp escape, folded his hands over his stomach, and told them a version of what he taught Guy.

"I have heard this tale's end." Lauressa signaled the head waiter to serve dessert. "Gilbreth built the first and greatest shrine to the One Who Fashioned All. I remember thinking that it must be magnificent since our own cathedral is superb, and I could not imagine anything grander."

Once they served the creamy pudding and fruit, Lauressa dismissed the servants.

"Now we can speak freely." She wrinkled her brow. "But I still do not understand how the wayposts come into it."

"The wayposts guided the pilgrims traveling to the shrine. Eventually waykeepers built inns on the pilgrim's road to accommodate the large influx of travelers. The rings allowed the wearers to move from one waypost to another." Usher unclasped his hands and removed his ring. He handed it to Lauressa, who after inspecting it, passed it to her husband.

"This is the reason I have come to you today. With only a handful of waykeepers left, most of the rings are lost. I'm concerned, because those of us who wear them are initiated in how to use them to travel from one waypost—or portal, as it's also called—to another."

After glancing at the ring, Alloryn handed it back. "Portals? Traveling by rings? I do not understand." Alloryn frowned at Usher.

"I think a demonstration is in order." Usher donned his ring and hefted his weight from the chair. "If you would please follow me, I have found a waypost in the palace grounds."

Prince Alloryn gave his wife his arm and they followed Usher out of the dining room doors that opened into the palace garden. They walked on the gravel path, past the fragrant orange trees and the kitchen herb garden, the air thick with the scents of rosemary and dill. Usher stopped at a gate connecting the inner palace grounds with the outer grounds.

On the other side of the gate the palace guards barracks and training area stretched to the outer walls.

Usher pointed out the doorway's edge. Upon closer

inspection, the doorway had one wooden lintel and one stone lintel.

"You see, the waypost has been incorporated into the wall at some point."

Usher reached out his ringed left hand. Mist gathered in the door gap, spinning in a spiral. Usher summoned an image of his home. The herb garden disappeared, and the road and familiar mountains beside his dwelling appeared in front of the three.

Lauressa took an involuntary step back, and Alloryn let out a surprised gasp. Alloryn turned to Usher, all friendliness gone, and gripped his sword hilt.

"What magic is this, old man? Do you seek to harm the Reina?" Alloryn placed himself in front of his wife.

Before Usher could reassure them, Lauressa moved beside her husband. She grasped his arm and spoke, "Calm yourself, Alloryn. He means no harm." Her eyes narrowed. "Vague memories stir in my mind. I have seen this before, in my childhood."

"I didn't mean to alarm you." Usher stepped away from the portal. The image faded into the mist, which dissipated. In a moment the birds in the garden began chirping again.

"My ring activates the portal. But over a dozen rings are missing, Your Majesty. Thankfully, I found some of them in your own archives." He somberly glanced from one to the other. His usual humorous patter had dried up at the situation's seriousness.

Reina Lauressa touched her medallion with her right hand. Prince Alloryn stood with crossed arms.

Usher continued, "I fear there is grave danger to Valdeor." And he proceeded to tell them about Donella and the foreign conspirator in the woods, the horse trader with a ring, and the plotters meeting at the Forest Deer Inn. When he finished, he added, "There is something else I would like you to see in the archives."

Lauressa dropped her hand. "This is disturbing news, indeed. Proceed."

Usher, Prince Alloryn, Reina Lauressa, and Libran the archivist stood in the archive center. Candles guttered low, barely throwing their light past the four gathered in the room, deep within the palace. Partly unrolled maps, dusty scrolls, stacks of books, and a box of rings haphazardly littered the table before them.

Libran rolled out a map and put a gnarled finger on it. "I count nearly fifty wayposts."

"But there is no knowing if fifty rings existed." Usher rubbed his bald spot. "I myself man three waystations regularly, and I know others do the same. Over my lifetime, I have hunted and found dozens of others. That is too many for one person to maintain." He shifted position. "Maybe one waykeeper has always manned more than one waystation. Most aren't full-service inns, but small dwellings on the pilgrim's way."

Lauressa shook the box of rings. "Thirty rings are a better number than you led me to believe existed, if each waykeeper ran two stations. But if each waystation required its own keeper—"

"—there are too many rings unaccounted for," Alloryn finished for her. He crossed his muscular arms over his chest, frowning at Usher. "But the ring numbers are academic. What we need is a count of conspirators with the ability to open your portals. You say not everyone who tries to use the rings is successful."

Usher pushed away the scroll. "It takes focus. If one doesn't have the inborn ability to activate or sense the nearest waypost, then the ring is just a pretty trinket. All but one waykeeper need to leave tokens in order to travel back to a waypost they find. So, no, the rings will not work for most people."

"I would like to be present at the inn where the conspirators gather. We desperately need more information." Alloryn turned his head to Lauressa and raised a brow.

Usher watched as the husband and wife communicated a silent question and answer.

Lauressa broke the connection and faced Usher. "Your description of the plotters sounds as if they come from the pagan nation of Canteor. For many centuries they raided the eastern seaboard. They even established a colony for a time in Samarantha, killing those who refused to bow down before their goat god. My great-grandfather defeated them and signed a treaty with them over a century and a half ago. But our realm has had no dealings with them since."

Lauressa's brow creased. "I would like to know the state of their government." She tapped a delicate finger on her cheek. "I must see to bulking up our navy. Even send a merchant ship to spy under cover of trade. There is much to do."

Alloryn leaned his fists on the table, his intense gaze meeting Usher's. "Tomorrow, you and I leave at dawn for Forest Deer Inn."

Usher nodded, straightening his spine. "I am at your service, Your Highness. We may have more information when we get there. I directed my fellow waykeepers to keep a lookout for strange things."

The next morning, Usher found Prince Alloryn eating breakfast alone.

"I am delaying our trip because Reina Lauressa is feeling ill."

"Oh, dear. What ails her?" Usher paused dishing up eggs from the bowl the servant held for him.

"I don't know. The Royal physician is with her now."

Prince Alloryn pushed aside his half-eaten meal. "I wanted to speak to you of an important matter. After yesterday's discussion, I spoke to Lauressa of removing the waypost and placing it beyond the outer walls. Is that possible? Will it still work?"

"I think the placement was well thought out. It allows a messenger access to the ruler in times of emergency yet being situated near the barracks allows it to be monitored at all hours. But I will research it this morning."

Usher could understand Prince Alloryn's concern that it was too near the palace. A nefarious person with a ring could use it to breach the inner walls. But Usher desired Prince Alloryn to keep the waypost in the palace enclave.

"I will consult with the Reina. She expressed a desire for its use as a courier system. It would save a great deal of time passing messages to strategic places." Alloryn departed.

Usher retrieved a cloak against the chill of the stone room and descended to the archives. Libran eagerly greeted him. They chatted a few minutes about yesterday's meeting with the Reina.

"The prince told me she is ill."

"I heard rumors among the servants that they either suspected an enemy's poison or food poisoning." Libran shook his head sorrowfully. "I hope she recovers soon."

Edo hunched over a table. He looked up as Usher's shadow fell upon the scroll he worked on. "The Reina asked for me to draw several copies of the map of Valdeor, paying special attention to the coastlines." A large map of Valdeor lay stretched open with piles of books holding it in place.

"She shows great foresight." Usher nodded and moved to the other table.

The archives fascinated him. The central table had the previous days research still scattered on it. Sitting, Usher picked a scroll at random. Details of a waykeeper's life, like his own experiences, filled the page. As he read other scrolls, he realized many ancient waykeepers kept journals. Some went back hundreds of years when waystations were popular, though few people made pilgrimages even that far back. Only fragments of scrolls survived from times even earlier.

One of these fragments described the great shrine the pilgrims sought as having "walls of sparkling gold. . . towering spirals of glass . . . the immense size dwarfing the penitent."

These words made Usher long to see the magnificent structure for himself.

Wondering if drawing the trinity symbol on a hewn rock would create a new portal, Usher searched for mentions of who built them. He read in a thick tome with faded print that the winged Guardian of Valdeor placed the wayposts a thousand years ago for the pilgrims to find the great shrine.

So the loss of even one post wasn't an option.

Reading further, he learned the waystation keepers' calling was originally a religious one. Somehow that didn't surprise him. It had devolved over time to an innkeeper.

In the next chapter, Usher read one could determine another person's previous destination using the ring that person wore. The book told of emptying one's mind of any images and concentrating on the ring's previous position.

That knowledge could prove useful.

Only insistent hunger pains finally roused him to seek food. He reluctantly left the archives and climbed the many flights of stairs into the main part of the palace.

No one was in the dining room, but a cold luncheon lay spread out, so Usher helped himself.

Strolling into the gardens, Usher soaked up the sunshine after his hours in the windowless library. Eventually his rambling walk led him back to the waypost. Desirous of seeing his dwelling, he touched the post. Closing his eyes, he concentrated. He imagined his home, which he hadn't visited in a month. His garden would be long dead. But catastrophes did not wait on the growing season.

He opened his eyes as the spiraling mist enveloped him. But

before his home fully coalesced, he felt another presence trying to access the portal.

He stiffened. This had never happened before! *If we had more waykeepers, this might become a common occurrence.*

Usher stared blankly at the post. *Maybe Guy was trying to come through!*

Usher emptied his mind so the boy could enter.

A black silhouetted figure appeared in the mist. Usher instinctively stepped back. The presence stepped out of the fog on the other side of the gate into the training grounds. Scimitar drawn, he quickly glanced around, assessing the situation. He called out in a foreign tongue, and eleven more men clad in black followed him through the portal in quick succession before it closed.

Usher fell back farther, heart pumping. He had not anticipated this.

The palace was under attack!

The invaders spread out, while soldiers who had been standing idle in the distance withdrew their swords. A horn's blare signaled 'To Arms.' The barracks erupted with soldiers cramming on their helmets, pikes or swords in their hands. The Captain of the Palace Guards led his men. Swords clanged. Pierced, men screamed. Both sides lost limbs and lives. Guards outnumbered the black clad invaders, yet the elite fighting group held its ground against the Reina's force.

Suddenly, another man joined the fray. Prince Alloryn's sword flashed like a golden arc of death. A chop to a gut. Swirl and lunge. Slash the back of someone's legs. Hack another's arm off. Grim and deadly. No other swordsman could move like a hurricane of force.

The last invader, though he fought well, met his death at the prince's hand.

Prince Alloryn commanded, "Captain Rodrek search the

bodies of the enemy and then dispose of them." The soldiers began separating several of their comrades from the invaders.

Usher opened the garden gate and stepped through. He approached the prince. "I am sorry, Your Highness. I should have foreseen this. My opening of the waypost may be the reason the enemy found this particular portal."

"It is not your fault." Prince Alloryn wiped the sweat off his forehead. "At least the waypost is situated near the barracks, as you pointed out earlier. Or no telling how many civilians would have died."

"Is there any word from the doctors? How does the Reina do today?"

"Ah, friend, that is the good news." The grim look left the prince's eyes. "I was coming to find you. My wife is not poisoned. Her condition is a time for rejoicing." He smiled at Usher's confused face. "The Reina is expecting an heir."

The emotionally charged air went from sorrow at the death and carnage the invaders had wrought, to joy. "That is good news, Your Highness."

Usher rubbed his chin. "I first thought these intruders invaded directly from their home country—"

Prince Alloryn frowned, interrupting, "How so? Is that even possible? I thought you said it was difficult to travel far distances unless you had visited previously?"

"Upon reflection, I think they must have come from somewhere in Valdeor itself."

Prince Alloryn's brow creased. "Does that mean you can trace where those men came from?"

"I can try." Usher walked over to the black-clad invaders. Overcoming his revulsion, he inspected each man's hands. Usher removed the ring from the leader.

Walking up to the post, Usher held out the conspirator's ring with his ringless hand, concentrating on the ring itself. It opened to its previous location—just as the archival scrolls described. Beyond lay a desert land, sand and scrub brush in endless waves, with bare hills in the far distance.

Usher made a move to step through when a hand grasped his arm.

"Wait!" The prince wiped the Crestin Sword free of blood on an enemy's black cloak. A ruby in the hilt caught the light as he sheathed it. "We will enter together."

"Put your hand on my shoulder," Usher told the prince, then pulled them both through the portal. Stepping onto the hot sand, Usher turned his head around to check if the prince remained with him as he no longer felt the prince's hand.

"Disorienting." Prince Alloryn straightened quickly from a half crouch and took in the bare landscape. "But where did the interlopers come from? There is nothing here."

Usher followed the prince's hand motion as it took in the uninhabited, desolate place where they stood.

"Good question, Your Highness." He searched his surroundings. This place's waypost leaned precariously over, its symbol barely discernible from the prevailing wind's scouring. A dusty trail led off to the distant nowhere. Usher could see no habitation in this barren land.

"What now?" Prince Alloryn asked, shading his eyes as he strained to see in every direction.

"I think they are untrained in the ring's use. They may not have been able to travel directly from their place of origin to the palace. This could be a jumping-off point." Usher rubbed his bald head.

"Then we have no way to know where they came from?" Alloryn squinted in the strong light, his hand straying to the Crestin Sword's hilt.

Without speaking, Usher held up the foreigner's ring again to the tilted waypost. He concentrated on the oval design, instead of forming an image of where he wished to go. After a few minutes of intense concentration, a bustling harbor materialized through the mist.

Usher's thoughts strayed to Donella and Guy. By now they should've headed to Tulken Harbor if they had no luck at the garrison. Surely, they had connected with Odem by now.

"Take my arm, Your Highness. This, I believe, is where they originated." Usher led them through the portal, wondering if they would all meet up and solve this dilemma.

Chapter 14

Fortunately, the raiders neither threw Guy to the sea monsters, nor did he have to pierce a water barrel and risk being discovered in the act of sabotage. Not a week passed before an opportunity presented itself for escape.

The weather turned rough. A summer storm blew in. Guy and Hiram spent four hour shifts in the rain and wind watching for shoals and rocks.

Pushing his hair out of his eyes for the dozenth time that hour, Guy squinted into the storm. *Was that a rock jutting out of the sea?* Heart pounding, holding on with a death grip to the rigging with his left hand, he signaled to turn starboard with his right by waving a white cloth. The wind tried to rip it from his hand, but he clung to it. His life depended on signaling the crew. If the ship hit the rock, all aboard would be lost.

The ship veered to the right. Slow at first, then making way faster as the mainsail below him caught the wind.

Guy clutched the rigging in the slashing rain. Occasionally he wiped the water from his eyes, keeping a sharp lookout for danger.

Hours passed, and the rain lessened, then ceased entirely. Drenched through to his skin, shivering, Guy longed for food and a warm bunk below decks.

Glad when his shift ended, he began his climb down. His foot slipped, and he clenched his hands, barely hanging on two stories above the deck. He sucked in his breath, heart racing, while feeling with his feet for the next rung. He exhaled when his right foot found a place to stand. His hands were slippery, and his body shook with cold and fear. He took much longer to descend than usual.

Wearily, he made it to his hammock below. Sleep claimed him the minute he shut his eyes.

A hand shook him, and a voice whispered, "Guy, wake up."

"I just got to sleep. Go away." Guy pushed the hand away.

"It's Hiram. Get up. You slept for six hours. We've made port unexpectedly."

Guy pried his eyes open. His whole body throbbed from the long hours standing in the storm.

"I'm telling you, this is our chance! Come on, lazy head, or I'll escape without you!" Hiram's face retreated as he stepped away from Guy's ear.

Hiram's words finally sunk into Guy's brain. He sat up with a start, all desire for sleep evaporating like dew in the hot sun. His pulse raced. "What's happening?!"

"I told you." Hiram stood at the base of the stair leading to the deck. "We came into an inlet. The captain and first officer are arguing whether to land. This is our chance."

The boys crept up on deck. Guy feared his rapid heartbeat could be heard ten feet away. The captain and the first mate engaged in a heated discussion in their language. Many crewmen watched the argument. Others seemed to be preparing for battle. A sword pile lay amidships, and officers passed them out.

No one looked their way.

Hiram put his fingers to his lips and edged behind some barrels and ropes. Guy followed. They scooted to the side away from shore and swung their legs over the ship's side. Lowering themselves as far as they could with their arms, the boys dangled for a few seconds, then Hiram dropped into the water. Guy's arm muscles screamed with the previous day's exertion of clenching the mast for stability in the storm. Guy sucked in a deep breath and let go. The water's warmth surprised him. It closed over his head, so he kicked his feet and surfaced. Hiram waited for him, floating a few feet away.

As soon as Guy broke the surface, Hiram stroked his way parallel to the ship's stern. Guy followed with powerful strokes, pushing through the pain, the taste of freedom giving him strength. He followed his friend.

Guy's shoulders tensed, sure they would be spotted any minute. They swam at a frantic pace toward the shore.

Gasping for breath, the rocky shore tore at their bare insteps. They scuttled quickly into the lush foliage amid a grove, panic still gripping them in its iron hand.

The air smelled of moist earth and decaying vegetation. Exertion and humidity made it hard to breathe.

They peered back at the ship to see if anyone observed their escape. The crew lowered a dinghy with four men in it, who rowed toward the inlet's opposite side.

"What do you think is going on?" Hiram swatted insects buzzing him.

"I don't know, but should we run the other direction, or wait and see what happens?"

"I vote we leave while they are distracted." Hiram wrung out his wet shirt.

"Agreed." Guy turned his back on the ship and struck out further into the grove. The underbrush soon enveloped them.

In half an hour, the two boys found themselves going uphill, deep in the trees. The sun's warmth didn't dry them off; instead, their clothes stuck to their backs. Sweat ran down Guy's face and back of his neck.

As they reached the crest, a clearing appeared. They instinctively turned to check the ship's position below them. It sat anchored in the inlet. But beyond the ship, sailors wound up a bare hill toward an outpost set over a ridge which they couldn't see from the shore. Soldiers moved on the outpost's wall, seemingly unaware of the approaching raiders.

This outpost could only be the eastern garrison, Odem's home base. Guy and Donella had approached the post from the opposite direction. Maybe the wayfaring soldier had returned. Guy had been over a month at sea.

Guy wanted to pretend he didn't see the danger. Walk away. Go back to the farm.

"Look! The crew must plan to attack the outpost. We have to warn them."

"What? We are too far away." Hiram put his fists on his hips. "And besides, they are better able to take care of themselves than we are. Haven't you noticed? We don't have any weapons!"

Ignoring Hiram's grumbling, Guy pulled off his shirt. It was no longer white but flapping it in the breeze might get the soldiers' attention. He barely waved it a moment when Hiram grabbed his arm and forcibly lowered it.

"Hey!" Guy angrily fought his friend.

"You idiot! The *Indomitable's* crew have seen us." Hiram's face paled, and his breathing came in short bursts.

Guy swung around as the deck master raised his spyglass, while another man pointed in their direction.

Hearing brush snapping, Guy turned to find Hiram running down the back of the hill, away from the sea. As if sensing Guy's eyes on him, Hiram turned and waved. "Come on! Time to get outta here."

Guy hesitated a few seconds. "Sorry, Hiram. If you do not want to go with me, this is where we part ways."

"Suit yourself." Hiram frowned. "Good luck. You'll need it."

And without another backward glance, Hiram was soon lost to sight in the thicket.

Guy bit his lip.

Maybe Hiram is right, and I should head away from here as fast as I can. What difference can I make?

But he pushed those cowardly thoughts away. *I can warn them and give them a chance.*

He raced for cover back the way he had come. As soon as he crossed into the dense wooded area, he headed inland at an angle. The heavy growth slowed him down. Glimpsing the blue inlet, he skirted it, still under cover of the trees.

He hesitated at the path the raiders had taken. It was probably a supply route and might be the shortest route to the garrison, but he would surely run into his captors that way. A cliff loomed close to his position. He had never done rock climbing before, but the minutes ticked by. He ran to the base.

The cliff was much steeper than it looked, but reaching for a handhold, he found places to put his hands and feet. Since he had lost his fear of heights, he kept going, one handhold at a time. He found it no more difficult than climbing the ship's mast.

Guy rested only a moment when he reached the summit. Now to get to the garrison unseen.

The sound of a fire shooter's boom reached his ears. *That isn't a good sign!* He jumped up and stared across the inlet at the ship. Fire belched forth as the ship fired another round at the garrison.

Guy advanced toward the outpost. The supply road wound fifteen feet below him. He followed parallel to it. As he drew closer, he could hear sounds of a battle. The pirates had swarmed the garrison and fought the soldiers. A giant hole blown in the garrison wall let Guy know what the ship had aimed at.

Guy was no soldier. He didn't even have a weapon. His only

chance to help the soldiers was to cause a diversion. He looked around for anything to create one. On the garrison's battlements, he spotted a fire shooter facing inland. If he could point it toward the ship, and fire it . . .

Guy clambered down to the main road. The invaders were all inside the walls. No one guarded their retreat. He cautiously peered around the blasted hole. No one nearby. Men fought all over the courtyard and battlements. He darted around the newly-made entrance and found the steps leading up to the catwalk.

Soldiers clashed with the *Indomitable's* crew in the courtyard, on the catwalk, and everywhere he looked.

As Guy crouched, one man, in particular, caught his eye.

The soldier looked to be ten years older than Guy. He wore fancier garb than the others—all black with gold thread in patterns along the edges, and a dragon insignia on his breastplate. His curved sword was a type Guy had never seen.

He was like a whirlwind with his unusual weapon. He advanced, thrust, danced out of the way and came in at another angle, dispatching his opponent. Without stopping, he lunged at another man, quickly impaling him, pulled out his sword and advanced to the next.

Admiration filled Guy as he watched the black-clad soldier's speed and precision. This man was definitely far superior to the soldiers and pirates battling around him.

A scuffle behind him made Guy swing around. The soldier nearest to him had slayed his opponent, and now had his sword pointed at Guy.

"You, there, boy!"

Guy raised his hands above his head. "I'm not one of the attackers. They kidnapped me. I'm a farm boy from Zendira way."

The soldier advanced and checked Guy for weapons. When he didn't find any, he asked, "What are you doing here then? Up to some mischief or they wouldn't have let you come."

"No, sir. I escaped in the chaos. I followed them from the ship. I wanted to help the garrison." Guy gulped and rubbed his nose with his sleeve. "Their ship is below us, and very few men are left on it. If you can fire on it with your fire shooter—"

"—we might force them to leave," the soldier finished Guy's thought. The man stared at him, then put away his sword. "Help me move the cannon. But any tricks," he pulled out a wicked, sharp knife, "and I put this through you."

Guy lowered his hands. The soldier made Guy walk before him along the catwalk to what the pirates called a fire shooter. Guy had never touched one before since the crew guarded their weapons from the boys. The squat, black destructor was very impressive up close.

Grabbing the ropes, Guy and the soldier pulled the cannon along the walkway. It was enormously heavy, but farm work and ship work had strengthened Guy's muscles.

The soldier got the cannon in position, directing Guy to help him. The soldier seemed to know how to use it. He loaded the weapon with powder. He had Guy pass him a steel ball from a pile on the catwalk. The ball's sheer weight would do a lot of damage if it hit the ship's deck, Guy thought.

"Stand back," the soldier ordered. "Cover your ears."

Guy obeyed. He had seen the shipboard fire shooters and learned from Hiram how they worked, but never saw one in action. Hope surged when it put a hole in the ship's deck, even as it left his ears ringing.

As soon as it went off, several more soldiers joined the first to reload it and do more damage.

Guy stepped further back. No one paid any attention to him. He glanced back at the courtyard and watched the swordsman assail two pirates at once. Guy wondered if he could be the famed Champion of Valdeor.

Guy glimpsed the ship's captain, who jumped up on a stone

from the blasted wall and called a retreat. Within minutes, the pirates disengaged and raced back the way they came. Some soldiers pursued them, the swordsman in the lead. But another, older man with an officer's rank on his tunic signaled a bugler and called a halt. The black-clad swordsman frowned but wiped off his blade. He, as many others, looked toward the cannon. Then his eyes locked on Guy.

An iron grip bruised Guy's shoulder. He turned.

The soldier he helped with the cannon confronted him. "You still have some explaining to do."

The soldier took Guy down the stairs to the courtyard. Guy studied the two men as he approached. The middle-aged officer had a crooked nose and a scruffy beard. He wore an insignia on his shoulder marking him as captain. The outstanding swordsman stood covered in gore. They grew silent and stared at Guy when the soldier stopped in front of them.

Guy found himself the center of attention. His hands became sweaty.

They might not believe my story. I'm sure I wouldn't in their place.

The soldier saluted the older man. "Captain, I found this boy on the catwalk, sir. He claims yon pirates kidnapped him."

"A likely story." The captain squinted at Guy. "Who are you? And why are you here?"

"My name is Gyfar. I left my farm to visit the city. But an enemy fleet pressed me into service." Guy had decided to tell the truth, but not all the details. "I've spent the last month aboard the pirate's ship. I have details to share with the garrison's commander. Are you the commander, Sir?"

Guy wanted to ask if he was Odem but realized knowing his name might look even more suspicious.

"I am the ranking officer here while our commander is away." The captain folded his arms over his broad chest. "You will tell me all you know."

Guy hesitated. He needed to find Odem. Usher had made that very clear. But he couldn't antagonize the captain. He decided to tell part of his story.

"The ship that attacked is no ordinary pirate ship. They are a scout ship from Canteor." Guy bit his lip, deciding how much to reveal. "Rumors in Tulken Harbor are that an invasion fleet is massing."

That ought to get their attention and make him credible in their eyes.

"What?" The swordsman interrupted. He turned his face toward the captain. "I can't believe you let them get away! You should have let me chase them and cut them down before they boarded their ship." He put his hand on his sword hilt. "Odem should have left me in charge. I would have destroyed them, leaving a few prisoners to interrogate."

"It is not your call, Your Highness." The captain's expression hardened. "Commander Odem left me in charge. I am a veteran of many skirmishes. Our strength lies in the defense capabilities of this garrison."

"Your strategy has left us at the mercy of an invasion." The swordsman turned to Guy. "What details do you have? Ships numbers? Men? A timeline for this invasion?" His intense eyes penetrated Guy.

"I picked up a little of their language, but they didn't discuss their plans in front of me. They addressed me in our common tongue when they wanted me to do something, Sir." Guy, not sure what to call him, didn't add a title.

"I thought you said you had details." The prince got into Guy's face and gave him a push in the chest that made Guy stumble backward into his captor's arm. "If it were up to me, I would lock you up." The prince hmphed, looked at the captain accusingly, and stalked away.

The Champion of Valdeor, Prince Alloryn, was his hero. Or he had been until now. Guy knew it might be irrational, but he expected them to believe him. Especially when he risked his life to bring word of impending danger.

"Never mind him, lad." The soldier spoke up from behind Guy. "After yer little trick worked, I believe you." He faced the officer. "With your leave, Captain, I think this lad could use a bite to eat."

"Very well, Farley. But don't let him out of your sight. I will speak with him later." The captain walked over to inspect the damage to the wall, calling out orders to fix it forthwith.

Guy trailed along behind Farley. His stomach rumbled. His last meal had been yesterday.

Soon Guy was seated at the soldiers' mess area. He gulped down the plain brown bread. But the brown ale made him choke.

"You cannot even hold your liquor," a voice said above Guy. Tears streaming from Guy's eyes prevented him from seeing who spoke as he bent over, coughing. "You should know better to waste it on a child, Farley." Fancy black boots stopped in front of him. "How old are you, boy?"

Guy cleared his throat, wiped his sleeve across his eyes, and gazed up into the prince's mocking face.

"Sixteen," Guy choked out, staring back at the prince.

"I am a prince. End your sentence with 'your highness' when you address me, farm boy."

Guy sat mute. His hero-worship of Prince Alloryn evaporated with those words. Even Guy's admiration for his skilled swordsmanship, which he had witnessed, diminished.

"Tongue-tied dolt." The prince moved away.

"Don't mind him, son. He has a problem with everyone. Thinks himself better than us. But he is a master with a sword, worth ten soldiers in battle." Farley winked at Guy. "But he has a wildcat's temper."

"What kind of blade does he use? I've never seen one like it."

"He calls it a scimitar." Farley glanced at the undrunk liquid in Guy's mug, so Guy offered it to him, and the soldier drained it in one gulp. "Fighting makes a man mighty thirsty."

Farley took a rag and began cleaning his blade. "Whereabouts did you say you came from?"

"My father owned a small inn on the road outside the village of Fister. We turned to farming when he died." The words brought his home before Guy's eyes. *How long I've been gone! Would I ever see home again?*

"I grew up on a farm meself once. I longed to escape and see the world." Farley got a faraway look in his eyes. "Left me da and ma and all the little ones. Never been back." He furrowed his brow and concentrated on his sword.

They shared a companionable silence.

"I didn't want an adventure, but it seemed to find me." Guy stared at his hands clasped between his knees.

"That is the way of life. Adventure and troubles find us, even when we aren't looking for them."

Guy indicated the prince, sitting apart from the others, cleaning his blade. "I heard stories about his quest to find the lost princess and how he became the Champion of Valdeor. I thought he would be more, well, champion-like." Guy scuffed his foot on the ground. "Having gone through many trials, I thought he might listen to me."

If the prince of the realm won't believe me, then all is truly lost.

"Him? The Champion of Valdeor?" Farley threw a look over his shoulder. "You've got it wrong. He's not Prince Alloryn." Farley leaned forward and lowered his voice. "No, he is Prince Gensard, the oldest son of Prince Xander of Samarantha. Mighty spoiled if you ask me. Sent here to gain experience." He grunted. "He'd rather tell everyone else how to do their jobs."

Guy's spirits rose. "I thought since he was a prince, and he fought so well . . . I mean, how could Prince Alloryn be a greater swordsman than he?"

Farley lay his clean sword across his knees. "I heard the two princes are well-matched. But the champion's quest was not laid on this one's shoulders. And Commander Odem had more sense than to leave him in charge, prince or no prince."

Guy perked up at Odem's name.

But before he could speak, a tall soldier walked up. "Captain is calling for all able-bodied men to repair the wall. The invaders are gone, but maybe they'll come with reinforcements next time."

Guy joined Farley and the other men as they shored up the sea-facing wall. Sure enough, the pirate ship's sails faded distantly on the horizon. At the sight, it was as if a weight lifted from Guy's heart. *I dreamt of this moment for weeks. I've truly escaped!*

"Wait till your commander finds out what happened in his absence." Guy threw out a line, and Farley took the bait.

"Aye, Commander Odem will be disappointed he missed the skirmish. And he would have taken a prisoner to interrogate."

"I don't know about that. Those pirates are wily." Guy remembered Drake's cold eye. "I think they might have preferred to die than to speak."

"Commander Odem is wily himself. Not much gets past him. He left a month ago on Her Majesty's business. Got a message in the middle of the night, I heard." Farley put his hand on his lower back as he straightened up. "I'm a soldier, not a mason."

He surveyed Guy's work. "Our cannon 'twas only introduced at the garrison a few years ago when Reina Lauressa took her throne. We've had practice with it, but I never fired it on an enemy before."

Guy sat with Farley over a bowl of hot stew after repairing the wall.

"Hundreds of years ago, the eastern raiders of Canteor habitually attacked this coast." Farley dipped his brown bread in the bowl. "The garrison had been one of many outposts built to defend the seaboard. But since the peace accords many generations ago, the outposts were mostly abandoned. Reina Lauressa sent troops to build up the presence at all the garrisons, but lacking funds, we are all short-staffed." Farley fished out the last pieces of meat and slurped the broth.

"But why did the scout ship come here? Why not attack a city or town with no defenses?" Guy finished his stew, his muscles aching in a good way after a hard afternoon's work. His good fortune in escaping, along with the satisfying manual labor, buoyed him up.

Farley stepped over to the stewpot hanging over the campfire and ladled more food in his bowl. He ambled back to the log he used for a seat. "Testing their enemy. Only this garrison is maintained and manned, because Canteor made frequent raids along the eastern coast, closest to their homeland."

And now the enemy threatened to raid it again.

That night, Guy bedded down in the barracks with the troops. Farley threw him an extra blanket. Two soldiers died during the skirmish. Relieved and thankful to have escaped with his life, Guy hoped the *Indomitable's* crew had no plans to come back.

Although sleep tugged at him, he lay awake thinking about his next move.

Odem must have gone to meet Donella in Tulken Harbor. But was Odem still there? He had not come back here. And should Guy follow him or seek out Usher?

I must tell someone in charge about the coming invasion. I'm unsure if the garrison captain believed me, and even if he did, it would take weeks by horseback to get the information to the palace.

And Guy knew they did not have weeks.

The sea raiders had attacked the garrison. They had gauged the strength of the defenses. If they had won the day, it would have given them a landing place to stage their raids or, maybe, all out war. Even so, now they knew the strength and number of this outpost.

Guy decided he had to use the portal and bring news to the capital.

So before sunrise, Guy made his way to the waypost half a league from the garrison. It seemed ages since he had last been here, accompanying Donella in their search for Odem.

Guy stepped up to the waypost, a water canteen slung over his shoulder. Unfortunately, he had lost the clump of moss Usher had given him. So Guy pictured Usher's familiar face. His hand tingled as he touched the post.

Fog emanated from the ground and enveloped Guy. Swirling in a spiral pattern, his mentor's snug home materialized in it. But the place looked deserted. No smoke from the little fire kept under the perpetual stew. The door was shut. Guy couldn't feel Usher's presence.

Guy hesitated, then withdrew his hand.

He drew out the clay bead he wore on a string around his neck. Fortunately, the pirates thought it had no value. Sailors, in general, were a superstitious lot so they hadn't taken it from him. They probably assumed it was a good luck piece. Many crewmen carried them, marked with the goat god they worshiped.

Guy drew a deep breath, closed his eyes and focused. This time he summoned up Donella's image—her black curls surrounding her elfin face, her dimples showing as she grinned, and the sparkle in her eyes. He reached out with his marked left hand.

He opened his eyes to cool mist touching his face. A waypost on a lonely road coalesced.

"You, boy! What do you think you are doing?"

Guy's heart raced. *No! I cannot be questioned. If they didn't believe me before, they will never believe me now!* Hastily, Guy stepped through the portal as a footstep crunched behind him and a hand fell on his shoulder.

Guy's weight doubled as up and down disappeared. He seemed to hang in between places for a longer time than his earlier forays into the portal.

Guy fell forward and hit the ground, grunting in pain. Something heavy lay on his back, pressing him into the dirt. *Someone had come through the portal with me!* Guy struggled to get out from underneath the weight.

Guy heard a retching sound and slithered out from underneath the body. He turned his head to see Prince Gensard getting onto his knees, his face pale.

Guy fought his own dizziness and nausea. He took stock of his surroundings. They stood on a hill with a town nestled in the valley below.

Guy raced toward the village, but he didn't get very far before the prince tackled him, arms around his legs, bearing him down into the dust.

"I knew you were a spy! What magic did you use to get us here? What place is this? Where are your pirate masters?"

Guy gulped. He would tell the truth, even if the prince wouldn't believe him. Guy must warn someone about the impending invasion. Someone who could act upon it. Being a prince, Gensard could command the ear of Reina Lauressa.

Gensard turned Guy over and leaned into his face. "Speak, dolt." The prince pressed a knife to Guy's throat, and Guy stiffened.

He encountered an unrelenting stare. No compassion, no weakness showed in Gensard's face.

Guy swallowed. "I am searching for Commander Odem. He

must be told about the raid. Don't you see? What if that ship is only the first of an invasion fleet? Weren't the eastern raiders a plague on the coast for centuries? Innocent farmers and villages will be pillaged if I cannot get word to someone."

Guy searched Gensard's eyes for a sign that he would listen. "Be a hero. Help me to find Commander Odem, or, even better, bring me before Reina Lauressa herself."

For an answer, Gensard yanked Guy to his feet and twisted Guy's arm behind his back. "Raving lunatic. Head for that town. No tricks, mind you."

Guy felt Gensard's breath on the back of his neck as they continued down the road. A cliff towered on their left and a steep drop on their right.

Suddenly a rope appeared before Guy's astonished eyes, and a man slithered down it from above. Guy ducked as a man aimed a short sword at his head.

Gensard freed Guy as he slid his scimitar out of his scabbard. Three bandits beset the prince.

Guy hesitated. He had no weapon, so he wouldn't be much use in a fight. Besides, Gensard's lightning moves already took down one attacker.

Guy's head told him to run for the town. He could always send back help, he reasoned. But his heart said he would be a coward if he ran.

"Hey, you big lug, over here!" Guy taunted. One bandit left the melee and strode toward him.

Guy imagined a desert wasteland as he raced for the waypost. He entered a white wall of fog, the bandit close on his heels. Guy threw himself on the ground just before the portal's edge. The bandit tripped over him and flew, arms spread out, into the desert sand on the portal's other side.

Guy quickly released the image in his mind and sat, amazed that it had worked. The mist dissipated, along with the bandit sprawled on the ground. Guy breathed again.

He looked back. Prince Gensard stood over two fallen men. As if sensing his gaze, Gensard met Guy's eyes, his face stern.

Chapter 15

At the break of day, Donella and Odem sat by a small campfire beside a rock outcropping, discussing their plans. Donella wrapped her cloak tighter around her in the chill morning air.

A distant rumble interrupted Donella as she finished eating her warm porridge. Scanning the area, she saw nothing alarming.

Across the fire from her, Odem paused in mid-sentence, his posture stiff.

A growing roar echoed around the valley and the ground began to shake. Odem leapt from his seat and pushed Donella flat to the ground at the foot of the boulders.

She covered her ears as the deafening sound came closer. Odem covered her body with his as a stampede swerved around the rock outcropping—the only thing standing between them and a hundred horses' hooves.

Trembling uncontrollably, she had the crazy desire to jump to her feet and run screaming in any direction to escape. Gritting her teeth and squeezing shut her eyes, she fought it down and remained still. She clenched her hands and made herself breathe in and out.

Keep us safe in the palm of your hand, O One Who Fashioned

All. Let it be over soon!

The wind rushed by as the creatures passed, hooves pounding like endless thunder. She peeked from where she lay prone and perceived a sea of horses flashing by, the dirt flying as their hooves churned up the earth.

The dust choked her, but Odem's weight on her back made it impossible to cough.

After what seemed an eternity to Donella, the last horse passed them. Odem released her and she sat up. She thought her heart would never settle back to its normal rhythm.

Donella stood up and brushed herself off. Wracked by a fit of coughing, she couldn't dislodge the taste of sand in her mouth.

Odem passed her his water bag. "Drink up."

She drank, greedily.

"Thank you for saving my life. That is closer than I ever want to be to a maddened herd." Her hands shook as she passed the water back to him.

Odem stood beside her, one hand shading his eyes, as he stared to where the herd of horses had come from. "The sky is dark above that mountain range. A lightning flash most likely started the stampede."

The crazed animals had trampled the remains of their little camp and their supplies beyond recognition.

Odem and Donella traveled as a father and daughter. She felt safe in Odem's company and found him easy to talk to. He was no longer a stranger.

They had been on the road several weeks. They had started at the Forest Deer Inn and trailed Lord Tastaver from reports they picked up on the road. They traced his route through tollgates and inns. He wasn't trying to hide his movement.

After journeying for weeks on horse, they had come to a fishing village by the sea. The storekeeper there directed them to crossing the moors till they came to a green valley.

"You canna miss it. An old orchard is at the valley's entrance. Go a little farther and you'll see lovely grass growing in abundance, with a stream meandering through the heart of it, and horses milling about as far as they can range."

The storekeeper scratched his head. "I don't rightly know what he plans to do with such a herd. We mostly fish along this stretch of coast. Farms are farther inland. Too rocky here, and the moors aren't good soil for growing. If he had any sense, he would take them to Mintala and sell them. Enough horses for an army of men."

Donella exchanged a glance with Odem at the news.

Odem chose to walk the rest of the way to the valley, so they left their horses at the town stable. Odem had insisted they travel the old-fashioned way. Jumping from portals wouldn't work for tracking, he had explained early on.

So now, here they were in the valley, lucky to be alive. Donella shivered, even though the warm sun climbed in the sky.

If Odem saw, he chose not to comment. "We are nearly there. And when we have enough information, we will use the waypost outside the fishing village and join Usher at the palace."

"You think he is still there?" Donella matched Odem's shortened strides.

"Usher will use the resources available to him. He will find the information we need regarding the number of waystations in the archives. I only hope he can account for most of the waykeeper's rings. The fewer conspirators who can jump from place to place, the better."

Donella pondered his words. Other than Tastaver, no one they encountered had seen anyone suspicious. Foreigners either did not frequent the inns, taverns, or markets where Odem and she visited, or they were infrequent travelers.

That was the good news.

Donella's thoughts strayed to the bad news.

No sign of Guy.

She didn't feel a pull when she tried to sense him through the few wayposts they had encountered. His unusually strong presence was absent. Wherever he was, he was out of range of a waypost. Fear for his safety nagged at the back of her mind. *Was he alright?*

Donella came back to the present when Odem stopped short and she bumped into him. He pulled her down in some bushes near the road.

Before them a rough wood-hewn cabin with a sagging porch sat low and squat to the ground. An extremely large stable that seemed newly built stood silent and seemed empty, as did the extensive corrals. But nothing moved.

"I think our foreign friend is busy rounding up his wayward stampede," Odem said as they studied the scene before them.

He put a hand on Donella's arm. "But tread lightly, he may have a guard on the lookout." He let her go and motioned her to follow him around the back of the cabin, which seemed as deserted as the front.

Using outbuildings as cover, Odem and Donella made their way to the yard behind the cabin. Odem waved Donella forward, and she ran low, zigzagging until she reached the back porch. Crouching, the rough wood against her hands, she slowly peeked through the open window above her. No curtain hung there. A bare table and rustic chairs were visible. The living area consisted of one room, a fireplace at the other end. One door led to what she assumed was the sleeping area. The fire was out, and the place seemed empty. She waited, listening.

She turned her head and spotted Odem near a rail fence. She put both palms up in an empty signal. He motioned with his hands for her to check the window around the side.

Donella bent over and moved, head below the windows on the porch, sneaking to the side away from Odem, where the inner door was located. She found a feed pail, turned it upside down, and stepped on it. Through the window, she saw a bedroom, uninhabited as the rest of the cabin.

Donella jumped off the pail and walked back to the porch, no longer worried that she'd be seen. She stepped on the porch and motioned for Odem to join her. She didn't wait for him but walked inside.

The cabin was sparsely furnished. Besides the table and chairs around it, another chair and a bench stood near the fireplace. Donella hoped to find some plan or map or something to let her know the plotters' plans.

Odem walked around the room's perimeter, his eagle eye on the wall, not the furnishings.

Donella realized he searched for hiding places, so she spun around looking for anything out of place. She checked the sugar and coffee tins in what passed for the kitchen and looked behind the rest of the supplies.

Odem checked under the rug, presumably for a trap door.

Donella opened the door to the sleeping area. The door creaked and she glimpsed an unmade bed, and clothes strewn about. Lord Tastaver dressed like a dandy, yet his things told another story. She hoped that meant he was as careless in his hiding place as he was in his belongings.

She rifled through pockets in his trousers and vests. She peeked under the bed. The floor was bare, but as she moved away, she glimpsed a cylinder tucked up against the taut strings that held the ticking in place. Holding her breath, Donella lay down and stretched until her fingers could reach it. Someone had tied it in place. She worked the knot loose, then pulled her find out.

She brushed off the dust bunnies and went back in the main room. She found Odem on his knees, working on a wood knot in the floor.

"I found something!" Donella rushed over to Odem and held out the metal cylinder.

"That's my girl."

Odem's praise was rare indeed, so Donella hugged it to herself.

Odem took the roll to the kitchen table in the better light, unscrewed the metal top and tipped it. Several tightly wrapped scrolls thumped onto the table. Odem unrolled them. The first one showed a map of Valdeor with little flags in a dozen places around the realm. The next two scrolls were written in a foreign language.

"Ah, this is just what I hoped we would find."

Before Donella could respond, they heard a rumble of hooves. Donella ran to the window facing the road they had traveled. "The herd is headed our way! I think I see at least two outriders."

"Quick, out the porch door, and run to the outbuildings." Odem swept up the cylinder in one hand and the papers in the other.

Donella raced out of the cabin and ran toward the farthest outbuilding. She saw movement in her peripheral vision. The first of the herd headed toward the open corral. Her heart thumping, she put on a burst of speed. She swung through a barn door. She smelled hay and clover and horse sweat.

She headed for a ladder leading to a loft. Stopped. *Not a good idea! Where else would the riders put horses, except for a barn?*

She backed out. There! A tiny, windowless building. She raced for it. As she neared the building's door, Odem reached it before her. The door stuck where weeds grew around it, blocking the entrance. Donella threw herself down and dug with her hands at the weeds. Odem yanked the latch. They ducked in as soon as the door swung open.

In the pitch black, the strong smell of mold and damp, wet earth assailed her. Donella found it surprisingly cool for a midsummer's day.

"Stop! Stay where you are. I believe we are on the edge of an old cistern," Odem cautioned her.

Donella froze. "Thanks." Not wanting to fall down a well, she knelt carefully. Placing her hands on the ground in front of her, she crawled until she found a wall. There she found a knothole where she could view the cabin and surrounding area.

Donella kept her eye glued to the slat where she could watch the horses mill about. She counted a dozen riders rounding up the horses.

When she grew tired of watching, she sat with her back to the wall and searched her dress pockets for anything to eat. She pulled out an ever-present apple, dried up and forgotten. Excitement made her hungry, so she ate it anyway.

If only they hadn't lost their packs in the stampede!

Her eyes had adjusted enough to see Odem crouching by the door, still keeping his eye on things.

"What is our next move?" Donella tossed the apple core toward the deeper blackness in the center of the tiny building and listened for it to plop at the bottom of the well. She shivered, more from nearly falling down the hole than from the chill, moist air.

"I want to open this door a bit wider and study these scrolls. Then, when things are quiet tonight, you and I are going to steal a horse and ride out of this valley." And with his words, Odem gently opened the door a crack. "Keep watch for now." He laid out one scroll on his knee.

Donella put her eye to the knothole and went back to counting riders. If only Seeker were here, she could ride him bareback any place in the realm. She longed for her little sheltered waystation in the woods. She would even be happy to be on the open hillside outside of Zendira, sharing her meal with farmers on the way to market.

The hours passed slowly.

"Rest a while, Donella, while I keep watch."

With a start, Donella realized the sun was going down in a pink sky. While her mind had been drifting, the afternoon had passed.

The riders congregated on the porch; the horses corralled for the night.

"What happens when Lord Tastaver finds his papers missing?" Donella remembered the sharp little dagger the man carried.

"My guess is, he is too busy to be thinking of that tonight. Or too worn out." Odem's disembodied voice hung in the quickening darkness. "They will have to ride out tomorrow and look for any stray horses in the hills and gullies. He might only be a courier. The maps mark some waystations, as well as all the garrisons and troop-strengths estimates." Odem's voice sounded grim. "Also, the best unguarded harbors where to land a contingent of ships."

"And the foreign writing?" Donella curled up to sleep, resting her head on her balled-up cloak.

"I'm afraid I only understand a few words. Otherwise, I would consider replacing the cylinder so no one would become suspicious. But we must take these plans with us to the palace in Mintala. Someone there will be able to decipher what it says."

The hooting of an owl penetrated Donella's dreams. She awoke, cramped in a ball, the smell of mold assaulting her. Remembering where she was, she sat up and saw Odem hunched in a corner of the cistern outbuilding. The moon broke over the horizon through the knothole as she put her eye to it, glancing around for danger. Donella groaned with stiffness as she tried to work out her cramped muscles.

"I could try to put the cylinder back under the bed where I found it." Donella stretched.

"Too dangerous." Odem shook his head in the moonlight.

"I have another idea. I can spike their water and make them sleep in late tomorrow. When I was exploring, I found another well off the back porch. A few drops of this," Donella removed a small vial from the pouch around her neck, "and they will sleep for hours."

Odem grunted. "Where did you come by that?"

"A girl alone has to protect herself." Donella heard the defensiveness in her voice.

"I'm not judging you." Odem tipped his head in her direction. "You remind me of your mother Janyssa. She was also resourceful."

Donella glowed with the praise. She was talented, even if she wasn't the Gifted One.

"One time she put a burr under the horse blanket of her unwanted suitor's steed. When he tried to impress her, his horse instead flew down the road, bucking madly, unseating her would-be-beau." She heard the smile in his voice.

Donella smiled back, even if he couldn't see it. In these weeks of traveling, she had grown very fond of Odem, even to the point of wishing he had become her stepfather. She would love to hear more tales of Mother as a young woman, but she pushed that desire away and went back to sharing her plan.

"I can put a few drops in the well's pitcher, and when they wake in the morning, after drinking all night, as they did, they will want a cool sip of water. But instead, they will slumber some more."

After a pause, when she was sure he was going to say "no," he surprised her and said "yes."

Donella crept from her hiding place. Her heart started beating fast, more thrilled than scared, if she admitted it to herself. She preferred action to waiting. She scurried from one hiding spot to another, always keeping an eye on the dark cabin for any movement. When she reached the porch, she nearly cried out when she tripped over a figure in the dark.

She bit back a cry, waiting for the sleeping figure to raise the alarm. After a heart-stopping pause, she leaned closer, to find a saddle had been carelessly thrown down and left on the ground.

Tension eased somewhat in her chest. She picked her way to the well and found the pitcher conveniently placed on the wall. She lowered the pitcher into the well and drew up some water. She drank some greedily. She carefully added a drop of liquid from her vial. Hopefully, the water would appeal to the first person to come for a drink, and they'd not think to lower the pail for fresh water. She added a few drops to the trough around the corner.

She hurried back to the cistern.

By dawn she would know if her plan worked.

As the sun rose, they watched for the men to stir. Eventually, a scar-faced man stumbled out of the cabin and made his way to the well. Donella held her breath as he took a long quaff of water. He rubbed his face, then headed to the corrals. He stumbled as he reached the fence. Reaching out to grab the rail, he pitched over and lay still.

Donella caught Odem's eye and used a hand signal meaning "success."

As the morning progressed, two others followed the same ritual, not slumping down until they reached the porch. The next man simply walked over them on his way out, having no idea that his comrades were drugged, not passed out drunk from the night before.

Donella stifled a giggle.

But her mirth faded away when Odem drew his long knife and motioned for her to follow him. Donning her plain brown cloak, she slung the cylinder's strap over her back and followed.

They crept through the yard, sometimes crawling on their bellies through scarce cover. Odem motioned for her to stay while he inched around the cabin, checking out each window. He rounded the last corner and signaled her to enter.

Donella stepped gingerly over the men on the porch. She slithered along the wall near the only bedroom. Loud snoring came from inside. She glanced through the open door. Lord Tastaver lay, one arm flung out of the bed covers. Odem's face showed at the window. He nodded encouragement.

Withdrawing the cylinder, she got down on her hands and knees, and crawled under the bed. She froze as the bed squeaked above her. Long minutes passed before she decided he must have changed positions. Then a big spider dropped on the floor in front of her nose. She squeaked and dropped the metal cylinder, which made a loud noise.

The bed above her heaved, and the occupant's face peered at her upside down. Leaping out of bed, he clutched Donella's arm and hauled her out.

"What are you doing, girl? How did you get here?" His eyes bored into hers. Glancing at the door, he bellowed, "Wyn! Jed! Get in here!"

Donella hoped he wouldn't see the cylinder still under the bed.

When no one answered, Tastaver, wearing only breeches and socks, yanked her into the empty living area. Seeing no one, her captor headed for the cabin door. Two men lay on the porch, unmoving.

The lord cursed and dragged Donella back inside.

Just as he pushed the door closed, Odem flung himself out of the bedroom, taking Tastaver with him to the floor. They fought, but Odem kept his position on top of his opponent, choking until Lord Tastaver stilled.

Odem stood, wiping blood from his mouth.

"Get us a horse. Quick!"

Donella raced to the stables, snagging a bridle, and put it on a horse in the nearest stall. She spoke softly and he followed her as she led him out.

In no time, Odem mounted and pulled Donella behind him. They rode away from the valley.

Shouts made her glance back. Several men staggered to the corral and mounted bareback.

Odem spurred their horse toward the main road. Donella's heart raced. They didn't have much of a lead.

Only when they approached the waypost outside the fishing town forty minutes later, did Odem slow the mount.

"Nice work." Odem brought them to a stop. "You will have to let me know where you bought that sleeping potion. I can see its usefulness."

"I make it myself from herbs in my garden." Donella gave him a wide grin. "I will brew you up a batch, if I ever get home."

"Witch!" He shook his head, but his eyes twinkled. He sobered as he touched his ring to the waypost. "We'll come back for our horses. Let's go to the palace with our important find."

Donella only hoped they were in time. Things were moving faster than she liked.

Glancing back the way they came, Donella perceived distant riders.

"The portal is somehow blocked!" Odem's voice was grim. "Hold on!"

Donella grabbed him tighter around the waist as he whipped the horse back into a gallop.

Chapter 16

Gensard strode over as Guy picked himself off the ground and brushed dirt from his clothes. Guy expected the prince to grab him again and to continue marching him to the town.

Instead, Guy thought he glimpsed embarrassment in the prince's face for a fleeting second, but it was gone so quickly, Guy wasn't sure if he imagined it.

"I may have misjudged you," the prince spoke begrudgingly. Then his face grew haughty again. "Not to say I trust you, wizard. Your magic dispelled that bandit, but I still do not know whose side you are on." Gensard narrowed his eyes and held up a hand as Guy opened his mouth to speak. "Your actions will impress me more than empty words. For now, I say we head to the town below and find horses to continue our journey."

Guy supposed that was as close as the prince would ever get to saying, "thank you."

Guy nodded. "Very well."

They tramped toward the town. Their stop provided them with food and horses.

Gensard seemed to know the way to Mintala. The days passed with monotony as they rode along the main route crossing Valdeor. They rode during the day and camped out among the stars at night.

Gensard kept a watchful eye on Guy, as if expecting him to vanish into the air. When Guy tried to talk or explain his ability, Gensard shut him down with, "Tell that to the authorities when we arrive at the palace."

Guy bit back a response. He resented the prince's treatment. Gensard acted like a jailer bringing a dangerous prisoner to trial.

But if Guy needed to ride the length of Valdeor with his unwanted companion to fulfill his mission, he would.

Pondering whether he would abandon the prince if given the opportunity, Guy kept alert for any sign of a waypost to hurry his trip. But in this scarcely populated province they found few inns or waystations.

Or should I use the prince's goodwill to gain an audience with the Reina? Guy didn't know the best course of action, so he bided his time.

The road traveled through valleys and woods, then through mountain passes.

Game had been plentiful, with rabbits and deer, and they were well-nourished.

The air grew thin and cold, even though it was late summer. They traversed the Blue Mountain Range's flanks, and now climbed up toward the barren mountain heights. The evergreen trees thinned out, exposing them to the elements.

Guy pulled his cloak tighter as the wind gusted. He contemplated all the twists and turns his life had taken in the last few months. It felt like years since his stepmother's harsh tongue-lashing was the worst thing he faced. He thought back to the day that changed his life, the girl whose arrival started it all.

Where was Donella now? Was she safe? Or on her own adventure? Knowing her, she was probably in the thick of things.

Engrossed in his thoughts, Guy didn't realize Gensard had come to a halt. He would have plowed into the prince if his horse hadn't stopped of its own accord.

They sat at an intersection of ways. The trail to the left led down and around a corner, while the right went up the mountainside, where Guy could see the switchbacks above him.

Gensard unbent from leaning over in the saddle. "Tracks. Five men traveling." Gensard stared down the trail on the left. "Most likely traders. They cross the Blue Range this time of year to trade in Domadaria."

"Which way?" Guy asked.

For an answer, Gensard turned his horse's head to the upper trail. Gensard expected Guy to follow, no questions asked. It seemed the prince couldn't waste his breath answering one so lowly in station. Guy glared at the prince's back. He bit back a sarcastic comment. Traveling alone would be so much easier.

Guy nudged his own horse to follow. He scanned the area for the tracks Gensard spoke of and found them. Guy grew rigid at a little clay bead laying along a hoof mark. Pulling on the reins, he stopped his horse. Ignoring Gensard, he slipped out of his saddle and knelt on the ground. He picked up the bead and examined it closely. He pulled out the string he wore around his neck with her bead. The one Donella had given him matched the one in his hand.

Donella rode one of those horses!

Even Guy could tell the travelers went downhill. That is the way they should go, too.

He pictured Donella's exuberance and black tresses. He longed to tell her of his adventures, how he eventually found himself on the path she urged him to take, despite his original reluctance.

"What are you doing, boy?" A hand grabbed the back of his shirt and hauled him upright.

Guy ground his teeth but kept the anger out of his voice. "Look!" He held up the bead for inspection. "I know the girl who wears these."

"We do not have time to chase after your girlfriend." Gensard's face wore a set expression. "According to you, we must make all haste to speak with the Reina."

Guy fought the blush spreading over his face and held his temper with an effort.

"But she journeys with Commander Odem." Guy didn't deliberately lie. She had been waiting for Odem and was probably with him by now. Although she was stubborn enough to strike out on her own if the commander didn't show.

"The palace is our destination, remember?" Gensard shoved Guy toward his horse, releasing his grip on Guy's shirt. "Commander Odem will not take the glory from me. I will be the hero in Lauressa's eyes if your wild story turns out to be true." Under his breath Guy heard the prince mutter, as if talking to himself, "She will regret choosing that shepherd boy over me."

Guy hesitated. He wanted to find Donella. He'd share his exploits and impress her with his escape from the pirate ship. As annoyingly direct as she could be, she was a far sight better company than this stuck-up prince.

But she couldn't hasten their trip. Guy wasn't sure the prince would take orders from Odem, who may, or may not, be traveling with Donella.

He reluctantly chose to go with Gensard. The Reina needed to know of a possible invasion. Even Commander Odem was only a link in the chain, not the ruler of an army.

Things Guy observed on the pirate ship now made sense. The port calls. The horses. The holy war.

Guy mounted his horse and followed Gensard as he started up the switchbacks. They went around the first corner, when a scream reached their ears. Donella was in trouble! Guy's horse shied at the sound. Guy stared down the trail they hadn't taken.

Abandoning his decision from moments before, he turned his horse back to the crossroads and goaded the animal to fly downhill toward the sound.

"Hey! Come back here!"

Guy ignored the prince's command.

Guy rounded the blind corner past where he found the bead and peered below him on the trail. Several horsemen attacked another. Guy urged his horse to go faster, while he scanned for any sign of Donella.

As his horse skidded around the next hairpin turn and almost lost its footing, Guy's heart leapt into his throat.

Back on the straightaway, he spied Donella standing on the slope above the fighting swordsmen, a good-sized rock in her hands. As he watched, she hefted and threw it. The rock hit one of the men squarely in the head, and he toppled off his horse.

What a girl!

Guy took measure of the uneven ambush—three men against one. Now two against one, with Donella's help.

Guy urged his horse forward and pulled alongside Donella. She glanced his way.

"Oh, Guy, help Odem!"

They both turned at a loud yell to see a rider race past them in a cloud of dust and descend on the melee. The dust cleared as Prince Gensard grabbed a horseman and tumbled to the ground with his opponent. The prince quickly got on his feet, stabbing the man trying to rise. The attacker rolled out of the way and rose. Gensard easily parried the man's blade, raining blows down hard and swift.

Guy was taken aback to recognize the aggressor as the thief Jed.

Guy joined Donella, picking up rocks and flinging them at their enemies. His aim was better than hers. *At least I do something better than she can.*

But the combat moved out of their range.

One on one, Odem defeated his opponent with practiced skill. He wiped his sword.

Jed lay in a pool of blood from a wound in his stomach. Now Prince Gensard faced the man Donella had hit with the stone. He slew him with a jab to the throat.

"Who is your friend? He is a hero with a sword," swooned Donella.

"He is not my friend." Guy's eagerness deflated. After all this time apart, Donella had no time for him. *Just like a girl to be impressed by a handsome prince with a fancy blade.* Guy forgot that he had been overawed, too, the first time he witnessed Gensard's masterful swordsmanship.

During their separation, Guy longed to share his adventures with Donella and win her approval.

No chance of that now.

"Your friend is amazing! He's even a better swordsman than Odem." Donella smoothed her hair. "Please introduce me." She came down from her perch above the others.

A flame of jealousy flickered in Guy's chest.

Ignoring her, Guy mounted his horse and searched for the other horses, which had trotted away from the skirmish.

Donella was perfectly capable of batting her eyelashes and introducing herself to Gensard, as far as Guy was concerned. But he doubted she would get very far with Prince High and Mighty. With a small feeling of satisfaction, Guy smirked.

When he returned a few moments later with the wandering horses, Donella wore a pouty frown on her face. She stood to one side while the prince and Odem were in deep discussion.

Guy had time to study Odem and noted muscled arms, a trim body, and short haircut of a soldier. Guy could easily imagine him in leather mail. Odem held himself with an air of patient command. Different than Gensard; not so condescending.

"—and they threatened to hold us for ransom." Guy heard Odem say. "But we never gave them the chance to search us, so the documents we bring Reina Lauressa are safe."

"Then you do know this boy? His story is true? Canteor is planning to invade us?" Prince Gensard held his scimitar at his side.

Odem glanced at Guy, who pushed his hair out of his face. "We've never met, but I heard about him from several trustworthy friends, including Donella." Odem nodded his head at Donella, who lit up at her name, but Prince Gensard kept his eyes on Odem.

Donella's pert smile died on her lips. Guy figured she hated being ignored. But she didn't jump into the conversation, as he expected her to.

"All the rumors point to an imminent invasion," Odem confirmed. "And I carry proof of it. I suggest we join forces and ride to Mintala. We could use your sword." Odem nodded at it with a slight upturn of his lips.

With a quick flick of his wrist, Prince Gensard brought his scimitar's tip up and pointed it at Odem's heart.

Odem's smile faded. Guy and Donella froze, confusion on their faces.

"I will be the one to bring news of this dastardly plot to Lauressa. I, alone, will have the glory. Give the documents to me." With his words, he touched the scimitar to Odem's chest. "Slowly," he commanded, as they all could read the growing anger in Odem's eyes.

Tight-lipped, Odem haltingly reached under his tunic and withdrew a roll of parchment. He laid it reluctantly into the prince's outstretched hand.

"No!" Donella cried. She glanced from one man to the other. She tensed, and Guy feared she would fling herself between them, or do something equally impulsive. Guy thrust out a hand in her direction to stop her.

"You, girl, get over here." When Donella didn't move, Gensard lifted his blade from Odem's chest to his throat. "Hurry. I do not want to hurt him, but I will."

"Do what he says, child," Odem advised her. He showed no fear, but in his eyes burned a simmering anger.

Shaking, probably more from fury than cowardice—as her eyes blazed, her expression grim—Donella moved closer. The prince grabbed her arm and yanked her to him.

Donella clenched her fists as Gensard held her tight against him. "Stay where you are, Commander, and I will let her go farther down the road. If I see or hear any sign of you following me in the next twenty minutes, I *will* harm her." Gensard backed up toward his horse, dragging Donella with him.

Guy stood dumbfounded. The prince could be obnoxious, but this was outrageous.

"We'll come for you, my dear," Odem called. "Just do what he says."

Gensard hefted a stiff Donella into the saddle, then mounted behind her. He kicked the horse and rode up the switchbacks.

The whole episode took only a few minutes. Shamed, Guy realized that he hadn't even made an effort to help. *How could I stand by, not even lifting a finger to rescue Donella?*

He gazed along the path the prince had taken.

Guy came out of his thoughts when a deep voice spoke, "You must be Guy. Donella has told me about you."

Guy swung to face the man standing beside him.

Odem must have seen the stricken look on Guy's face. "We will get her back, never fear." Odem laid a friendly hand on Guy's shoulder. "I don't think he means to harm her. He is driven by pride, like a beast on his back, prodding him to act thus."

Guy remembered that Odem commanded Gensard during their time together at the garrison. Guy recalled Gensard's claim after the pirate attack, "Commander Odem should have left me in charge." Obviously, Odem had been equally unimpressed with the arrogant prince or Odem would have trusted Gensard with the garrison's protection.

"I hope you are right, Commander."

Guy watched as Odem stripped the dead men of their money pouches, daggers and swords, which he wrapped in a bundle and strapped to his horse. Catching Guy's eye, he explained, "They are foreign made, and will prove our tale."

The dead had pointed beards and goat head amulets. He nearly forgot his original errand in the chaos of his emotions.

Fortunately for Donella, Gensard kept his word and abandoned her a league from the scuffle. A weight lifted from Guy's chest at the sight of her. Guy and Odem found her pacing on the trail, muttering under her breath.

"I simply cannot believe that all Odem and I risked recovering the scrolls is undone by this prince's need to prove himself. He wants glory! What about the fate of his country? I told him what I thought of him! 'You might be a prince, but you are the rudest man I ever met. I hope the Reina throws you in her dungeon!'" Donella shook her fist.

Guy could easily imagine her blistering tirade against the prince's character. She still crackled with angry energy.

"What did he respond?"

Donella curled her lip. "Nothing. He ignored me. He put me down here and he spurred his horse away.

Calming down, her eyes focused on Guy.

"I'm glad you came to our rescue, Guy. I've been worried about you for weeks!"

"I was kidnapped."

"What?!"

"Night falls swiftly in the mountains," Odem interrupted. "Set up camp and then we'll talk."

They rummaged through the saddlebag of one of the men who followed Odem and Donella from the valley of the horses. Four men had ridden bareback. They found one full waterskin, a blanket for Donella, and a flint, which they used to start a fire.

"I don't think much of your friend. Why did you bring him along?" Donella added sticks to the fire.

The little fire blazed like a beacon of light on a cloudy night. Insects hummed in the background. The tied horses stood in the shadows. Small gleaming eyes winked under the nearby trees.

"I didn't bring him on purpose. I fled the eastern garrison early in the morning. But I guess I wasn't early enough. He grabbed me as I stepped through the portal and came through with me."

"I had that happen to me once," Donella admitted. "But what were you doing there? I thought you said you were kidnapped?"

Guy shared his small store of food. Some dried jerky and a couple of hard tack biscuits.

Over their meal, Guy informed Odem and Donella about his kidnapping, living aboard the pirate ship, and escaping it. He had got to the part where he and Gensard appeared in the valley above the town when Donella interrupted.

"He has terrible manners for a prince. He never even acknowledged me, not until he used me as a hostage." Donella tossed her black curls. She poked a stick with unnecessary violence into the campfire.

Girls were odd. Why would she want someone to pay her attention when he treated her so badly?

"Let me tell you about Prince Gensard." Odem sat cross-legged on the ground, his back against a log. The firelight washed him in an orange glow.

"Five years ago, Gensard failed to secure the hand of the Princess Lauressa. Now she rules Valdeor. He is under the impression that it should have been him, not Alloryn, ruling at her side."

Donella threw the half-burnt stick into the flames. "Why? Alloryn is a prince, too. And he rescued Lauressa and brought her home."

"At the time, no one knew that Alloryn was a prince. Not even himself. And he didn't have a kingdom, wealth, or connections." Odem stretched out his legs and crossed his ankles. "If Gensard's homeland of Samarantha allied through marriage to Lauressa, the high ruler of Valdeor, his countrymen would've acknowledged him as true heir to his father and rightful leader of his people. He is one of several sons of Prince Xander."

Guy slid from the rock where he sat and propped his back up against it. "So now he must win the Reina's favor by alerting her to the danger facing all Valdeor," Guy summed it up.

Donella spread a blanket over herself. "I still don't like him," she huffed.

The next day on the road, Odem led them along a winding mountain path. Evergreen trees surrounded them. Lush undergrowth proved a lot of rain fell in this area. A thick carpet of pine needles made for a quiet ride. Birds flit from branch to branch.

"I haven't seen any wayposts on this journey. Are there any ahead?" Guy sat astride his horse keeping pace with Odem.

"That is why you found us on the road." Donella pulled her horse abreast of them as they entered a meadow. She squinted in the sudden sunshine. "We did try to use a portal, but something, or someone, blocked the way." Her pert nose sniffed. "Very odd."

"I felt someone's presence using the palace's portal. It could've been Usher." Odem's expression grew thoughtful.

Guy looked from one to the other. Donella bit her lip in a

worried gesture, while Odem stared into the distance.

Guy's shoulders tensed. So many strange things. He felt powerless to stop them. They desperately needed to get to Mintala and warn the Reina, but time was against them. Guy itched to do something.

Odem glanced up and caught Guy's eye. "We could not get through, even after a second try." He rubbed his hand over his eyes, and Guy realized how tired they must be after weeks on the road. "I fear the palace may be under attack."

The worried look on their faces made his heart sink. All this trouble for nothing. The month on the ship, the week traveling with the prince, even leaving his farm—he had accomplished nothing.

And yet, Guy wasn't the same. These last weeks, his worries and trials served a greater purpose. Striving for a goal, something greater than himself, had given him confidence and determination. Working for his stepmother had been like a horse doing a job under the whip. Beaten down. Plodding along one day at a time. He had lived to avoid confrontation. Since leaving home, he learned to take risks and pursue opportunities that presented themselves.

He wouldn't give up so easily.

Odem pulled ahead and took the lead as they left the meadow and headed into the steep hills.

Soon they climbed higher in the mountains, single file as the trail narrowed. Ancient trees closed around them. So tall that they blocked the sunlight, crowding out the undergrowth. Silence pressed them from all sides.

Eventually they reached a plateau, three sides open to the air. A spectacular view spread out below them. The Blue Range mountains and valleys marched across the horizon. A stiff breeze had them all pulling their hoods over their heads.

They rode until they came to a sheltered area with a steep cliff rising above them.

"We had best make camp and get some sleep. Tomorrow is another day of hard travel."

They dismounted and Odem went in search of food. Guy took care of the horses and Donella gathered wood and made a fire. After a meal of cooked rabbit, Odem pulled blankets from his saddlebag and tossed one to Guy.

Guy settled down and used his saddle as a pillow. The stars twinkled coldly in the black sky above. But sleep eluded him.

The other two settled in for the night. Guy thought about his mark. He stared at it in the firelight. Closing his eyes, he imagined the symbol. He grew it in his mind until it became as big as a house.

What did the symbol mean? Seeing it in a different way, he imagined it as a path, looping round and round the center point. He walked it in his mind's eye. What would he find at the center?

He opened his eyes, only to find himself standing inside the maze. What happened? He fought panic as he ran this way and that, finding nothing but walls around him, and a curving path. He gasped with fright.

It is nothing but a dream, a vision. Take a deep breath. Guy slowed his breathing and put out a hand to touch the wall. It wavered, as if he touched water. Jutting out his jaw, one step at a time, he followed the path.

Round and round he went, the maze's walls reflecting his own image. When he turned the final bend, he found himself in a garden, with a fountain tinkling in the center. Butterflies fluttered around, and birds tweeted merrily.

But Guy's attention was held by the creature of light standing beside the fountain. Winged and so beautiful, it made him ache with a strange longing.

"The heart of the maze is the heart of the world. Find the One Who Fashioned All Things' shrine, that men and women's hearts may be full of beauty again."

The glowing figure faded, and with it, the garden grew dim. Guy found himself floating above the maze, seeing the trinity shape. His body floated higher and higher, the maze becoming a glowing speck on a map. Then he saw a speck of light far to the left, and more, winking to the right. Floating higher dozens of lights blazed below him, as if Guy gazed down on the world. Then very far to the right, a lone light stood out, like the shining star of morning, brighter than the rest.

He blinked and found himself back at the campfire, staring at his birthmark. The fire had burned low, and the stars had changed positions. How much time passed? Was it only a dream? It felt so real.

Guy, not sure what to think, yawned. Nothing he could do now. He would figure it out in the morning.

Donella never thought she could wish for Prince Gensard's presence. He was a royal pain. But right now, she would hug him if he appeared.

The day had started out the same as usual. Along with Odem and Guy, she broke camp for the day, eating a handful of fruit to break her fast, since they didn't spare time to hunt. After feeding and watering the horses and saddling them up, they set off through the woods.

How she longed for a real meal, rolling hills of grass, apple orchards, town markets, and people. She was heartily sick of evergreen trees and chill mountain air. Once, she desired to see the realm from end to end—coastal towns on the sparkling sea, placid lakes, and majestic mountains touching the heavens—but now she would be satisfied with a soft bed, a luxurious bath, and a hot meal.

Adventures were fun, until they weren't anymore.

Guy was unusually quiet on the ride. Granted, he was never garrulous at the best of times. But he had been so full of his experiences, words tumbling out since they met, as he shared each incident since they parted. But today was different. He seemed unaware of his surroundings and his companions.

The sky darkened, a heavy feeling in the air. Silence replaced the birdsong that greeted her this morning. Gray clouds shrouded the higher peaks.

When the trail forked, Guy's preoccupation disappeared. "This way," he announced, taking the lead, authoritatively. Though up until today, he seemed content to follow Odem. Guy rode on, not even looking back to see if his friends followed.

Odem exchanged glances with Donella, as if to say, what's come over him? She shrugged and urged her horse forward.

Several times as their path diverged, Guy seemed to know, unerringly, where to go. Donella marveled at his new confidence. She wondered what happened to change him.

At the afternoon's end, a waypost leaned beside a cave in the hillside above them. *How could Guy have known of it? Was it part of his gift?*

The mission's end drew near. She imagined she could smell the steaming food awaiting them and feel crisp sheets underneath her clean body. *It would be so easy to use the waypost and go directly to the palace . . .*

They rounded the corner and her heart stopped.

. . . except for the pack of wolves between them and the portal.

The path went along a ridge, a sharp drop hundreds of feet on either side. Their horses stood on a wide ledge with nowhere to go.

In the previous spring, probably during the snowmelt, rocks and boulders had tumbled down the mountainside, now partly blocking the path to the waypost.

The rockslide keeps the wolves at bay. But how I wish for Prince Gensard and his sword.

The lead wolf raised up its head and bayed. The sound echoed weirdly. She had never heard, or seen, a wolf this close. She wished she still hadn't. Goosebumps ran over her body and her blood raced. She had the primal urge to flee.

The pack closed in.

Odem had his sword at the ready. Guy, although weaponless, kept Donella behind him. The horses danced nervously, ready to bolt, if their riders failed to keep them in line.

The alpha wolf leapt for Odem. Turning his horse to the side at the last moment, Odem slashed at the lead wolf as its paws raked him. He cried out. Blood streamed from his right arm. His blade still in motion sliced through animal's throat and it fell.

Praying under her breath, Donella's heart leaped with gratitude, but the feeling was short-lived as the rest of the pack hastened hard on the leader's heels.

A heavy drop of rain hit Donella, followed by another. A blinding flash hit a lone tree beside the trail, followed by a thunderous crack. Her horse reared, sending her tumbling.

Donella landed on the hard ground. She couldn't breathe as panic surged through her. Expecting fangs to sink into her at any moment, she forced herself on her hands and knees, flexing limbs and muscles for any injuries. The lightning's afterimage clouded her vision, but upon clearing, she glimpsed the pack disappearing back the way they came.

Lightning crackled above them, from cloud to cloud. Big, heavy drops followed.

Guy's horse stepped beside her. He reached down a hand. Donella rose and took it, and he pulled her up behind him. She yanked her hood over her head and clasped her hands around his waist.

The rain came down faster and harder.

Guy urged his horse next to Odem. The commander held his injured arm close to his body, his face white. Donella glimpsed a long, bloody gash. Was that bone? Faintness swept over her.

Wrapping the edge of his cloak around his arm, Odem urged, "Lead on." Guy grabbed the other horse's reins and led them around the rockslide to the waypost.

"What about my horse?" Donella leaned forward and shouted in Guy's ear.

"Whether from fear of the wolves or the lightning, he bolted and lost his footing. He disappeared down the steep slope. You are lucky you fell off, or you would've tumbled down with him."

Heart stuttering at the realization of her close call, she sent up a prayer of thankfulness she was alive. And a prayer for Odem.

Chapter 17

$\mathcal{U}$sher led Alloryn through the portal in the desert to the harbor port. They appeared in a dead-end alleyway. A humid sea breeze tickled Usher's nose, wafting a fishy smell. Walking to the corner, they entered the dockyards.

The wharf hummed with activity. Dockworkers loaded and unloaded ships. Crates and animals blocked the decks. A horse shied at being dragged up the gangplank, neighing and stomping. People barely stopped to stare at the spectacle. Passengers in silk dresses and linen robes boarded big ships. Smaller boats brought in loads of fish, making the salt air pungent. Alongside the chatter of people and crying of gulls, they heard the creaking and groaning of the mighty ships themselves.

No one spared the old man and the warrior a glance.

"I know this place. We're in Laketown Harbor. See the houses rising up the hill?" Alloryn nodded toward the town above them.

"I thought it would be Tulken Harbor. That's where Odem was to meet Donella and Guy." Usher frowned. "It seems the Cantcorans are in this port as well."

"That's not good." Alloryn glanced sharply about. "Let us search for their vessel." The prince entered the stream of people and goods, Usher in his wake. Men stripped to their waists loaded heavy wooden crates. A harassed mother shooed her wayward brood out of the way of a wagon of baggage rolling by. A runny-nosed urchin ran up and begged for coins. Alloryn flipped a coin and moved on.

It didn't take them long to find the Canteor ship with its goat-head prow, plus the fact it rode lower in the water than the Valdeoran ships docked nearby.

They strolled by, scrutinizing it surreptitiously. The prince stopped before a passenger ship berthed beside the pirate ship. They pretended to watch a fancy carriage lifted aboard. Alloryn probably counted cannons and men, while Usher noted the sailors' dress and heard the foreign language they shouted. Usher quickly averted his glance when he observed they drew attention from a tall, one-eyed man aboard the ship staring at them.

Continuing their saunter, they surveyed all the ships tied up at the wharf but found no other suspicious ship.

They circled back, passing it by again. Alloryn stopped on a distant corner of the docks. "No doubt it is a warship. The low water draft allows for greater maneuverability, and the two mainsails give it greater speed.

"Let us see what we can learn in the taverns." Alloryn gestured toward the town.

The two men agreed to split up and Usher spent the rest of the afternoon canvasing the drinking establishments. He eavesdropped on many conversations. When he finally heard a group speaking the Canteor language in a hushed tone, he took the booth nearest to them. He sat facing away from them and leaned back to hear the conspirator behind him. The man didn't keep his voice down.

Spilled ale made the tavern's floor sticky. Usher's waitress wore an apron that looked as if she hadn't washed it in ages. He drank warm ale and ate greasy meat and potatoes. He inwardly sighed at the need to patronize such a low establishment.

He leaned as close as he dared to hear the conversation. Unfortunately, they spoke mostly in Canteoran.

Usher flinched when a cloaked figure sat down across from him. The stranger lifted his hood and revealed the prince. Usher silently approved of the cloak, as it hid the fine linens the prince wore underneath it.

Alloryn tilted his head and raised his eyebrows, as if asking whether Usher eavesdropped on the table behind him. Usher gave a tiny nod in return. Wanting the prince to listen, knowing he might understand Canteoran, Usher clumsily upset his drink. In reaching for the mug under the table, he seemingly fell drunk out of his chair.

"Let me help, old man." Alloryn came around to his side of the table.

Usher whispered, "See if you can understand them, for I cannot."

Casually, Alloryn helped Usher into another chair and took Usher's former seat. Alloryn waved to the barmaid for a round of ale. After that, the two sat silently, as if contemplating the dregs of their drinks.

The Canteorans wrapped up their business and eventually left together.

Alloryn leaned forward and spoke softly. "Those men boasted of the easy conquest of Valdeor. As far as they knew, the local inhabitants have no idea a massive fleet is planning to sweep across the sea." Alloryn clenched his jaw, anger sparking from his eyes. "They spoke of magic that their leaders have harnessed to travel inland." He gripped his mug with both hands. "You were right about the rings, it seems. They mostly talked about what they'd do with their share of the spoils."

Usher knew how serious the situation was. Reina Lauressa ascended the throne only a few years ago, and Usher didn't know the state of her navy, or even if Valdeor had one to mobilize.

"What can we do, Your Highness?"

"If we do not act immediately, the realm will be an easy conquest." Alloryn lifted one arm off the table and signaled the barman, while speaking to Usher in a low voice. "I need you to deliver messages. First to the eastern garrison, then to the lesser princes. We need their support."

The barman came over, wiping his hands on his greasy apron. "What can I do for ye, gents?"

"We need paper and pen. And a quiet place to discuss our business." Alloryn deftly flicked the man a coin.

"Ah, right this way, good sirs." He led them to a back room, shooing out two old men playing a board game. The barman gave a swipe of his rag over the table and stepped in the hall. "Raz! Where has that boy gone?" A lad of about ten appeared in the doorway. "Get these gents pen and paper. And be quick about it!"

They made themselves comfortable in the private sitting room and discussed the situation while waiting for the boy to fetch the items. When Raz returned, Alloryn wrote letters to the garrison captain and the princes of each of the provinces, putting their names on the back. He folded the scrolls up with the names showing and tipped the lit candle, dripping a little wax on the seam. He removed his signet ring with his royal seal of a rampant lion and pressed it into the hot wax as he finalized them.

He handed them to Usher. "Deliver these as quickly as you can. Wait for their answers, then travel to the next. Lauressa will approve of the steps I am taking when she hears the news."

The two somberly retraced their steps to the waypost on the wharf's farthest end. Except for the men on watch, the docks stretched emptily. Lights and sounds spilled forth from the taverns in the distance, but they stood in a pool of silence.

They ducked into the dead-end alley. Usher opened the way to the newly installed portal near the soldiers' quarters outside the palace.

"Thank you for all your help." Alloryn grasped Usher's forearm in a soldier's grip, then stepped through, swirling cloak disappearing into the mist.

Usher glanced around again, and seeing no one, he summoned Odem's garrison on the east coast and stepped through the portal.

The lightning had successfully chased the wolves away, and Donella rode with Guy through the portal.

Soldiers surrounded them as they appeared outside the palace walls.

Odem slipped from his horse as he dismounted. His limp form lay on the ground, his gray cloak dark with blood.

A burly soldier grabbed Donella when she jumped off Guy's mount and headed for her friend. "Can't you see he's hurt!" She vainly struggled.

"He'll be attended to. But any intruders are to be held, by the Reina's orders." She fought against her captor as he dragged her away.

She could hear Guy resisting behind her. "We have important news for the Reina! We must see her!"

"I don't have that authority. You must wait for the captain."

She turned her head back for one last glimpse of Odem, but the soldiers around him blocked her view.

The enormous gemstones set in the embrasures of the palace tower gleamed above them in the late afternoon sun. This wasn't how she imagined entering Mintala.

The guards marched them into a holding cell and left them. The hours passed slowly. Tired and hoarse from begging to be heard, Donella let go of the bars. As she slid down to a sitting position, she muttered to Guy, "If Gensard had only come with us and not stolen the scrolls, this wouldn't have happened."

Guy sat hunched on the floor. "Since we have time on our hands, I want to tell you something." He stared at his mark, seeming reluctant to continue.

Donella watched him with concern.

Finally, he met her eyes. "I had a vision the other night. I entered a maze in the shape of the interlocking ovals. When I reached the center, a being of light stood there." Guy ran his hand through his hair. "I know it sounds crazy."

Donella touched his arm. "Not really. I have always believed you were the Gifted One." She withdrew her hand and hugged herself. "I've always been envious. I wanted to be the one to perform great feats." Admitting it aloud was like releasing a burden she didn't realize she carried.

"You envious? Really?" Guy stared at her wide-eyed. "But you are so confident. Everything you do is successful, unlike me."

"More like full of myself. Too often I want my own way. But you were saying?"

Guy leaned forward. "The Guardian of Valdeor, for that is who he must be, told me to use the portals to find the Isle of Origin. He said, 'The heart of the maze is the heart of the world. Find the One Who Fashioned All Things' shrine, that men and women's hearts may be full of beauty again.'"

"Wow!"

"There's more." Guy rubbed the back of his neck. "After he disappeared, I found myself floating above the world, each portal a pinprick of light below."

The old bite of envy rose in her heart, which she quickly squashed. *I'm glad for Guy. Truly.* Her talents lay in another direction.

She refocused on his conversation. "That's how you knew where to find the portal in the mountains."

He nodded.

"Thank you for telling me. I don't think you're crazy. I think you've been given a quest."

His surprised expression made it clear he expected her to react differently.

Voices outside their cell claimed their attention. They both stood as Captain of the Palace Guards and their jailers approached their cell.

"Are you the two who accompanied Odem?"

"Yes!" they both exclaimed.

"Let them out, Sergeant."

Inserting a key in the lock, the sergeant opened the heavy iron door.

"Sorry you've been imprisoned so long. I just arrived at the barracks for my evening meal. Odem has been in the royal physician's care. He'll recover. Come with me. The prince awaits."

Torches lit their way through the palace hallways.

Donella glanced around the Great Hall. Winged human faces coated in gold topped towering columns. The marble floor tiles made intricate patterns. Dwarfed by the size of the magnificent antechamber, she felt like an insect.

"Your Highness, these are Odem's companions."

Handsome in a green tunic and gold-edged cape, Prince Alloryn listened courteously, unlike Prince Gensard's impatience.

Prince Alloryn's face was manly with chiseled features. His dark, shoulder length hair was brushed back. His brown eyes were intelligent and kind.

Waiting as the prince summoned his wife from her chamber, Donella's heart beat nervously at finally meeting the ruler of the kingdom. She ran her fingers through her hair for the tenth time, trying to tame her wild curls. No time to eat or clean up before delivering their news. She wondered if Gensard had beat them to it.

Would Reina Lauressa dismiss them haughtily?

From another door, Odem joined them. His face looked

strained, his arm bandaged and wrapped in a sling. His face lit up at the sight of them. Careful not to touch his injured arm, Donella hugged him.

When the men at arms opened the doors and ushered them inside, Donella followed her companions and made a curtsy to the royals. When Odem introduced her, she glanced shyly up at the Reina arrayed in a pleated silk gown of royal blue. Lauressa's chestnut hair was done up in an elaborate twisted braid, topped with a delicate, gold filigree tiara. Lauressa wasn't imposing or stern-faced. Her eyes caught Donella's stare, and she gave her a slight smile, the skin around her eyes crinkled with laugh lines. The Reina's eyes seemed to penetrate her with intelligence and wisdom. Donella's tension faded away.

"Please be seated." Lauressa gestured to a long table bearing several lit candelabra. She wore a dark red ruby ring on her slender hand. Prince Alloryn pulled out a chair for his wife and the three sat around the table. Two servants entered, carrying platters of bread, cheese, and fresh fruit for their consumption. "Partake of the snack while we speak." Lauressa motioned to them.

Guy reached out for the food. "Thank you, Your Majesty. Quests can be very difficult on the stomach." A gurgle from his abdomen punctuated his words and his face turned bright red.

Donella suppressed a giggle.

Even Lauressa's eyes twinkled as she agreed, "Yes, I seem to remember that." She shared a look with her husband.

Prince Alloryn spoke and Donella turned her attention to him.

"I passed through your portals today, else I would be skeptical of your tale. Even you, Commander Odem, as much as I esteem you, well, it would normally be hard for me to swallow the idea of traveling instantly between places." Alloryn paced around the room, hands behind his back. "But I was in Laketown only a few hours ago." He proceeded to tell them of his travels with

Usher, and the conversation he had overheard.

"But where is Usher?" Donella blurted out when the prince finished his report. She winced inwardly at speaking out of turn in the royal presence.

Odem spoke before she could embarrass herself further. "I, too, was hoping to see my old friend."

Prince Alloryn turned to him. "I sent him on an errand to find you at the garrison. Or, at least, warn them of the invasion."

"They already know of it." This time it was Guy who interrupted. His face reddened when all eyes turned on him. He hastily put down the bread in his hand and swallowed convulsively. "I was there when the pirates attacked the eastern garrison. They had been holding me captive until then." Guy explained his escape and adventures at the garrison. He dwelt on how the well-placed shots from the cannon overcame the marauders.

While Donella listened to the exchange of news and information on what they each had observed in the last months, and occasionally chimed in, the candles burned lower and lower.

Lauressa spoke very little but asked pointed questions about details. Lauressa's eyes seemed to measure each person as they spoke. Not suspiciously, but as if she read between the lines and pieced a puzzle together. Noticing every flicker of an eye and every gesture of a hand, it seemed as if the Reina saw deeply inside them.

Lauressa finally spoke when the stories wound down. "It seems to me we face an imminent threat of invasion from Canteor, the eastern realm across the sea. Many times, in the distant past, they raided our shores.

"It's my belief Lord Tastaver is getting organized for a cavalry effort." Lauressa glanced around the table. "Odem, you are correct that the garrisons on the seaboards are unprepared to defend against a fleet of ships. I have not had time in these few years of my reign to petition for or fund troops to man the posts. The realm was so poor and beaten down with constant civil war that I concentrated all our troops on routing out the bandit strongholds left over from that time."

Glancing around the table, she added, "I am afraid I did not anticipate war from beyond our shores."

Last, she turned to Guy. "Gyfar, I think you have an important role to play in this, but I cannot see my way clear just yet. May I count on you when the time comes?"

Guy gulped. All eyes were on him. From the beginning, he had resisted getting involved, and yet here he sat in the great palace with the ruler of Valdeor asking for his help. He wet his lips before answering her plea. "Please, call me Guy. I would be honored to serve you in any way, Your Majesty." He just hoped he wouldn't let her nor any of the others down.

It grew very late before the group broke up and pages showed the visitors to their rooms.

The next morning, Guy's limbs felt heavy. He wanted to turn over and bury himself back under the covers. He had tossed and turned half the night after the meeting. He worried that his fledgling powers would not be enough in war time to make the difference everyone expected.

He groaned and dragged himself out of the bed. He washed the grit out of his eyes, just as a tap came at the door. A servant carried in a washtub, followed by other servants bearing hot water cans. But Guy didn't luxuriate long in the warm water, as much as he desired to. A long soak, he feared, would make him sleepier.

When he finished, he found new clothes laid out for him with a servant ready to help him dress. Embarrassed with the unnecessary attention, he dismissed the boy, first asking the way to the dining hall.

Here he found the others already assembled with half-finished plates of food before them. He wasted no time piling his plate high with eggs, bread, bacon, and fresh fruit. When the Prince and Reina joined them, he tried to swallow a large mouthful and ended up choking. He could swear Lauressa held back a laugh, before tears welled in his eyes and Odem hit him hard on the back with his good arm.

"Please finish your meal. We have much to discuss, but minds think better on full stomachs." Reina Lauressa's lips twitched as she darted a glance at Guy's full plate.

"I sent messages to our allies through your friend Usher." Prince Alloryn addressed the group. "Some of them may join us in person. I will need you to tell the pertinent facts of your findings as we work out a plan to combat the enemy."

Lauressa leaned her clasped hands on the table. "I wish I could summon a fleet out of desire. It will take time to build ships and train sailors."

"Fishermen and small ships are found in every harbor." Odem gestured with his good hand. "Their livelihoods, as well as their families, are at risk from the enemy's ships. I am sure you can enlist their help."

Prince Alloryn stopped his pacing and faced Odem. "You have a valid point, Commander, but they are not trained to fight." He shook his head, adding, "And their ships could not handle the rough seas far from shore." He turned his attention to his wife, an odd look on his face. "There is one fleet prepared to besiege our enemy and win . . ." He looked a question at her.

Reina Lauressa stared back at him, her eyes widening.

Ignoring the others, she asked the prince, "Do we trust them to stay the course? Our alliance is still tenuous. They would find themselves in a position to attack our coastline, unhindered." Her brows drew together. "Do we dare?"

"What choice do we have?" Alloryn crossed his arms, his face stern, as if he didn't like his own answer.

Odem's eyes flashed from one to the other, a light dawning on his face.

Guy frowned and glanced at Donella, who also wore a baffled expression.

"The Nyrmidions." Silence met Odem's statement as they all contemplated what that meant.

Guy swallowed his surprise. *How could the Reina even consider them as allies?* The Nyrmidions were dread pirates. Rumor was they caused shipwrecks in order to plunder the goods ships carried. They had a bloodthirsty reputation of sparing no one. They were the most feared enemy on the seas, worse than any sea monster tale.

Into the silence, the head Chamberlain entered. "A message has arrived for Your Majesty—one you were waiting for." Lauressa excused herself and left the dining hall.

They all looked expectantly at Prince Alloryn. He swung a chair around and sat with his arms on the chair back. "It is not as dangerous as your expressions seem to fear. Let me tell you about our encounter with the islanders."

His face took on a distant expression. "After I found Princess Lauressa on the island continent of Hamleor, we set sail for Valdeor. Nyrmidion pirates chased our ship toward their islands. When our ship, the *Silver Spray,* was shipwrecked, I thought my quest had ended before it hardly began. I could not defend us against an island of savages.

"They captured us and brought us to their town built with pieces of salvaged ships—hold hatches for doors, masts for poles, rigging for their laundry lines. They dress oddly, wearing helms with horns, arm or leg braces, breastplates of steel or wood of many different styles from all the peoples they conquered. But the mishmash is only on the surface. They are fierce fighters, as I found out, when their strongest, young warrior fought me for Lauressa.

Alloryn shook his head. "I beat him, but barely. After that, they cruelly imprisoned us in a cage, which they then pulled up to dangle in the air. We waited for them to kill us with other prisoners at the Death Goddess's celebration. That is if we didn't starve first." Alloryn's expression was grim as he remembered.

"How horrible!" Donella burst out. "How did you ever escape? And why would you ever trust them?"

"We did not escape." Alloryn gave her a half smile. "Lauressa healed the headman's son of a deadly fever. In gratitude, he let us go. Later, he paid his debt, joining us against Warlord Feornson. His pirates sailed into this city and took it while the main battle raged near the Warlord's stronghold."

"Would he form an alliance with Her Majesty again?" Odem leaned forward.

"That is the question." Alloryn rubbed the back of his neck. "And could we trust him to stay on target and attack only the Canteor invaders, and not plunder our towns and villages? I am not even sure if Marjek Red Horns is the headman of the island we were shipwrecked on, or the ruler of all the islands. How much influence does he have if he is only the leader of one island?"

The Chamberlain came back at this point and whispered in the prince's ear. "Excuse me. I have important business with the Reina. Make yourself at home in the palace. The servants will see to all your needs."

When the door closed behind the prince, Donella turned toward the others. "I hope this is not the only plan the Reina considers. I don't like the odds at all."

"It is risky, I agree," Odem nodded. "But she cannot conjure a navy from untrained peasants and fishermen. Only a concerted effort will beat the force we fear is coming." He turned to Guy. "What is your assessment of the Canteor raiders, having lived among them?"

An image of the harsh deck master flashed across Guy's mind.

"They are cruel, but very competent at what they do. An untrained group of fishing boats have no chance of defeating them."

"That's what I figured." Odem stroked his chin. "May He Who Fashioned All help us through this."

Guy contemplated the bleak-sounding future. No longer hungry, he pushed his plate away.

Chapter 18

$\mathcal{I}$n a castle perched high above Forestown, Usher had a magnificent view of the city from the window. He stood in the great hall outside the throne room awaiting an audience with King Stepan of Domadaria.

Usher had traveled first to the eastern garrison. There he delivered Prince Alloryn's message to the captain of the garrison. Having helped the prince to compose it, Usher knew the contents. Prince Alloryn praised the captain for his defense of the outpost against the scout ship and promoted him to garrison commander. The message also noted that Commander Odem had been transferred.

Truly, Lauressa needed Odem's special skills elsewhere. Odem was the best spy in the land, although Usher personally thought Donella would soon equal him.

The letter to the captain contained further instructions on what do if the sea raiders returned. The captain must send all sightings or information the garrison gathered to Evodia at the Forest Deer Inn by swift courier. Usher would visit her next to let her know she must immediately pass it on to the palace.

Usher wished there were more waykeepers. He determined to do something about it as soon as he returned to the palace. He would petition Reina Lauressa to allow him to start a program to train new apprentices. If multiple waystations around the country could be manned, news could travel faster and safer than the courier system in place now.

Usher tore his thoughts away from the past when the master of ceremonies beckoned Usher and led him into the throne room. Upon seeing another contingent of courtiers and citizens waiting to speak to the King in this chamber, Usher pursed his lips in frustration.

He tapped the master of ceremonies on the arm. "My business is urgent!" Usher waved the scroll with Prince Alloryn's seal in the man's face. "I come on Prince Alloryn's behalf."

It seemed he spoke the magic words, because the master of ceremonies himself crossed the room to whisper in the King's ear. King Stepan followed the man's gesture and scrutinized Usher. The King nodded and said something, before turning back to the supplicants before him.

The master of ceremonies returned. "If you will step into another room, sir." He then beckoned another servant who led Usher into a private room off the throne room. Usher paced about for a bit, swinging around as the door opened. But instead of King Stepan, a younger man entered.

"I have urgent business—" he began again, his tone sharp and impatient.

"I know, and that is why my father sent me. Prince Talud, at your service." The prince held out a hand for the message. He smiled, "I am well acquainted with Alloryn. We rescued the princess from Feornang together."

Usher relented and handed over the letter. In this message, Prince Alloryn asked for Stepan's help in raising a navy against the looming threat of an overseas invasion. The kingdom of Domadaria lay along the southeastern coast of Valdeor. Tulken Harbor was the biggest seaport of King Stepan's province.

Prince Talud raised his eyebrows and his smile receded as he read. He was of medium height, but broad-shouldered. He wore soft clothes in colors of muted brown and green, with his sword's scabbard strapped over top of them. He frowned and re-rolled the scroll, gripping it in his right hand.

"You have seen these pirate dogs?" he demanded, staring at Usher over the scroll in his hand.

"Yes, Your Highness. As you have read, we overheard their plans the day before yesterday." Usher hoped Talud wouldn't ask how he had gotten this message to the castle so quickly. But he knew Alloryn had written in the letter that the king could trust Usher absolutely.

The prince tapped the scroll on his open palm. "Of course, my father will help in any way. He is related to Lauressa and was instrumental in defeating Feornson, the warlord who usurped her throne. It is providential timing, actually, as we have spent several years upgrading our fleet."

Usher lifted his eyebrows at the news.

Talud must have seen the surprise on Usher's face, because he explained further, "Not, as you might presume, against any attack on our shores, but to carry our goods to every port. Reina Lauressa, as well as my father, knows that trade is the only way to make the kingdoms prosperous again."

"Of course. She will be most pleased to receive your support."

Prince Talud walked toward the door. "I will send servants with food and ale. You may take your rest while I speak with my father." Talud waved Alloryn's letter. "We will give you a swift answer, never fear."

The prince was as good as his word. Several hours later, after Usher had satisfied his hunger and had a chance to clean himself up, a page summoned him to the King's private chamber.

Torches lit the wide halls. Though not as grand as Lauressa's palace, the castle had many wood-carved details showing off Domadaria's skilled woodworkers. Upon entering the chamber, Usher first noticed the huge, finely carved mantelpiece which dominated the room. Fantastical animals peeked out from the vines that covered the piece. Beside it, on a wooden chair made in the image of a griffin, sat King Stepan.

The king had a brown beard going gray. He wore forest brown leggings and a green over-tunic with long laced boots. He looked more like a forester than a king, except for the gold crown on his head. Short and muscular like his son, he had piercing, blue eyes. Usher thought he would be a formidable enemy.

"My son has shown me the letter from the Prince Consort. I wish you to tell me the story in your own words."

Usher bowed, then sat on the chair provided for him. His spirits brightened when the prince fetched him a jug of ale and a mug and put them on a table at his elbow. Talud leaned against the fireplace mantel.

"The story does not start with me, but with a young girl who is a very good spy. Now suspend your disbelief while I tell you about the waykeepers—which are not legends, as I myself am one—and how the foreign plotters are using our own rings against us."

Usher began the story with Donella searching for a powerful waykeeper and stumbling upon the conspirator in the woods. Her subsequent enlisting other waykeepers to find and determine his plans, Odem's involvement, and Guy's kidnapping. Usher told of enlisting the Reina's help, Alloryn's eavesdropping, and ended with the plea for help from the palace.

Usher quenched his thirst with the last of the ale and sat back.

King Stepan had listened, interrupting occasionally, to clear up a point. Now he sat silent, digesting the news.

Usher glanced at Prince Talud, his brow crinkled, staring off into the distance of his own thoughts.

"If Alloryn had not written to trust you implicitly, I wouldn't give credence to your story. But as it is . . ." The king stood up and paced, his hands clasped behind his back. "The situation you describe is very grave. You may reassure Lauressa that our small fleet is at her disposal. Talud tells me you have other provinces to alert. I will write a letter to each, adding my weight to the seriousness of aiding the Reina at this time. I will have them at the ready tomorrow morning."

The king retook his seat.

Sensing the audience was over, Usher stood and bowed. "Thank you, Gracious King, for your help. One other thing, Your Majesty. There is one here in the city that you can use to ferry messages to the Reina. Brodyn is the potter's son in the Forestown marketplace. He is also an apprentice waykeeper."

"A waykeeper in my realm?" King Stepan leaned forward, grasping the arms of the throne. "Why did I not know of this?"

"We became a secretive group as our numbers dwindled, even before the Myrkr Revolt against Lauressa's father, King Arness. Let us just say we continue to be cautious in a changing world." Usher pinched his chin with his fingers. "Just as the invaders are using the portals for nefarious reasons, we fear the enemy might exploit our weaknesses. Imagine if they could coerce us into transporting illegal goods or evil men across vast distances. Better to stay in the shadows than let them manipulate us."

The king grunted, then sat back and said, "You have valid reasons. I will seek the boy out. This will cut down enormously on time from using couriers. Thank you for the invaluable information. I will keep the secret you have entrusted me with, as will my son."

Talud stepped forward. "I would like to accompany him, Father. Even traveling secretly as he does, he could use a swordsman by his side. Bandits still lurk on the roadways, watching for easy targets. These conspirators might watch over the wayposts, too."

King Stepan glanced from one to the other. "Very well, son. Go with my blessing."

Chapter 19

*D*onella jingled the coins in her pocket as she walked, abstracted, through the Mintala market. The market's smells greeted her nose—roast meats, fresh bread, and spices. Its familiarity comforted her.

Who knew a palace with everything one could desire would become boring? Did luxury make her weary? After all, in the last weeks she ate well, slept well, and indulged in a bath whenever she wished. Her hair elegantly styled and a new gown to wear every day was every girl's dream. Yet she went in search of something to do.

She contemplated all the people hurrying along with a purpose. *That is what I lack. Purpose. No one needs me at the palace.*

Donella enjoyed sharing her meal with travelers, exploring new waystations, singing for her bread. Now she received all she wanted without lifting a finger. *Who knew life could be so dull when you didn't have to work?*

Donella thought about finding a spot and singing. But what if Reina Lauressa found out? Would she be hurt that Donella tried to earn her way?

Odem often attended meetings with the Reina and Prince

Alloryn and their generals as they worked on strategy.

Guy spent his time in the archives, furthering his understanding of the portals and his gift.

If only I could find something useful to do. Planning a war is not one of my accomplishments. Dusty scrolls couldn't teach me any more about my talent than experience already has.

She realized she stood before a stall with crystal pendants. She reached out and touched one with her fingertip. It spun and caught the light, shooting rainbows. She watched idly, when a conversation penetrated her self-absorption.

"—a pearl in his ear. He offered it to me if I would tell him the number of soldiers in the palace barracks and when the shift changed."

"Ooh," a second female giggled. "I'd take the pearl. Imagine how much it'd be worth!"

"You'd sell out the lovely princess for a bauble?! For shame, Merryn! What is the younger generation coming to?"

"Well, I wouldn't give him the *real* number of men. Just a portion, so as the foreigner would believe me. Then expecting fewer, they'd overwhelm him. And I would be the proud owner of a lovely pearl. No more washing the garrison laundry for me."

As the voices moved away, Donella peered at the washerwomen so she'd know them again.

Here was one of her accomplishments. One that the Reina could use in her arsenal against invaders. Gathering information.

A plan formed in her head. Her boredom evaporated, replaced with the tingle of excitement.

She tailed the washerwomen as they made their way to the area near the barracks outside the palace walls. When they separated, Donella followed the younger one, Merryn. The girl went down an alleyway. Women sat in doorways nursing their babies, while other ragged children helped their mothers as they worked over steaming washing tubs. Laundry lines of soldiers' uniforms and nobility's finery hung everywhere, swaying in the breeze.

As Merryn was about to enter a house, Donella increased her pace and called out, "A moment of your time!"

Merryn swung around. The girl stared a moment before making a deep curtsy. Donella realized she must look like a fine lady because she wore a borrowed lace-trimmed gown and a jeweled headband held her tamed ringlets in place.

"Does your ladyship require a new laundress? My family offers very good prices and exceptional service."

Donella studied the girl as she rattled off her services. Not much older than herself she had mousy brown hair and a thin, pointed nose. She wore a clean dress too big for her, tied with a colorful sash tightly around her waist. That and the gaudy red ribbon in her hair reminded Donella that Merryn spoke of craving fine things.

When Merryn paused for breath, Donella stepped closer. "I wish to learn your trade. Will you take me as an apprentice?"

If Donella had offered to fly Merryn to a distant land, the girl couldn't have looked more shocked. Her mouth gaped open, resembling a fish.

Donella leaned in closer. "It's for a bet. With my boyfriend. He thinks I am only good for embroidery."

Donella smiled, encouragingly. She pulled a coin from her pocket and put it in the girl's unresisting hand and closed it over. "And for your personal trouble . . ." Donella removed her sparkling headband and offered it.

Actually, it wasn't hers to give. She supposed it came from the royal treasury. But she figured this was a worthy cause.

Merryn's eyes grew wide, then she snatched the headband and held it close. "Anything your ladyship wants, I'd be happy to help."

"First, though, I'll trade you dresses." When Merryn did the fish out of water routine again, Donella gestured at her own attire. "I cannot wash clothes in this finery!"

Donella spent her afternoon chatting and working with Merryn at her family's laundry, learning more about washing than she ever wanted to know.

Hot, sweaty, and smelling of soap, she walked back to the palace hours later, satisfied that she could put her plan in motion come morning. Humming, she barely registered a few odd looks she received as she walked into the palace and down the halls to her assigned room.

"My goodness! What happened to you?"

Donella registered her maid's shocked gaze. As the girl laid out an evening dress for dinner, Donella realized the maid saw her leave for the day dressed as a lady and return as a peasant.

"Do you wish to have a bath?"

After all the time she spent with her arms in the laundry vat, Donella had no desire to get wet. "No, I'll just brush my hair. You can leave."

A gentle tap came on Donella's bedroom door. She got up from brushing her hair, walked over, and opened it. Evodia stood there. Without her plain brown homespun and apron, she was almost unrecognizable in an emerald green dress, her plaited hair over one shoulder.

"Evodia! What are you doing here? Come in!" Donella opened the door wide and welcomed her friend inside.

"My dear, it is so good to see you." Evodia gave her a big hug. She smelled like flour and vanilla.

Donella led her to a settee at the foot of the fourposter bed.

"What news? Tell me while I dress." Donella moved behind the changing screen.

"Usher came to visit me."

"I wondered where he went."

"He asked me to take a letter from the Reina to the mayor of Zendira. She wanted volunteer troops to train at the palace. Imagine my surprise when Usher said to bring them with me through the portal. But he hinted at war and told me of great urgency.

"The mayor made a proclamation throughout the region. Men gathered from the city and the surrounding area in the last weeks. I opened the waypost in the center of the market. You should've seen the amazement on everyone's face. I'm sure I now have the reputation of a witch." She chuckled. "Anyway, here I am."

Donella came out from behind the screen. "Could you button up the back? I sent my maid away." While Evodia worked, Donella told her of her adventures since they last met.

When Evodia finished, Donella studied herself in the full mirror. Her black curls tumbled down the back of her lilac gown. The sleeves were tight to the elbow, then widening to her wrists. She turned this way and that, smoothing her dress.

"Now I understand Usher's haste." Evodia frowned. Then her face brightened. "Oh, and I brought a friend of yours."

"Really? Who?" Donella spun to face her. She couldn't think of who it could be.

"He sells rugs."

"Rongel? He's here!" Donella's eyes widened. "Of course, he told me he was a prizefighter in his youth. He would volunteer. There's time before dinner. Will you take me to him?"

They left the palace and wound through town. Evodia led her out of the city gates to a tent town full of volunteer troops. Asking around, they eventually located Rongel eating a bowl of stew.

"I'll leave the two of you. Dinner is calling." Evodia patted Donella's arm and walked away.

"Any left for me?" Donella teased him.

"What are you doing here?" Rongel's astonished gaze traveled over her.

"Same as you. I came to help the Reina." Donella twisted a piece of hair around her fingers. "I could use your help."

"I know that look. You're up to something." He sighed and put down his spoon. "What is it now?"

Donella outlined her plan. Rongel shook his head, but eventually agreed.

She arrived at Merryn's hovel before dawn. Donella had Merryn's mother set up her vat at the parade ground's edge, near the barracks. Merryn and her siblings followed, carrying jugs of steaming water and filling it up. Donella drummed up business by indulging in flirty banter with the soldiers. All the while she kept an eye out for a man with a pearl earring.

Arms crossed, Rongel stood at the corner of the training yard.

Merryn and her widowed mother did most of the washing, freeing up Donella to keep an eye on potential customers.

As the morning wore on and became afternoon, she realized it might take days for her plan to work. Sighing as she wrung out a pair of trousers, she noted Rongel signing to her. She followed his stare. A man stood nearby, his profile to her. He displayed a pearl in his left ear. Something about him was off, as if she had seen him before. He turned slightly and she recognized him.

The conspirator from the cave! Harban.

Her pulse sped up at the sight of him here.

She followed Harban's gaze. He observed the soldiers.

Donella nudged Merryn and hissed, "Is he the one?" Merryn looked up, using the back of her hand to push the hair out of her eyes. "Yes! That's him," she whispered back.

Cold fear pooled in Donella's stomach. She recalled Evodia's advice that he would not remember their first encounter. What about a barmaid months ago? She had to take the chance he had forgotten her face.

Donella passed the trousers to Merryn's mother and boldly approached the man. "Looking for exceptional service? We offer the best rates and cleanest clothes in Mintala."

He turned his full gaze toward her. A glint caught her eyes and she observed he wore a goat head amulet.

She had her man. Now to keep him.

She parted her lips and stepped closer. She made her voice husky. "I'll even throw in a free bath for such a fine fellow as yerself." She winked at him. "I know every soldier in this place, and none have your dreamy chocolate eyes. Bet the girls chase you mercilessly."

He thrust out his chest and rubbed his goatee. "Well, you're a pretty little maid. Where is this bath of yours?"

She smiled on the outside, but her hands were clammy.

Rongel strolled by.

She led Harban to the bathing stalls belonging to Merryn's family, gave him a bar of soap and a towel. She tossed her hair and sashayed back to the vats while he watched. When he disappeared inside, Rongel stepped up and bolted him in the stall.

Returning, Donella heard loud whistling coming from inside the bathhouse, so she didn't think he heard the bolt slip into place.

Rongel crossed his arms and stood guard.

She could barely contain her glee as she hurried toward the palace to seek out Odem. He would know what to do next.

A growing crowd pushing their way beyond the barracks distracted her. When she glimpsed the spectacle drawing everyone's attention, she stood gaping like Merryn had yesterday.

Two portals stood open, one on either side of the waypost.

She joined the others racing that way. As she got there a space opened in the crowd and she spotted a familiar face.

Chapter 20

*I*n the flickering candlelight, as his stomach rumbled, Guy realized he had missed another meal. But the scrolls, laid in heaps around him in the archive room, occupied him for the last weeks to the exclusion of all else. Libran, the archivist, retrieved for him all the documents about the waykeepers and their rings.

"No trouble. No trouble at all. I recently found them for Usher."

Guy rubbed his hand over his eyes, tired from reading. But he knew much more about his calling. Because whether he wanted it or not, it was a calling. Few knew how to open the portals with the rings, and no one could do it without one. Except him.

He stared at the imprint on the back of his hand. He received occasional stares when people saw it. He could understand their fear, especially since the attempt to breach the portal at the barracks. Seems no one had known a thing about the old post in the palace garden until Usher came. Now rumors of invasion circulated daily among the soldiers and servants.

Guy's dream, or vision, or whatever it was, fueled his desire to read accounts of waykeeper's lives. Many had kept journals or logs, some intact, while others were only fragments with cramped handwriting. Most writings contained everyday transactions and glimpses into ancient times, but once in a while, a nugget of information caught his eye.

Such as today's scroll. It told of one waykeeper who opened two portals at once when the thought of seeing his dying father distracted him. One doorway opened to his father's home and another to a pilgrim's destination. Other waykeepers learning of the anomaly had tried to duplicate the feat, but they abandoned their attempts, lacking the ability to focus.

I wonder if I could do it?

Excitement tingled along his arm as he thought of trying. Pushing back his chair, he strode out of the archives and took the stairs two at a time.

He marched toward the barrack waypost, past bakers carrying baskets of pastries, and washerwomen plying their trade just beyond the training yard.

The soldiers nodded familiarly at him. Guy had visited several times. First with Prince Alloryn to look at Usher's work, another time to show his ability to the curious Reina, and on other occasions.

Reaching the waypost, Guy forced all distractions aside—the soldiers' conversation, the sword practice in a nearby field, the chirping birds in the garden. Instead, he focused on his farm's details.

He thought of the stable and the smell of hay and horses. Once he burned the image firmly in his mind, he envisaged himself standing in the stable. With eyes closed, he reached out and touched the waypost.

Then he tried to imagine a totally different environment, the garrison by the sea. Pretending he stood in his stable, he tried to smell the sea air and hear the waves crashing and seagulls crying. Soon a massive energy surge hummed around him, as if vibrations from two directions pulled at him. Startled, he opened his eyes.

On either side of the waypost, different landscapes opened.

His old farm seemed rundown, weeds growing in the field. Next to it, the majestic sea blew a storm toward him. He could feel the humid storm air ruffling his hair and his clothes.

Sudden light-headedness swept over him.

I did it! Only the second waykeeper in history to open two portals simultaneously! He grinned from ear to ear.

Someone bumped his arm. Guy turned to see who touched him. A crowd had quickly gathered around him.

"How did you do that?!" Guy blinked at Donella's sudden appearance as she grabbed his arm. He did a double take at her brown sackcloth gown. Were those soap bubbles in her hair? But he had no time to answer her as soldiers and other palace staff gathered round them, yelling and pointing.

The Captain of the Guard pushed his way roughly through the crowd, using his pike end to make headway. "Move along. Let me through, clods. You, soldier! Quit staring. Alert the prince. Two invasion groups confront us!" he shouted. The storm blowing through the portal carried his voice away.

Moments later, soldiers with pikes pushed Guy and Donella back and took up attack positions, pikes pointed into the wind from the sea. Guy's focus faltered, but he put more effort into it. The portals scaled back in size but remained open.

Donella let go of Guy and grabbed the captain's arm. "It's not an attack!" she yelled over the wind. "Guy's doing it!"

The confused captain was soon joined by Prince Alloryn, the Crestin Sword at the ready. "What is the status here, Captain Rodrek?"

Donella transferred her gaze to Alloryn and spoke before the captain could. "Guy is doing it! He opened two portals! This has never been done!" She sounded as elated as Guy felt.

The prince put his free hand on Guy's shoulder. "Is there any danger? Why did you do it?"

Guy's mouth went dry. *How to explain why I caused an*

uproar? Just because I wanted to prove I could do something that was only done once before!

Donella saved him. "The danger is not here. I've captured Harban, a foreign plotter, for you to interrogate." She wore a smug expression as Guy, Prince Alloryn, Captain Rodrek and others swiveled to gaze at her with astonishment.

Guy had been losing concentration for some time, the portals shrinking in size, and at her announcement he finally let the images go. The storm winds disappeared and the unsettling, vibrating hum with it.

The soldiers dispersed the crowd at Prince Alloryn's command. They left with much murmuring.

The four stood alone.

"Hurry! There's no time to lose! I've got a spy who's been observing the soldiers."

Staring at Donella, Guy noted her odd attire. She wore not only a sackcloth dress with an apron, but her rolled up sleeves showed her bare wet arms, and her pinned-up hair was damp. She smelled strongly of laundry soap. But she seemed oblivious to her appearance.

She, too, it seemed, had done the impossible.

Odem trotted up and joined the group trailing behind Donella to the laundry vats. "Quite the accomplishment." He quirked an eyebrow at Guy.

Heat rose up Guy's neck. *Why do I do things that make me stand out in a crowd? But if I do not grasp my abilities now, learning them in the time of danger wouldn't do much good.*

Prince Alloryn confronted him. "Next time, let Odem or me know when you plan to experiment with your power."

Guy nodded, shoulders slumped.

Ahead of them, Donella stopped before a bathing stall. A

burly man with crossed arms stood outside it.

Pounding came from inside. "Let me out! Help! Can anyone hear me?"

"Step aside, Rongel." Donella pulled the bolt from the latch.

Harban popped out. Quickly assessing the situation, he grabbed Donella, his knife at her throat. He faced Guy and the others as they approached, still too far away to help. They froze.

Quick as a cobra, burly Rongel clasped him in a wrestler's hold. He bent Harban's wrist until Donella heard a snap.

Freed, Donella jumped aside as her friends rushed over.

Prince Alloryn and Odem, whose sword arm had healed, drew their weapons. Harban, white-faced and clutching his arm against his middle, stared at Prince Alloryn's ruby-hilted sword. His gaze darted around seemingly looking for escape. Captain Rodrek's pike joined the other weapons and the man reluctantly put up his good hand in surrender.

"I've done nothing wrong, gentlemen. I assure you." His gaze caught Donella hovering in the background. "Whatever the girl told you, I can explain."

Guy spoke in the language he learned aboard ship. "The jig is up. We know who you are."

The man tensed, his eyes narrowing at Guy.

Guy nodded at the prince. "He understands me. He is one of them."

Gathering a contingent of soldiers, Captain Rodrek led the man to the barracks for interrogation.

Excitedly, Donella told them how she heard about a man interested in learning the number of soldiers and their schedule. Then how she set out to catch him and recognized him as a conspirator.

"Well done, little one." Odem squeezed Donella's shoulder, then followed Captain Rodrek and Prince Alloryn.

"That was very clever." He didn't know what else to say. Guy didn't think she could preen anymore, but she did.

"You too," she responded, bouncing on the balls of her feet.

From the barrack doorway, Odem motioned for Guy to join him. "You can help the prince translate what the prisoner says."

Guy made an apologetic face at Donella as he shuffled after Odem. He did not want to partake in an interrogation. Shipboard life had somewhat toughened him. He attended several whippings. *But torture?* He wasn't sure he was up to it.

Chapter 21

onella didn't witness Harban's interrogation. She did her part handing him over to the authorities. *Not that I am squeamish. Well, maybe a little.* She could handle blood. *But pulling out fingernails . . . even if he threatened her with a knife once.* She shuddered at the thought. Maybe she wasn't cut out to be a spy.

"If you're done with me, I'll head back to training with the Zendirans."

"Thank you, Rongel. Working together is like old times."

He grinned and shook his head side to side, with an exasperated expression.

She left the barrack area and laundry vats and headed toward the palace. As she debated what to do next, someone tugged on her sleeve. She glanced over and perceived a young boy. Ready to shoo a beggar away, she realized he wore the royal page's uniform—a deep, royal blue tunic with a seven-pointed, gold embroidered star in the center, with black leggings underneath.

He had a thatch of light brown hair, his bangs hanging down over his enormous eyes. He impatiently pushed the bangs aside. "Please, mistress, come with me. Her Majesty wishes your attendance."

After getting her attention, he entered the palace, Donella following. He confidently led her down hallways.

"Do I have time to change?" she asked as she hurried to keep up with him.

"Only if you're quick. Me sister takes half the morning. Are you like that?"

"No, I won't let the Reina wait so long. But my dress is splashed, and my hair is damp. That is no way to make a good impression, you know."

The boy guided her to the guest quarters.

"What is your name?" Donella turned to face him as she opened her bedroom door.

"Jimzy."

"Well, Jimzy, I will try not to take as long as your sister."

"Sisters," Jimzy corrected her. "I have five. And they all love fancy get-ups." He sighed with the weary air of all men, though he looked to be about ten.

Donella suppressed a giggle and hurriedly changed. She stood before the mirror in a rose-colored frock that contrasted well with her dark hair and brought out the apples in her cheeks.

She sighed at her bedraggled hair. No time to fix it up properly in one of the new styles the ladies-in-waiting wore. Not just because Jimzy waited, but she would need her maid's help, and that would take half the afternoon. Her eyes watered as she ruthlessly pulled a comb through it. Her damp curls exploded wildly, so she put in a few pins to at least keep it off her face.

A dab of perfume and she was ready to meet with the Reina.

Jimzy gave her the once over when she joined him in the corridor.

"How was that for speed?" Donella fell in beside him as he set off.

He sniffed. "Not too bad. For a female, that is."

Donella didn't think she could ever find her way around these passageways, but Jimzy was like an ant scurrying for his anthill. He stopped before a large, carved door where several guards stood at attention.

"Her Majesty awaits us." Jimzy told them, morphing into a haughty little courtier. When the honor guards opened the door, the boy swept his hand out, indicating for Donella to enter. "This way, mistress."

Donella cocked a brow at him as she passed, but he ignored her. Putting his chin up in the air, he walked up to the table where Reina Lauressa sat, sheaves of papers strewn before her.

Her gown's beautiful shade of green complemented her eyes and contrasted with her chestnut hair swept back in a loose bun at the nape of her neck. She wore no jewelry except an intricately woven gold wedding band. Her casual attire signaled a less informal meeting.

Jimzy announced imperiously, "Mistress Donella, Your Majesty." He bowed stiffly, then stepped backward as he straightened.

Donella thought a twinkle gleamed in Lauressa's eye, but the Reina spoke seriously, "Thank you, Jimzy. You may go to the kitchen and receive your afternoon refreshment."

At her words, Jimzy's formal manner disappeared. "Thank you, Your Majesty." He sketched a quick bow and happily skipped out a servant's door.

"Wherever did you find him?" Donella burst out, then blushed at her temerity. She curtsied, hoping her bowed head hid her embarrassment.

Reina Lauressa seemed not to notice her bad manners of speaking first in the royal presence. "On the streets. His mother is a widow, who takes in laundry for a living."

"Is his sister named Merryn?" Donella recalled Jimzy's description of his finery-loving sisters.

"Why, yes. Do you know her?"

"Uh, we've met."

"Well, anyway, he struck me as such a lively little thing. Alloryn calls him my folly. Says I will never make anything of him. But you can see the intelligence in his eyes." She pushed her papers away. "Before becoming ruler, I dreamt of helping orphans. Now I am in a position to help Jimzy and others in harsh circumstances through no fault of their own."

Donella admired the Reina's compassion.

"Warlord Feornson and the others who squabbled over the throne thought only of themselves. True leaders must be public servants. I've dedicated my life to improving my subjects' lives.

"But I ramble on." Reina Lauressa smiled and gestured to a chair opposite hers at the table. "Please be seated."

Donella sat, her back as straight as the woman she faced.

She understood now why the Reina was so popular among the people. Lauressa looked to be only a handful of years older than herself. Only her eyes were old and wise. Her demeanor was calm, rather than stern. The suppressed grin at Jimzy's exit showed her humor. In other circumstances, Donella would have sought her as a friend.

"How can I be of service, Your Majesty?"

"I wanted you to tell me how you continue to find enemies when my own spies cannot."

For a moment, the seriousness in the Reina's face made Donella's heart speed up. *Surely Lauressa didn't suspect me of being part of this?*

Lauressa leaned back in her seat and tucked one fist under her chin. "For instance, I heard something about a bathhouse?" She raised one eyebrow and the corner of her mouth lifted.

Donella supposed she shouldn't be surprised that Valdeor's ruler had the most up-to-date information.

Embarrassed at first, Donella related the whole tale, including her costume and the soap which she had to wash off just before her appearance.

Donella held nothing back, as Lauressa proved to be such a good listener.

"Usher was correct when he said you are quite the spy, after Odem."

"I don't know about that, Your Majesty. But I have had some experience." And with a little encouragement, she told the curious monarch how she came to be a waykeeper and then a spy.

"But most of all, I wish I had Guy's talent," Donella found herself admitting out loud. "I always hoped I'd be chosen to be the Gifted One."

"Donella, I'll share what I learned in a long lifetime." The Reina clasped her hands in front of her and leaned forward. "Life is a tapestry and we are the threads. Trust in the One Who Fashioned All to weave your story in as He wants it to be. Seek His glory, not yours. Search your heart to discover what your true talents are. Not what you want them to be. Do what you do best."

Donella wandered the palace halls after leaving the Reina. She peeked in a fancy drawing room, empty except for richly carved furniture, sumptuous rugs and thick curtains. She waltzed in, imagining she wore a dress with a long train which she flipped to one side as she sat on an overstuffed chair and pretended to pour tea.

"Lady Frump, how good of you to come." She nodded her head to her invisible guest while she fanned herself with a fan she found lying on the coffee table.

"Girls." The word whispered in the air, making Donella jump. She spun around, seeking the source.

Jimzy stood in the doorway.

"Is the Reina holding another meeting?" Donella spoke quickly, embarrassed. *Thank goodness it was only Jimzy, and not*

Guy who found me pretending to be a grand lady.

"Nots that I know of. I'm off duty." He seemed in no hurry to leave. She wondered if he was lonely. She had seen only a few other pages.

"Do you like horses? Let's go to the stable." Donella stood. She desired to befriend this boy, not much younger than herself. She could use another friend, too.

"I guess so."

She joined him. "Come on then. Lead me to the kitchen and we'll get my horse carrots to munch on."

Jimzy knew his way around the palace, leading her down halls and back staircases.

"I would take twice as long to get here," she commented as they arrived at the enormous kitchen.

He sniffed. "That's 'cause I know all the shortcuts."

Donella breathed in the smell of roasting pork mixed with spices. The head cook and assistants worked at a huge worktable in the middle of the room, some rolling out dough, others polishing silverware, while still others stirred pots over the giant fire.

Donella's mouth watered.

After cajoling an assistant cook for the treats, Donella led the way to the stables. Evodia had brought Seeker to the palace saying that he might be more useful here than at her inn.

Entering the stable, Donella relished the sweet smell of hay and manure. Jimzy copied her deep breath and promptly sneezed.

It took a moment for her eyes to adjust to the dim light. She glanced in each stall, searching for the proud stallion.

They found the giant wolfhound, Trekker, guarding his mate and a litter of squirming puppies. His threatening growl warned them not to touch his offspring.

"They are so cute, but I think we'd better leave them be for now." Donella longed to snuggle one.

A boy leaving the last stall turned around, holding a brush, and to her surprise, he wasn't the expected stable hand, but Guy.

"Jimzy and I came to visit Seeker, but I see you beat us to it." Donella walked up and the horse snuffed out at her when she stroked his bristly nose. "See what I brought you, old friend?" She fed a carrot to the magnificent black beast. Seeker gently took it from her hand with his big, square teeth.

Guy grinned. "I just got back from riding him. He needed the exercise, and I guess I needed the fresh air after spending time in the archives."

Donella gave Jimzy the second carrot. "Here. Hold out your hand and let Seeker take it." Jimzy looked doubtful. "He's gentle," she reassured him. As the horse leaned down and took the carrot from his outstretched hand, Jimzy rewarded her with his big smile.

"Did you find anything interesting?" Donella leaned back against the stall gate and faced Guy. She absently wrapped a strand of hair around her forefinger.

"I found a record of fifty known portals. At least a dozen rings are missing." Guy ran his hand through his hair, further mussing up the windblown locks. "But Usher already told us that. What I didn't expect was several more portals located outside Valdeor."

Donella stopped twirling her hair and stared. "Really? You mean the conspirators can travel from their land directly here?" Her eyes widened, imagining hordes descending on them.

"No." Guy shook his head. "It's too far. But other lands do have them. Islands to the east of us have portals. I'm not sure about the Nyrmidion Isles, but Hamleor has several. As best as I can determine, only lands where the One Who Fashioned All is worshiped have portals. But not pagan lands, nor Valdeoran provinces that never had the faith. Although I found one or two in Canteor."

Glancing at Jimzy, who petted Seeker's nose, Donella refocused on Guy. "Do you think the portals have something to do with the faith?"

Guy rubbed the back of his neck. "I'm thinking it must. The Gifted One is meant to find the lost shrine to the Almighty. The pilgrims used the portals in ancient times, visiting the shrine to worship Him." He put the brush on the shelf beside him. "Unfortunately, the older scrolls are in the worst condition. I'm trying to reconcile my vision with known maps."

Jimzy grew bored and interrupted the conversation. "Hey, do you think he'd let me ride him?"

Donella stood up straight. "Well, maybe we should let you sit on him first." She winked at Guy, and his worried expression cleared.

"Ooh, can I?"

Guy got the tack, while Donella showed Jimzy the symbol branded on Seeker's side. "You see, it matches my ring and the mark on Guy's hand."

Jimzy inspected each one intently. "What's it mean?"

"It means he can travel through the portals, even without a rider." Seeker seemed to know they spoke about him, as he chose this moment to push Donella's hand with his nose. "Seeker can go anywhere he wants."

"Is he yours?" Jimzy watched as Guy saddled the horse.

Donella stroked the stallion on the blaze between his eyes. "Seeker belongs to no one. He is his own master. Treat him well. He is the only animal who has this ability."

"Really? He's special!" Jimzy stared up at Seeker, his face curious.

Jimzy swallowed nervously as Guy lifted him up on the horse's back. "Gracious, he's as tall as me mom's house." Jimzy's fists gripped Seeker's mane.

"You'll get used to it. Just hold onto the saddle horn." Donella took the bridle and led Seeker into the stableyard. Jimzy held on for dear life. White-faced, the boy showed courage. Donella and

Guy walked Seeker until Jimzy gained a little confidence.

"See, you can do it."

That evening, Guy, along with Donella and Odem, joined the Prince and Reina for dinner in their private dining room. Not as large as the main dining hall, it boasted sunny yellow draperies over deep window embrasures. Candelabra on the table gave the room a warm, intimate glow. A fireplace flickered against the chill night.

After succulent roast pig and the many varied and delicious courses, talk turned to the day's events.

Reina Lauressa waited until the servants removed the last dish and left the wine decanter for the men. Only the five remained as she dismissed her honor guard to remain outside the doors.

When the doors shut behind them, Reina Lauressa turned to her husband. "Did you learn anything from the prisoner?"

Prince Alloryn poured himself a glass of wine. "Although he was reluctant to give us any information, we did get the outline of a plan. He is a major player and has full knowledge of the operation. You were right about the enemy we face, Lauressa. The man behind the plan is the Canteor monarch, Prince Pashmi.

"Roughly, the plot is to land a dozen ships in several spots along the coast, overwhelm the citizens and get to key wayposts. A wealthy Canteor trader has enough horses to supply the troops—"

"Troops, not sailors?" Reina Lauressa interrupted.

Prince Alloryn turned his eyes on Guy for confirmation.

"The word he used was troops, Your Majesty." Guy tried not to dwell on his part in the interrogation, the bile rising in his throat. Not that he hadn't seen cruelty while aboard the pirate ship—men's backs whipped raw and salt applied to the wounds afterward. But he had never taken part in causing another's suffering. Not that he himself had done anything more than translate today. The thought of Harban threatening Donella's life gave him courage to see it through.

Guy tuned back into the conversation to hear the prince say, "Then once mounted, they would head for wayposts known to them. And spread out to different targets Prince Pashmi identified." Prince Alloryn glanced at Odem for verification.

"It is the only thing that makes sense." Odem nodded. "Foreign troops riding across Valdeor would alarm the citizens. News would spread long before they reached Mintala. Our enemies are bold. As we heard at this very table, they already tried to breach the portal once."

That's when Usher opened the portal. Guy mentally kicked himself for his own stunt yesterday. *It could have led to disaster!*

Odem absently fingered his wine glass stem. "Long before an army can be assembled, they will strike here, at the heart of Valdeor. I fear the danger is very great." Odem transferred his eyes to Lauressa, his gaze intent under his lowered brow. "Especially to you, Your Majesty."

Everyone turned toward the Reina as the room grew silent. Guy supposed they were all thinking of the risks, as was he.

"If only we had the plans and maps we found at the hidden cabin!" Donella blurted out. She had been unusually silent till now. "Why anyone ever trusted that arrogant prince is beyond me." Her look burned with frustration as she glared at Guy.

Guy took a breath to defend himself, but Prince Alloryn spoke first. "Do not blame Guy. I myself sent Gensard to the eastern garrison to learn how to be a leader."

"And it was my job to teach him," Odem grunted with dissatisfaction. "But I, obviously, did not get through to him." Odem returned his gaze into his wineglass as if looking into it for answers.

Lauressa put her hand over Guy's for an instant, to his great embarrassment. "And I gave him a chance to serve me when his father, Prince Xander, asked me to give him a leadership position. He wants Gensard prepared to rule over Samarantha after he's gone."

She pulled her hand away and transferred her gaze to Donella. "So, you see, we all misplaced our trust."

Rebuked, Donella blushed and lowered her eyes.

Lauressa folded her hands together. "We must outmaneuver the enemy, whether we have maps you speak of, or not. Guy, I hope you can reproduce the feat you accomplished today. I received word from King Stepan that his fleet is at my service. Usher sent a waykeeper from Forestown to bring me the news."

Guy and Donella exchanged surprised glances. *Another waykeeper?*

Guy whispered at her, "Did you know of another?"

Donella nodded "yes" in reply.

Lauressa must have seen their expressions because she added, "You may talk with him tomorrow, before he returns my message to King Stepan.

"Guy, I am depending upon you to open the way to the southern garrison and to Tulken Harbor. That way we can quickly funnel troops to multiple locations."

Lauressa shifted her gaze. "Commander Odem, I put you in charge of the southern garrison. It is the most likely place for an attack. Until now, it has been lightly defended. With Guy's help we shall divert a large contingent of soldiers to it. Guy will join you there when he is done here. He will relay communications between the different positions."

"Alloryn will support Stepan's troops at Tulken Harbor." She nodded at her husband.

An expression of sorrow was stamped on Donella's face as Lauressa gave everyone assignments except her.

As if sensing Donella's humility at being left out, Lauressa finally addressed her. "Donella, you shall be my eyes and ears at

Laketown. If the assault force doesn't land at the southern garrison or Tulken Harbor, that is the most likely landing spot. And with your ability to contact Guy or Odem, we can quickly transport troops to your post if needed."

Donella's expression brightened.

"And where shall I serve you, Your Majesty?" A voice suddenly rang from the room's far corner.

All eyes swung in that direction.

In a fluid motion, Prince Alloryn shoved his chair back and drew the Crestin Sword at the ready.

Prince Gensard stood there, a tapestry partly covering him. It swung behind him as he stepped through a secret door.

Varying degrees of shock on everyone's face mirrored Guy's own. The silence stretched out for several heartbeats. Gensard stared back at them with defiance.

Gensard's deep brown eyes focused on Lauressa—his face a mix of entreaty and pride.

She broke the spell. "Since you heard what we said, we will take your desire to be of assistance into consideration. You must first swear to obey orders. And deliver to us the invasion force maps."

Guy hadn't seen her look so regal and frosty since his arrival.

For the first time since Guy met him, Prince Gensard didn't look his usual haughty self. His once-resplendent clothes were covered in dirt, with ragged tears in various places. He looked unwashed and in desperate need of a shave. But his wild curls only enhanced his good looks. He ignored everyone except Lauressa.

"I thought the invasion plans likely to fall into the wrong hands if I did not intervene. They are too important to be entrusted to children."

Guy bristled with the injustice. He heard Donella snort with indignation. *Trust Prince Gensard to make the whole incident about himself. As if he had a hand in capturing the plans.*

"And I? Am I not a worthy emissary?" Odem challenged Prince Gensard.

Not answering, Gensard crossed the room and drew out the wrapped scrolls that Donella and Odem had taken such risks to steal from Lord Tastaver.

Prince Alloryn put out his hand before Gensard reached Lauressa. Gensard scowled but reluctantly handed it over.

Alloryn spread them out on the table before the group and they all craned over the map it contained.

Guy saw why Donella and Odem had placed such importance on it and stolen it. A dozen flags marked spots along the eastern and southern coastlines—some port cities, and some not. The bulk of the sites marked looked like natural harbors and river deltas.

Guy recognized the coastline he had sailed.

The next scroll contained a chart with numbers; the third was written in a foreign language.

Prince Alloryn picked up the chart, while the rest discussed the map. "This is a tide table," he announced after a short while.

"At least we know where they plan to attack." Odem tapped the garrisons marked.

"And this is a letter from Prince Pashmi, Canteor's ruler, authorizing money to buy horses for his troops." Lauressa stared at the scroll scribbled in the foreign language.

Gensard looked over her shoulder and concurred. When she gave him a puzzled glance, he gestured at it. "It's very similar to Samarantha's ancient writing."

"It seems King Stepan has pledged his help none too soon." Everyone gave Lauressa their attention. "Be ready to take your posts tomorrow."

When Gensard acted as if he would speak, Lauressa gestured to him. "Prince Gensard, I expect you to join Donella in Laketown. I need your negotiating skills there." She regarded him with a no-nonsense stare until he nodded acquiescence.

Her gaze swept the room. "Meet here tomorrow at dawn."

"Great, I get stuck with Prince High and Mighty," Donella moaned. She walked with Guy and Odem to the guest rooms in the far wing. "Why doesn't Reina Lauressa just banish him back to Samarantha and be done with his sneaky ways? I don't trust him at my side."

Odem put a hand on her shoulder. "It is not that easy. Seven provinces, or kingdoms, comprise Valdeor. Domadaria is a strong ally ruled by King Stepan, one of Lauressa's most trusted advisers. Her mother, who was born there, was King Stepan's relative. Winterhome is also very loyal."

Donella chimed in, "Once the royal summer residence. Now it's Preedim's kingdom."

"Yes. Then there are the tribal nomads living in the Motari Desert region. Their culture hasn't always welcomed other nations' interference. But Reina Lauressa saved a whole tribe caught in a deadly sandstorm. For that she won the desert dwellers' gratitude. But their lands are not fruitful, and their numbers are too small to send many men for defense.

"The Eastern lands have no ruler—"

"—not since Lauressa's first fiancé Prince Jarell died," Donella finished.

"Right, so she has no one to turn to for help there. Since defeating Feornson and regaining her rightful throne, the region around Feornang has also gone ruler-less. Laketown region is very independent, barely recognizing the High Kings of old. The region around Mintala already makes up her standing army, along with men from the other kingdoms."

Odem paused in the hallway outside their rooms. "So who is left that has a fleet and the ability to help stop a sea invasion?" He stared hard at Donella.

"Samarantha's ruler, I guess." Donella reluctantly answered.

She knew where he was going with this history lesson.

"And whose son is Gensard?"

"Prince Xander of Samarantha," she said in a small voice.

"Exactly. Reina Lauressa must make alliances where she can. Samarantha has some of the best soil and farmland on the continent. They are self-sufficient and independent. They don't need to rely on Lauressa's trade or army. She only has her diplomacy to work with since she rejected Prince Gensard's hand for Prince Alloryn." Odem tilted his head. "Now do you see why we all need to work with him, as much as he tries our patience?"

Donella nodded, seeing the truth, but not liking it.

"Sometimes we have to put aside our own feelings and think of the greater good." Odem squeezed her shoulder and gazed into her eyes until she gave another small nod of agreement. "Good girl. Both of you need to get some sleep. Tomorrow we go to battle."

Guy made no move to leave as Odem departed.

Donella squirmed. *Why did he have to witness Odem taking her to task? Even if she did deserve it.* So she changed the subject.

"What made you try it?"

Guy stared at her uncomprehendingly.

"The two portals today. What made you think of doing that?" She genuinely wanted to know.

"I read about it in a journal." He proceeded to tell her the story. "No one else has opened two." He exuded confidence.

"I knew you could do amazing things. You are strengthening your powers." She smiled with encouragement. "Wait until Usher hears of it. I wonder where he is."

Chapter 22

$\mathcal{G}$uy slept poorly since he lay awake half the night fretting over the morrow. Running late, his unsteady hands making it take longer to dress, Guy was the last to arrive in the dining hall. He stopped in the doorway trying to get his breathing under control. There was an addition of some members. Odem spoke to a group of generals decked out in mail, bristling with weapons. Prince Gensard was surrounded by courtiers in colorful silk robes.

Captain Rodrek of the Palace Guard stood just inside the door. Rodrek cornered Prince Alloryn nearby. Guy unwittingly overheard part of their conversation.

"Let me come with you. You know our swords are better together."

"I need you here." Prince Alloryn put out a hand to forestall Captain Rodrek when he would speak. "There is no one else I would trust with Lauressa's safety. If I cannot guard her, you are the one I trust the most."

Captain Rodrek bit his lip. His shoulders sagged. "Very well. I will guard her with my life, old friend." Rodrek cocked an eyebrow at the prince. "Be careful not to fall in the sea. You aren't the best swimmer."

Guy thought Rodrek smirked as he said it, but he couldn't be sure.

Someone behind Guy cleared his throat. Startled, he turned to see Usher smiling at him. "What are you doing hanging around outside the hall? Enter! We have things to discuss."

Usher had two men in tow, one a teenage boy, and the other about thirty. Prince Alloryn broke off his conversation with Captain Rodrek when they entered.

Alloryn strode over and greeted the stranger near his own age, "Talud! So good of you to come!" Alloryn clapped him on the back.

Talud was medium height and stocky, while Alloryn was taller and leaner. Alloryn wore a surcoat with a rampant lion crest over his chain mail, while Talud's surcoat had a red griffin on gold. With their muscled arms and their sword scabbards buckled over their chain mail, they stood ready for battle. They were a handsome pair.

Alloryn gestured the other prince aside and began talking in undertones. They motioned Odem over and were soon in deep discussion.

Guy tried to overhear their discussion, but Donella made a beeline for Usher and hugged him unabashedly, Evodia in her wake. Donella launched into an account of her adventures. Her prattling drowned out the princes' conversation, "—and then I had the brilliant idea of becoming a washerwoman."

"You must be Guy," a male voice said from behind him.

Guy turned around to see the teen who came with Usher. He looked a year or two older than Guy, his hair an untidy mop of brown, dry straw. He wore a simple homespun tunic of forest green over brown leggings.

"I'm Brodyn. I've heard a lot about you from Usher. I'm another of his students." Brodyn's glance traveled from Guy's face to his marked hand. "Is it true you can travel anywhere you wish?"

"Uh, nice to meet you." Guy put out his right hand, which

Brodyn gripped tightly and shook up and down at least five times in his enthusiasm. When he finally let it go, Guy surreptitiously flexed it.

"I brought messages from King Stepan to Reina Lauressa. I've never been in the presence of royalty before." He gulped visibly, his large Adam's apple going up and down. "If only my father, the potter, could see me now. Two palaces within a week!"

Guy felt sorry for Brodyn. Guy realized that he had been the same. *Was it only weeks ago?* And now the august company no longer awed him.

"How'd you get the mark on your hand, if you don't mind me asking? Better than a ring. Not so easy to lose. I'm always hunting for mine. I've rarely used it since Usher taught me how. Too busy helping my father. And it doesn't do to disappear in front of customers." He laughed at his own joke.

Guy caught Donella's eye. Reina Lauressa had drawn Usher, Evodia, and the princes into conversation. Donella walked over and raised one eyebrow in an inquiry.

"This is Brodyn. I'd like you to meet Donella, who's been a waykeeper much longer than I have." Guy reached out and drew Donella close. "She is much more experienced than I."

"I'm happy, uh, super pleased to meet you again! I thought you were one of the royals. Maybe we can work together? It'd be more fun than partnering with Usher." Judging by Brodyn's enthusiasm, he was smitten with the black-tressed Donella.

Brodyn was laying it on thick. And they'd met before?

An odd stirring in his chest caused him discomfort. *Could it be jealousy?*

Soon Reina Lauressa called the group to order. "I think it only right to pray to our Almighty Father before heading into battle. Father Dismas will lead us in prayer."

Lauressa's companion dressed in the black robes of a priest. From behind, Guy had thought he was a general.

Father led them in a short prayer. They knelt before him for a blessing.

Afterward, the Reina sent them to their posts.

Guy stood again at the palace barracks where he had performed his two-doorway opening feat, hoping that he could pull it off again on demand.

Archers with longbows and quills of arrows mingled nearby. Soldiers in armor and carrying swords, pikes, and mace gathered in the courtyard. They spilled into the nearby training grounds, through the open gate and into the city beyond. Cavalry horses danced with excitement to one side. He recognized the Reina's royal blue colors, but not many of the others. Her pennant flew above the others, a seven-pointed gold star on a deep blue background.

Guy knew Reina Lauressa had sent out a call to arms across the realm, but he gaped at the force's size.

Usher joined him. "Those are several hundred men from Winterhome." He pointed out the tall, fierce-looking warriors in red and white carrying longswords. They gathered under a red banner embroidered with a silver snowflake.

"And the archers in brown and green came with Prince Talud from Domadaria." Their gold banner with a red griffin flapped in the breeze.

Prince Gensard stood alone under a purple pennant embroidered with a gold dragon, which Guy assumed was the symbol of the Samarantha royal house. The prince was clad in black with gold thread outlining the sleeves and down the trouser seams. Guy thought he would've dressed more ostentatiously.

How am I supposed to transport so many men?

No matter how many times Guy wiped his sweaty hands down his pant legs, they remained damp. He stood before the waypost, waiting for instructions. Surely Commander Odem must hear his heart pounding, even standing five feet away.

I hope I don't let everyone down. This is what I get for pulling a stunt in front of a hundred witnesses. Almost as if Odem read his mind, the commander glanced at him and gave him a slight grin of encouragement.

Prince Alloryn stepped on a dais before the crowd. "Line up!" he ordered the gathered host, and two columns formed.

Reina Lauressa, dressed in a gown of gold and white, a sparkling crown on her head, came to stand beside her husband. Prince Talud stood on her other side.

Prince Alloryn raised a hand and the crowd hushed. All eyes turned toward the Reina.

"Many of you fought alongside Prince Alloryn, Champion of Valdeor, when he defeated Warlord Feornson, five years ago. You fought then for my cause, because you believed I would be a virtuous ruler. Now I ask you to take up arms again. Not for me. Not for the glory. But for your homes and your families."

Lauressa's gaze encompassed all gathered. "A new enemy faces us from across the seas. Canteor's ruler, Prince Pashmi, wishes to conquer us for his pagan gods. Today you strike for continued freedom for all your brothers and sisters in our great land of Valdeor."

Cheers erupted from hundreds of throats as Lauressa finished her speech. As the men beat their swords against their shields in support, Reina Lauressa caught Guy's gaze and nodded.

Guy's heart rate spiked. Determination rushed through his veins. Now he'd use the One Who Fashioned All's gift for the good of his homeland.

Maybe I was born for this very reason.

Donella, Usher, Odem, and even Brodyn, gathered around him.

"If anyone can do this, you can." Usher put his hand on Guy's shoulder.

Donella caught his elbow. "We're ready to add our power to yours." She beamed encouragement.

Their faith brought a lump into his throat.

Odem reached out first to the waypost. The mist gathered at his feet, spiraling, and a portal opened on the southern garrison. A bluff overlooking the calm sea emerged.

Those gathered gasped at the spectacle.

Taking a calming breath, Guy focused all his pent-up energy on the waypost. Stretching forth his marked hand, he put it over the waypost's symbol. A tingle moved up his arm as he concentrated on the scene before him. He heard the gulls cry and the slap of the waves. He breathed in humid air, pressing against his face.

Then Usher moved to Guy's right and placed his ringed hand on the stone post below Odem's and Guy's. Usher closed his eyes.

Guy could feel the hum of the first portal vibrating through his bones, soon joined by a hum in a different pitch that seemed to start in his toes and work its way to his head.

A view of a dockside and a ship at anchor wavered in the second portal. Sea breezes wafted through the crowd. The ship creaked at her mooring. The whitewashed houses of the town shone with their emerald green roofs.

The thrum of the soldiers' swords beating against their shields increased in volume, joining with the vibration and causing Guy to feel as if he was caught in an earthquake.

Over the noise, Donella cried, "You can do this, Guy!"

Guy concentrated, gritting his teeth with the effort, and the second portal grew to equal the size of the first. Guy focused until they grew big enough to step through.

Prince Alloryn signaled the two columns to march forward. Odem nodded to Guy, dropped his hand, and led his contingent through to the southern garrison. Prince Alloryn, mounting his steed, led a similar line through the portal to Tulken Harbor.

For half an hour, the army streamed through the portal. First in line came the cavalry, then the archers. Finally, the foot soldiers made up the greatest number of men.

Guy could feel the sweat pouring down his back as he strained to keep the two entrances open. The thrumming vibrations pulsed up his arm and through his body. They sapped his power to think, echoing like a bad headache.

When Guy's concentration waned and the portals began shrinking, Usher stepped back, his face pale. Donella replaced him, putting her ringed hand over Guy's, lending him her power. She smiled and winked.

After another half an hour, Donella's face wore a strained expression. Guy's legs wobbled like jelly. Brodyn gently pushed Donella away and replaced her. With a fresh surge of energy, the portals grew wider and foot soldiers marched through in pairs. Guy relaxed fractionally, as Brodyn helped uphold the doorways. Guy had held open the portals for over an hour.

As the last of the line approached, Usher approached and leaned his hand against the post. "I will keep Tulken Harbor in view, as I am familiar with it."

Brodyn left to sit with Donella on the sidelines.

Guy, with only enough stamina to nod back, focused the last of his energy on the southern garrison.

When only Reina Lauressa, Prince Gensard, Usher, Brodyn, Evodia and Donella remained, Guy let the waypost close. He dropped to the ground with exhaustion. *I did it!*

Donella came and knelt beside him. She dropped her clay bead at the waypost's base. "Be safe, Guy. And be careful! Don't get yourself pressed into the pirate's service. I—we can't lose you again." She leaned in and quickly kissed his cheek.

Guy's cheeks flamed. Too tired to react, he sagged against the waypost.

Standing up, she gathered her belongings.

"May the One Who Fashioned All keep you in His hands." Lauressa touched Donella's arm. The Reina beckoned Prince Gensard to stand beside them. "Take care of her."

Gensard scowled but spoke formally. "I'm at your service."

Donella tossed her mane of black hair, "Come along." She gripped Prince Gensard's arm, opened a portal to Laketown, and stepped through.

Guy put his head on his knees and rested for a few minutes. He should have wished Donella a safe journey, but his limbs felt like lead and he struggled to keep his eyes open.

Lifting his head, Guy realized Usher had disappeared at some point in the proceedings. Now he came from the palace with a servant following.

Usher stopped in front of Guy and the servant offered Guy a drink and a half a loaf of bread. Not caring what anyone thought, Guy drank every drop of the flagon of wine in one enormous gulp. Fire spread from his throat to his stomach, and through his weary limbs. His eyes tearing, he choked. He wolfed down the bread and wiped his sleeve across his mouth.

"There, there, lad. You should get your energy back now." Usher reached down and gave Guy a hand standing up.

Guy's tiredness slightly abated. "What was in the flagon, anyway?"

"Ah, that's my own recipe for times when focusing drains the life from me." He winked.

Usher glanced at the Reina, conversing with Brodyn and Evodia. Seeing his gaze, she broke off her conversation. "Is he ready to travel?" She asked Usher.

"Yes, Your Majesty. I think he is up to it now."

"I know I asked a lot of you today, Guy. You performed a great feat, and I am grateful." Lauressa's expression tensed. "But this is war, and I need you at the southern garrison to handle Commander Odem's communications. I do not need another soldier."

Relief, followed by guilt, bubbled through him. *I'm not a coward for not wanting to face the Canteoran pirates again.*

Guy nodded. "I will do my best, Your Majesty."

"Usher, join Alloryn. Evodia will remain here with me. Brodyn, you'll deploy to the western garrison, just in case the stolen papers didn't indicate the whole plan. This is a multi-pronged strike, my friends. We need to stay coordinated, able to move troops quickly. Our force is likely much smaller than Canteor's." Lauressa gazed earnestly at them.

"May the One Who Fashioned All bless you." She stepped away.

Usher gave Guy a waterskin. "Just water this time." He smiled, then grew serious. "You must block the Canteor conspirators. Have faith and courage, my boy."

"Thanks." Guy took a breath. He opened a way to the southern garrison and stepped through.

Up and down were indistinguishable. He clenched his teeth in an effort to calm his dizziness. His tiredness made it hard to focus.

A glowing light hurt his eyes. *The sun must be setting.*

The light grew brighter and closer. *But it's white, not yellow or orange. Something isn't right.*

Light coalesced into a young man in pure white raiment.

Guy blinked rapidly. Even squinting, the features remained blurry.

The apparition spoke. "Wayposts are not meant for war. Search out the pilgrim's way. Find the way, the truth, and the light."

The ground rose to meet Guy and he collapsed. He pushed

himself up and looked around for the man in white, but only observed the gray wall of the garrison before him. Soldiers were setting up camp outside of it.

Guy rubbed his eyes. *What just happened?*

As he stood gazing about, a soldier approached him. "Commander Odem wishes to see you. He bade me to watch for your arrival."

Pushing the vision from his mind, Guy followed the soldier.

They wove through men assembling the tents, past the tantalizing smell of a stewpot simmering over a cook fire. They passed a line of picketed horses shuffling as they passed. The sweet smell of hay and manure reminded Guy of his farm's stable.

They entered the garrison's gate into a beehive of activity. Here men fletched arrows, others honed their sword edges, a few pulled fire shooters into position and stacked heavy balls beside them. Blacksmiths worked over their forges making more weapons or shoeing horses. The pounding of metal was the beat underlying the hum of the men assembled. As he walked past their forges, smoke assailed Guy and he tasted acrid metal.

The soldier led Guy into a quiet room in the barracks where Odem and several warriors pored over maps.

"Ah, Guy, here you are." Odem made introductions. "Guy is our communication officer." Odem raised an eyebrow. "You can read and write, I hope?"

"Yessir." Guy nodded.

"Good. You will find parchment and quill over on that table." Odem gestured to the corner where a table and chair was set up. A lantern was ready to provide extra light. "You'll write out my missives and deliver them to the palace, or wherever I specify." Odem waved him toward the writing area. "You are to stay out of the way of the fighting. No heroics. Your job is important enough."

Guy's neck muscles relaxed.

Guy sized up the warriors as they re-gathered around the

coastal drawing and resumed their discussion. Every one of them looked to be battle hardened. They sported their weapons strapped across their chests and at their hips. The smell of sweat and leather hung heavy in the stifling space.

I can handle myself in a street scuffle, but I can't pretend I'm as capable as seasoned soldiers. My skills are different, but also needed.

The recent vision loomed in his mind. *If the portals were not meant for war, might that include messages?* But he couldn't worry about that now. Valdeor was in danger. Reina Lauressa and the others counted on him.

As soon as this is over, I promise I will search for the pilgrim's way. But if Canteor unbelievers overrun Valdeor, then there will be no pilgrims left to journey to the Isle of Origin's shrine. Guy directed his thoughts to the being of light in the place between wayposts, as if he could hear Guy's thoughts. Maybe he could.

Chapter 23

Along a sweeping crescent of beach and rock, Laketown overlooked the sea. In the shallow harbor the inhabitants had built great wharfs extending into the water. Many ships rode at anchor. The houses nestled above the harbor on the hills and cliffs leading up to Lake Genesay on the plain above the city.

Laketown was a very old merchant city. Domadaria sent its lumber for millers to make them into planks for building and furnishings.

Gazing with wonder at the beautiful city, Donella wished she could see it under better circumstances.

As soon as he recovered from the disorientation of traveling, Prince Gensard took control, of course. "The governor is a man known to me. He has visited my father's palace many times." Gensard strode at a fast pace into the town. "Try not to get lost in the winding streets," he said over his shoulder. "I'll need you to send messages back to Lauressa."

Donella clenched her teeth rather than say what she thought. She was more than a servant. And she wasn't a child to get lost in an unfamiliar place. Reina Lauressa counted on her. They all did. Donella tried to practice Odem's advice from last night. Lauressa needed allies, needed Prince High and Mighty, to win this battle.

I'll be patient if it kills me.

They made their way from the wharf up a winding, cobblestone thoroughfare. The houses were quarried stone, but instead of being drab, the inhabitants painted them with bright colors.

Since space was at a premium, townspeople planted gardens on rooftops. The air was fragrant with the scents of herbs and flowers. Donella slowed down, breathing deeply. She delighted in the riot of flowers and vines. *How enchanting!*

Steeper and steeper they climbed. Just when Donella thought her calves could take no more, she and the prince entered a level plaza with a marketplace. Donella tried to take it in all at once. The citizens dressed better than most of the towns she had visited, excepting Mintala. The ladies' gowns were embroidered at hem and bodice and their hair elaborately coiffed. The men wore patterned vests over their plain robes and tall cylindrical hats. The town was obviously prosperous.

Stalls of fine linen, flax, and delicate lace caught her eye. She recalled Lauressa telling her how she revived the trade in nearby villages, which now wove the finest fabric fit, for royalty.

The spice trade flourished here. Donella sneezed with the aromas mingling in the air: cinnamon, cardamom, nutmeg, and cloves.

Prince Gensard set a grueling pace, or Donella would've lingered.

People moved out of Gensard's way. Not only did his quick pace and disregard for others blocking his path set him apart, but his black garb stood out starkly against the multi-colored citizenry. Not to mention the scroll-worked scabbard he prominently displayed.

No doubt he wants to strut his importance before the governor of the city. At some point I'll come back here without him and listen for information. He could never blend into a crowd the way I can.

Let him win the governor to Lauressa's cause. But without me, she'll never hear of it.

Prince Gensard met with the pale, little, rotund man of business who governed the city and nearby environs. Ethreday was a born bureaucrat, Donella soon learned. Her annoyance rose each day at the amount of tit for tat he expected from Lauressa in order to ally with her. The conversations were endless concessions for goods and troops and promises of trade deals, all in Laketown's favor as far as she could discern. Donella privately nicknamed him "Ever Ready for Profit."

Gensard wore an expression of impatience at times but seemed to draw on experience in negotiation. She wished he'd hurry the little man along.

Donella's gaze drifted about the elegant office in the governor's mansion. An enormous mahogany desk dwarfed Ethreday, who shuffled papers around importantly. Prince Gensard sat with one leg casually crossed over the other, at his ease. Donella was banished to an uncomfortable stool in the corner. The Laketown map hanging on the wall across from the desk held her attention. She longed to explore the city.

After three days of negotiations, she had grown tired of sitting at meetings.

So during Ethreday's daily siesta, while the prince pored over trade compacts, Donella sneaked out of the governor's mansion and headed back to the plaza.

Sellers called out their wares, chickens clucked in cages, customers haggled. Familiarity settled over her at the busy marketplace. She ate a cinnamon bun slathered with butter. She bought herself a lace scarf which she draped over her plain blue gown.

Only after she sampled all the stalls had to offer, did she climb to one of the rooftop teahouses and sit overlooking the harbor.

She spotted strange ships sailing toward the harbor. Ships suspiciously like the one that captured Guy. Their goat head prows became visible as they drew closer.

Her tea forgotten, Donella's heart hammered in her chest. *Invaders! Approaching the coastline!*

Odem had extrapolated the approximate invasion day from the tide charts at one of the palace meetings. Donella assumed Prince Gensard made note of it, but either he hadn't, or he forgot, or the day changed.

She raced back to the provincial governor's villa, oblivious to the steep climb as the blood raced through her veins. She burst in on Prince Gensard and Ethreday documents spread before them.

"They're here!" She gasped, trying to catch her breath. "What are we going to do?!"

Prince Gensard swung around to face her. "Is that the way you make an entrance? Have you no manners in front of your betters?" Gensard frowned at her and pointed to the stool. "You may sit quietly in a corner until I am ready to send a message."

Donella's impatience boiled over. "Enemy ships are sailing into the harbor! Should I politely wait until they take over the city before I curtsy and let you know? Bah!" She stamped her foot but restrained her desire to just turn and leave. Instead, she crossed her arms and waited.

"Invaders?!" Ethreday's bulk seemed to shrivel in his chair. His bulging eyes sought Gensard. "You guaranteed our safety if we agreed to help you. Clause six of document nineteen. What are you going to do to protect the city?" Ethreday pulled out a giant handkerchief of lace and wiped sweat from his brow.

"The ships in the harbor and soldiers stationed in your city—give them to me and I will deal with the dogs!" Gensard jumped to his feet. He removed his scimitar from its scabbard and fastened it to a strap that held it in place at his side.

Donella gave Prince High and Mighty credit for bravery.

Towering over the governor, Gensard looked formidable all in black, like wrath unleashed.

Ethreday still insisted Gensard sign and put his seal on their latest treaty. Donella wanted to scream at the wasted time. With great effort she held her tongue. She played with the clay beads in her pocket, running them through her fingers over and over.

Prince Gensard noticed her long enough to thrust a few scrolls at her, keeping ahold of one. "Deliver these to Lauressa. Ethreday wants them signed and sealed by her, too, or he will pull back his offer of help."

Ethreday directed guards outside his office to sound the alarm. "Alert General Lunn to meet me in the courtyard, immediately."

Running downstairs and out the door, Donella and Gensard burst into the courtyard. Soldiers gathered. Huffing, Ethreday joined them. A bald man in high-ranking uniform, who Donella assumed was General Lunn, stepped forward. He had a gray beard and a scar over his left eye.

"General, you will liaison with Reina Lauressa's representative, Prince Gensard. He will command our forces against the Canteor ships. Give him all the help he needs."

The two men seemed to take each other's measure. Gensard broke off eye contact and took a moment to visually inspect the men. "To the harbor!" He motioned them to follow him.

Finally! She trailed after them, gripping the scrolls, as they raced through town.

When they reached the wharf, Gensard commandeered several seaworthy ships, flaunting Ethreday's document in their faces. Everything must run on paper here, she thought, as the sailors accepted them.

The foreign ships grew closer. The goat head prows leered evilly. From the masts flew what Donella assumed was the Canteor flag, a gold scimitar on a black background.

People on the docks stopped to watch the soldiers scrambling aboard the ships. General Lunn pressed other able seamen into service on the spot.

Gensard spared her a glance. "Don't stand there! Get those to Lauressa. Be Quick!"

She ran through the gathering crowd, pushing aside those in her way.

At the least he could have thanked me for sounding the alert!

Panting, she arrived at the wharf waypost. She leaned over to catch her breath. She spared a glance back at the Laketown ships launching to meet the incoming invaders. Then, summoning the palace waypost and gripping the bundle of scrolls, she stepped through the portal.

Donella landed next to Captain Rodrek, who stood on guard duty at the post.

"Laketown is under attack!" Donella cried and ran toward the palace door.

"I'll escort you!"

Servants and courtiers gave way before them as they pounded down the hallway to the throne room.

The guards stationed at the door opened it as Captain Rodrek approached.

Donella didn't stop and stare as she usually did at the ruby, emerald, citrine, azure, amethyst, and topaz gems which twinkled high above their heads. Instead, she rushed to where Reina Lauressa sat on the throne, the medallion around her neck sparkling against her dark russet gown.

Curtsying briefly, Donella burst into speech. "Your Majesty, the invasion has started at Laketown! I left Prince High—Gensard leading Ethreday's forces to meet the enemy."

"So soon!" The Reina stood and gave orders to Captain

Rodrek. "Secure the city gates. Set double the guards at the portal."

Donella waited until she gained Lauressa's attention again.

"Prince Gensard sent me to convey the demands—uh, terms of the treaty to you with all haste. Unless Ethreday gets them back signed, he will deem them null and void."

Donella had heard the phrase "null and void" tripping off Ethreday's tongue every time he did not think the terms were to his advantage.

"That's all right, child. I know what Ethreday is like. I deal with bureaucrats often enough," a quick lift of Lauressa's lips before her frown returned. "Get yourself something to eat and Jimzy will call you back when all is ready."

For some odd reason, when Lauressa called her "child," Donella didn't mind one bit. Lauressa didn't say it in the derogatory tone Prince Gensard habitually used.

Jimzy the page stood so silently in the background that Donella hadn't observed him. He escorted Donella down the servant's stairs toward the kitchens.

"How are your sisters?" She grabbed the rail to keep from falling down the steep steps.

"Same as always. Gossiping about the royal heir." Donella could hear the disdain in his voice. "A real war going on and they coo about babies that aren't even born."

"Well, war isn't always pretty. The blood, the gore, and the fear surrounding you on every side—"

Jimzy stopped suddenly and Donella almost tripped over him. "You mean you've been there?" His eyes gleamed. "What's it really like?"

"I just told you."

Jimzy waved his hand. "No, I want the real details. The pirates—do they chop off their enemies' heads and decorate their ships with them?" His lips parted as he eagerly awaited her answer.

"What? No! Who told you such outlandish stories? You shouldn't listen to such tales at your age."

Jimzy snorted, then continued down the last flight of stairs. "Just like a girl. 'Mind your manners.' 'Sit up straight.' 'Act like a gentleman.' How is a boy supposed to grow to be a man when he's surrounded by women trying to make a sissy of him?" Jimzy stomped up to the kitchen door, but before he opened it, Donella touched him on the arm.

"You'll be a man someday. We women just want you to be a child while you can."

His look of discontent remained.

"War is not all glory and gallantry. Good men are dying to save us all. We must all do our part."

Fearing that she wasn't getting to him, she sought for something he could do to help. He was intelligent for his age. "You have an important job right here in the palace. Reina Lauressa needs you to—"

"—act like a good little page. I know." He scowled.

"No, I was going to say, use your wits. Listen to conversations around you. You are already good at blending into the background. Use that. Reina Lauressa needs you to be her eyes and ears."

Jimzy's scornful expression became thoughtful.

She hoped giving him a purpose would help him. Although her conscience pricked her for putting him in harm's way. But dangerous conspirators were unlikely to come his way, she reasoned.

Donella let him open the door for her, passing into the welcoming kitchen. The smell of baking bread made her mouth water. But as she sat at the rough-hewn table eating, her thoughts went back to the harbor and the glimpse of ships preparing for battle.

War has truly come to Valdeor from over the seas! Is the attack only at Laketown, or are the invaders hitting many ports simultaneously?

She hoped her friends were safe, especially Guy.

The ship pitched up and down as it raced across the swells, all the sails unfurled to catch the wind.

Gensard stood at the forecastle with Captain Malek, who sported a long, curly, black mustache. Half the Laketown troops stood below them on the main deck. They were not Gensard's father's elite troops, unfortunately, but they fought under his command. They would have to do. He hoped the incentive of protecting their homes would spur them to do their best.

On another Laketown ship, off their port bow, General Lunn commanded the other half of the troops.

The Canteor ships sailed just ahead of them, the Laketown ships gaining fast. He chose this ship for its cannons. Gensard had seen what they could do at his time at the eastern garrison.

Closing with the enemy ship, his ship's cannon shot a volley and a blast of fire spurted. The ball burst through the sidewall near the enemy's prow. But it landed well above the waterline and didn't cause much damage.

"Archers forward," he commanded. The first mate yelled the order.

Men bearing longbows swarmed the prow.

"Take out the cannon's crew!" Gensard squinted as the arrows flew through the air. The sailors around the weapon fell. More took their place.

The next cannon ball went wide. More men working the cannon died, arrows protruding from their chests and necks. But others took their place and got off a few shots of their own. Only one ball landed on Gensard's ship, smashing through the deck and injuring several men.

So the sea battle went on for half an hour. Screams arose from the injured as arrows pierced them. The smell of blood mixed with the acrid smoke of the cannon. The two ships danced around each other—Captain Malek turned to maintain a front-on assault, protecting the ship from damage to her sides. But that silenced the cannons, leaving the archers wide open.

Gensard leaned toward Captain Malek and raised his voice to be heard over the battle noises. "My men are ready to board at your command." He descended to the main deck.

"Ready grappling hooks!" the black-mustached Captain commanded.

Two dozen soldiers and sailors stood along the starboard side, waiting for the sloop to turn. The rest of the fighting men readied themselves, drawing their swords and knives. Gensard plucked the scimitar from its strap. His pulse sped up. Exhilaration pounded through his veins.

In preparation for close battle, Gensard removed the little dagger, hidden in his blade's hilt, with his left hand. He placed it in a specially made wrist holder. Then he took his shield from his back and gripped it in his left hand.

"Turn hard port!"

The sloop obediently swung around, exposing her starboard side to the enemy cannon.

Gensard held his breath, but no blast followed. He grinned. *The enemy ran out of balls to shoot. Now let me teach these pirates a lesson they will never forget. If they survive.*

"Away grapple!"

Men threw the ropes and hooks, which arced over the distance between the ships. When most of the hooks connected, the men heaved on the lines, drawing the ships close enough together to board.

Gensard raised his scimitar. "Attack!"

He jumped easily from the sloop to the other deck, swinging and slashing his way toward the Canteor captain's position. He heard, rather than saw, the men follow him. He focused on the enemies within his range. The scimitar—an extension of his own arm—thrust through a man's chest, broke the helmet of the next, and knocked aside another man's sword. His world narrowed down to watching for an advantage as he met foe after foe. Time seemed to stretch into one long moment of glorious battle.

Suddenly, a giant dark-skinned warrior entered Gensard's field of vision. He had a broad nose, flaring nostrils and a shaved head. Meeting Gensard's gaze, the giant battered all before him, making straight for Gensard. Three men stood between them, which he scattered like twigs with his spiked bat.

The giant reached him. Strange diagonal slashes stood out on either cheek. "Die, Valdeor dog!" he snarled and attacked.

The giant swung his bat at Gensard's head. Gensard ducked below it and slashed with his scimitar. But the giant moved out of the way. The giant aimed for his chest, but Gensard blocked with his shield. The blow sent a shiver of pain up his arm. Swinging his scimitar at the arm wielding the bat, he managed to disengage and gain space.

"Bring it on, if you want a real fight!" Gensard challenged.

They fought a deadly dance. But as hard as Gensard tried, the giant's long-armed reach kept him at bay.

Gensard bared his teeth and growled with irritation.

He made as if to swing wildly in frustration. And when the giant countered, he met air. Gensard dove on his knees and slashed upward. His scimitar hit below the ribcage. Bleeding heavily, the giant dropped his bat, which landed on the deck, as he grasped his mid-section.

Giving an enraged cry, the giant threw himself on Gensard in the process of rolling out of the way. He knocked Gensard's shield from his grip, then wrestled for the scimitar with one hand. Gensard found himself in the embrace of a bull, as the giant tried to squeeze him and break his back with the other brawny arm.

Gasping, Gensard used his left hand, released the spring holding the mini dagger, and stabbed the giant in the eye. Howling, the giant grabbed his left wrist, trying to break it. Gensard butted him in the nose with his head. The giant's hands convulsively loosened enough that Gensard let go the scimitar, useless at such close range. Instead, he poked the black man in the eyes with his right fingers. The giant dropped his left hand to protect his eyes. Gensard stabbed him in the throat.

Gensard managed to push the bleeding man off him and staggered to his feet. His men had gained control of the ship while he fought.

Pain radiated up his left arm. He bent to pick up his scimitar.

The first mate of the Laketown crew saluted him. "Your Highness, what are your orders?"

Wiping the blood and sweat from his face on his right sleeve, he reckoned their position. "Have your men toss the bodies overboard for the sea monsters to feast on. Leave enough men aboard to man this ship. Raise the Laketown pennant. Then join the battle and aim for the nearest sister ship." He pointed to their next target.

"But first—" Gensard chopped the head off the giant, lifting it by its hair. The first mate blanched but awaited orders. "—send this from our cannon to her deck as a warning."

The first mate saluted and grim-faced carried out the order. Gensard used the mounted spyglass on the foredeck to watch the reaction of the crew when their champion's head hit the deck and rolled at their feet. He detected revulsion and fear as the sailors moved back from the evil omen at their feet.

Let them fear me. Fear is a good tactic.

Chapter 24

A few mornings later, Guy ate his lumpy oatmeal when the 'To Arms' bell sounded. He ran with the others to a vantage point on the rampart walls. He froze at the sight of the approaching ships on the horizon.

He could just make out a black flag with a scimitar. Recognizing them as Canteor, like the one enslaving him, Guy's heart hammered against his ribs.

"Where's your weapon, boy? This isn't a sideshow on festival day," Odem's grizzled lieutenant barked at Guy as he inspected the troops.

Guy raced back down the stairs and joined the line for weapons.

The defenders' numbers had swelled in the days since Guy arrived at the garrison. Fishermen and villagers volunteered their help. Determination shone on the faces around him as they readied to defend their families and their livelihoods.

Guy dutifully took the weapon handed to him from the armorer and headed back to the ramparts. He hunkered with a crossbow, waiting for action.

Cannons thundered, drowning out the cry of the seabirds and the crash of the waves. Soldiers hurried to and fro in controlled chaos, reloading the weapons. Smoke enveloped the southern garrison catwalk as the cannons' sulfurous gas blocked Guy's sight of the ships in the harbor below. The acrid smell burned his throat.

He had no idea how long he had crouched beneath the rampart wall. It felt like hours. He longed to stretch his cramped muscles.

"Fancy meeting you here!" a familiar voice spoke. Guy gasped as Hiram knelt beside him on the catwalk, a huge grin on his face.

"Hiram! How did you get here?" Guy's spirits lifted at the thought of a friend by his side.

"My fishing village is over yon hills." Hiram pointed to the west. "I came with me Da and brothers. 'Tis a chance for me to get revenge on those pagan pirates."

Hiram held a longbow. He inspected Guy's crossbow. "Where'd they get that contraption?"

"Princess Lauressa found this prototype deep in the ruined fortress of her former fiancé, Prince Jarell. Good thing she had seen their usefulness, ordered copies, and stockpiled them for the future. I sure hope this makes a difference in repelling the attack today." Guy described how it worked.

"Interesting." Hiram fingered his longbow. "We'll see who can shoot farther. Look! The fire shooters seem to be stopping the Canteor ships from landing."

His foot numb, Guy changed position. "That day we escaped—I shot our ship with a cannon."

"What? Tell me more!"

So as they watched the sea battle between the foreign ships and the outpost cannons, Guy described the previous battle he participated in.

One ship lowered a dinghy which approached the shore. Men disembarked and swarmed toward the garrison.

"Archers, fire!"

Guy and Hiram stood, aimed their bows, and let loose. The

archers picked the raiders off.

"Ha! Got one!" Hiram crowed. "I only wish it were the deck master, Drake."

Several approaching enemy ships blazed with fire, and one sank. Even as they watched, another ship settled deeper in the water while her crew abandoned her and swam to the nearest sister ship.

"They sure are taking a beating."

Both boys watched as a listing ship limped back to the main force.

"Lily-livered cowards."

Guy frowned. He thought the ship's move prudent. Following his friend's gaze, he realized Hiram spoke about the other two ships which, until now, held back. All their sails unfurled, they caught the wind, and headed down the coast.

The garrison bell sounded. Guy stood, stretching his cramped legs and trying to loosen his stiff neck muscles.

After the captains called the men to order, Commander Odem stood on the rampart. "Scouts, ride to the east and find those ships. Form up, Company B. Load the wagons. Get the teams hitched to the movable cannon. The invaders know many spots along the coast to land between here and Tulken Harbor. We must stop them. Company A stays to guard the garrison."

Odem leaned to say something in grizzled lieutenant's ear, who then hurried over to Guy. "Commander Odem wishes to speak to you."

Hiram gave Guy an odd look before following the rest of the men surging down the steps to the courtyard.

Guy followed the lieutenant to where Odem marshaled his leaders. He motioned for Guy to step aside with him. "I want you to get word to Alloryn of what transpired here. Cannons proved very useful. Tell him I'm sending a contingent of soldiers his way. And if he has any men to spare, send them to meet ours."

Guy recognized the honor in carrying an important message to the prince. His chest swelled with pride.

"Can you sense any waypost between ours here and Tulken Harbor?"

Guy emptied his mind of the chatter and movement around him. He concentrated on the sound of the sea endlessly beating the earth with its timeless rhythm. He stretched his senses out, but couldn't discern any portal closer than Usher's presence in Tulken Harbor.

Guy opened his eyes. "I sense nothing, Commander."

"Good. Then get going. Turn in your weapon." Commander Odem turned away.

"Commander?" Guy clutched his bow with both hands. "May I take a friend with me? He knows the coast and the language better than I."

"Very well. And Guy," Odem gripped his shoulder, "watch your back." He narrowed his eyes. "You, more than any of us, know what we're up against."

Guy nodded, his life aboard the pirate ship surfacing in his mind. "I don't plan to get caught again."

Guy found Hiram with a tall, lanky man who he introduced as his father. Two other tow-headed boys towered over Guy, their hands scared from working fishing nets.

"The commander says you can come with me on an errand." Guy pulled Hiram away from his family. "We go to warn Prince Alloryn about the invaders headed his way."

"You've risen in the world!" Hiram swung in step with Guy with a quick wave back at his father and brothers. "The commander himself sends you on such an errand. Are you a courier now?"

"Yes, that's one name for it." As the two boys approached the waypost outside the walls, they passed men hitching the cannons to oxen teams.

Guy took a calming breath, ready to show Hiram his true self.

Hiram touched his arm. "Hey, we passed the stable. Don't tell me we're going to walk all the way to the prince's position. Where'd you say he is?"

"Tulken Harbor. And we don't need horses." Guy smirked at Hiram's grimace. "I've a faster method of travel. Watch!" Guy walked up to the waypost, stretched out his marked hand, and focused on Usher's presence. Mist formed and swirled around his feet. Those nearby stopped working to watch. A city gate with a looming watchtower appeared.

Hiram's jaw dropped, and he backed away. "Magic doors? Are you some kind of wizard?" Hiram's eyes flickered from the symbol on the waypost to the symbol on Guy's hand.

"It's safe. I promise." Guy gestured. "Go ahead."

"I'm not going through there!"

Time pressing on him, Guy grabbed his friend's arm and pulled them both through.

An arrow whizzed by Guy's ear. He threw himself to the ground, dragging Hiram with him. Stepping through the portal, he had failed to perceive the forces gathered on rocky hilltops on either side of the road. The two opposing sides shot arrows. And Guy and Hiram appeared in the center of it.

"Can't you conjure us away from here?!" Hiram yelled in his ear.

"It doesn't work that way!" Guy crept into a ditch, Hiram close behind.

Guy's stomach roiled, not only from the trip through the between places, but from the new danger. *Think. There's got to be a way out of this.* The waypost stood in the open with no cover around it. Guy didn't know which side was which, since the archers hid among boulders. The only way to determine the prince's location was to crawl up the nearest hill and search for the prince's livery.

"Stay here," Guy hissed. Keeping himself flat on the ground, he slithered up the hill on his belly. The tall grass hid him but tickled his face. On reaching the summit, he sighed with relief. The soldiers on this side of the road wore Prince Alloryn's rampant lion crest.

He crawled back quickly to where Hiram still lay. "It's alright. We're close. The prince's men are just over the hill." Both boys scrambled up the hill, then raced down the other side.

"Halt, or I'll shoot!" A sentry stood up from behind a bush. Guy put his hands out in the universal sign of surrender. "I bring a message from Commander Odem for Prince Alloryn." Guy waved his hand, showing the new courier's signal.

The sentry led them through a field and across a stream, to a tent city outside the Tulken Harbor walls. Hundreds of men swarmed the area, prepping arms, grooming their horses, and sharpening their weapons. The three stopped at the main tent, larger than the rest, flying the lion pennant. The sentry passed them onto the guards posted there.

"Couriers with news," he reported before departing back to his post.

Guy repeated their business. One guard inspected them and demanded their weapons. Only then did he lift the flap of the tent and escort them in.

"Couriers from Commander Odem, Your Highness," he announced.

Glancing up as they entered, Alloryn motioned the generals and Prince Talud to silence.

Alloryn put down the report he held. "What news?"

Guy bowed, nudging Hiram to do the same, as the other boy seemed dazed to find himself before a prince. "Your Highness, I bear news from Commander Odem. Our cannons were successful.

We sank two ships and put two more out of commission. But the remaining three are headed down the coast this way. The commander asks that if you have any troops to spare, please send them west to meet his force."

Prince Alloryn asked more details, which Guy supplied.

Alloryn gestured to a barrel-chested man clad in a breastplate with a silver hammer emblazoned on it. "General Rishidan, gather your contingent and be ready to march west when we break the line."

Alloryn gave orders, while Guy and Hiram watched from the sidelines, forgotten now that they accomplished their mission.

Guy's gaze was drawn to a map pinned on the tent wall. He studied it intently.

Usher entered the tent, and seeing Guy, headed his way. "Ah, I see you suffered no harm. War is a bad business, a very bad business."

His mentor ushered them from the prince's presence. "Two lads like you must be hungry. A little cookpot of hearty stew awaits at my tent." They followed him through the maze of tents, until he stopped at one.

"Not much to look at, not like my snug home, but you are welcome to stay with me." He wagged his head side to side. "My poor garden back home is neglected; I've been gone so long. I'll need to buy rutabagas and onions from the market when I get home, or I'll have nothing to eat this winter."

Guy introduced Hiram. "Hiram is the only reason I survived my time on the pirate ship. He taught me the ropes."

Usher clapped Hiram on the shoulder. "I'm very happy to make your acquaintance. If not for you, we would've lost a valuable asset. Guy is destined for great things."

At Hiram's puzzled look, Usher grinned. "I see he did not tell you. Guy isn't one to boast. No, no, not like some we know, who will remain nameless. Your friend might be the greatest waykeeper in the long history of our order." He prattled on while he made Guy and Hiram comfortable in front of his campfire and dished up stew.

Eating hungrily, Guy informed Usher of events. He included Hiram's aptitude in Canteor's language.

"A very useful skill. I'll inform Prince Alloryn. He'll need you, son."

After defeating the archers along the road, Alloryn and General Rishidan took all but a skeleton crew to meet Commander Odem.

Waiting was not what Guy expected during battle operations. But Prince Alloryn insisted the boys remain safely at the camp.

Guy and Hiram sat in Usher's tent, playing a board game by lamplight. Guy's thoughts wandered as he waited for Hiram to make a move. He studied the board in front of him. The game of strategy made him wonder about Canteor's scheme.

He thought about the map in the prince's tent. Having sailed this area of the coast, he knew it had many inlets deep enough for a ship to pull in close and send dinghies to shore. Beyond Tulken Harbor to the east the shoreline grew steep, with areas of hidden rocks and shoals all the way to Laketown Harbor. If the Canteoran ships wanted to land, it would be between the southern garrison and Tulken Harbor.

But something about the situation nagged Guy. *Why drop a handful of archers against a larger force with no backup?*

The more he thought about it, the stranger it seemed.

What had they hoped to accomplish? The archers must have been a diversionary tactic. But a diversion from what?

"It's your move." Hiram snapped his fingers in Guy's face.

Guy came back to the present.

"Something is wrong. I have an odd feeling." Anxiety fluttered in his gut.

"Yeah, what's wrong is you take way too long to make a move. I'm waiting." Impatience laced Hiram's voice.

Guy stood. "Forget the game, will you?" He paced in his anxiety. "What did the archers defend? Why have no ships been spotted in this area?"

"I dunno." Hiram stared at him. "Just because you have a special gift of travel, doesn't mean you have greater insight than the prince. Let him deal with it."

With Hiram's words, the pieces of the puzzle fell into place. "The portal! That's what the raiders are after! What do they gain by taking Tulken Harbor? Nothing, that's what. Mounted on horses, they'd have to travel through the Domadarian forest. It'd slow them down."

At Hiram's blank look, Guy explained. "There is no strategic reason for the Canteorans to hold this position. But if they captured the portal, they could use horses and go anywhere in Valdeor."

Hiram got to his feet, frowning. "You mean like the capital?"

Guy's heart stuttered. *Of course! Where else would they hold the advantage?*

"We've got to warn Prince Alloryn or the Reina herself. Come on!" Leaving the brightly lit tent, Guy blinked in the dwindling twilight as his eyes adjusted.

Guy headed in the direction of the waypost. Prince Alloryn had posted sentries around the camp with one at the waypost. But as Guy got closer, he observed several men holding torches and standing around the portal.

He slowed his pace. *Of course, the prince posted a contingent around it!* Maybe Guy *was* becoming overconfident.

But then he tripped over something in the dim light. He looked down to see a soldier's dead eyes staring at him, his throat slit. Hiram bumped into Guy, causing Guy to fall over the dead man. Bile rose in his throat as he cried out.

Guy instinctively glanced at the waypost to see if anyone reacted. As he watched, torches began disappearing.

They were entering the portal!

"Warn the company," Guy hissed to Hiram, who stood gawking at the corpse. Rising, Guy pushed a stunned Hiram back the way they had come. "The enemy has taken the waypost!"

Hiram ran.

Three invaders remained.

Guy broke out in a cold sweat. A chance to prove himself. Not knowing what else to do, and fearing they'd notice him, Guy stretched out his senses toward the portal, the palace's image wavering in it.

Two of the assailants approached when they noticed him.

Guy held his ground, struggling to gain control over the portal. Sharp pain assaulted him from his shoulder and side as they attacked.

Staggering back, Guy willed himself to compartmentalize the pain of the wounds and concentrate. He searched for a place to send them. Dozens of waypost locations scrolled open, one after another.

The ring bearer fought to reopen Mintala's portal.

There! A giant storm off the coast of an island. Guy expanded the portal into the whirlwind. The strong winds buffeted the group, as the doorway grew two-stories high. The hurricane winds sucked them all in the maw.

Power emanated from the portal like a deep thrum. Guy wrested it to his will, staying in the between places while the men were ejected at the other end. He closed it behind them.

He floated in the nowhere, having no destination imagined. Lightning arced in the mist. Vistas and possibilities popped up all around him. Instead of fear, he felt calm. The portal was his to command.

He registered Canteorans opening gateways from several

locations around Valdeor. Their end goal was the palace.

No! He connected with each opening and bound all the wayposts to his will. No one could pass without his permission.

He felt Donella's presence reaching out and loosed her waypost.

Pain and weakness shot through him. Then the mist wavered, the connection broke. Finding himself back on the ground at the camp, he focused his mind on blocking the portals.

But spots floated before his eyes as he crouched on his knees. Something warm dripped from his shoulder and his side. He didn't know how long he could hold out.

"Dulee firth!" Guy cried out the words Donella taught him long ago to call the other waykeepers.

He gritted his teeth and willed himself to stay alert. But the blackness eventually won.

Guy floated. He opened his eyes but still saw only blackness. He couldn't feel the ground beneath him. Fear choked him. Where was he?

His side and shoulder no longer throbbed with pain. Was that good or bad?

A light flashed in the darkness. It grew bigger and Guy squinted as it burned the back of his eyes. He threw up his hand to protect himself. Feeling a presence, he glanced at the brightness which abated.

A being of light stood before him. "I come from the One Who Fashioned All to give you a mission. He asks you to find the Great Shrine. Humans have forgotten who He is. You are the one tasked with opening the portals so the pilgrims may come again. If not, war will come from pagan lands and enslave the remaining faithful."

Guy gazed at the winged man, his mind numb. The being

expected him to save Valdeor?

"Who are you? How am I supposed to find the shrine?" he blurted out the questions foremost in his mind.

The other's gaze scrutinized him. The intensity in his eyes made Guy think the supernatural creature could read his very soul. All of Guy's failings made him feel small before the glorious creature before him.

"I am Virtue, the Guardian of Valdeor, servant of the Most High. I showed you the way to the shrine the last time we met."

"My dream of the maze." Guy's mind again saw the layout of the portals as glowing dots. A map of Valdeor superimposed itself over the vision. Guy was unsure if the guardian was helping him connect the two, or his recent map studying made it clear. One dot grew in size, pulsing with light.

"Find the Isle of Origin. Open the portals. Lead the pilgrims."

The guardian opened his wings and faded away.

Guy limbs grew heavy. He gave into the blackness once again.

Chapter 25

Returning to Laketown with Reina Lauressa's signed documents, Donella made her way to the governor's mansion. The city was a ghost town. The inhabitants had barricaded their streets against invaders. It took her a long time weaving around the blocked streets to reach the mansion. She found it deserted except for one gray-haired retainer with stooped shoulders brandishing a cane until he recognized her.

"Where is everyone?" Donella asked him, glancing around the grand entryway.

"Laketown citizens hide in their homes. Ethreday fled in fear of his life. But I am too old to run like the others," the rheumy-eyed servant answered her. He shuffled to a hall bench and sat.

She headed for the governor's office on the third floor. Entering, she glanced around. A massive mahogany desk dominated the masculine room. Behind the desk stood a large cabinet. Across the room hung a map of Laketown and surrounding areas. Opposite the door she entered were doors to a balcony overlooking the city.

Finding no one there, she stepped out on the balcony. The governor had a spyglass mounted on a stand overlooking the harbor. She used it to watch the end of the sea battle play out.

Unfortunately, she couldn't tell which ship held Prince Gensard.

She knew the harbor ships by their shape and the pennant of the wavy blue stripes denoting Laketown. As she watched, the pennant of a scimitar on a black background of one ship was lowered and a striped one took its place. Gensard and his men must have overtaken a Canteor ship. She searched for him but couldn't pick out his black outfit at that distance.

I'm surprised he didn't wear red since he loves to draw attention to himself.

A twinge of guilt assailed her at the thought. The longer she spent in Reina Lauressa's presence, the more she was reminded of the virtues she should practice. Such as forgiveness and charity. She may not like Prince Gensard, but she need not despise him. After all, he was helping Lauressa win this war.

While in the palace, she'd heard stories of how he and Prince Alloryn were equally matched swordsmen five years ago when they dueled for the Reina's hand. Donella almost felt sorry for the men at the other end of Gensard's scimitar today.

When the battle finished, Ethreday's staff trickled back into the mansion. Last to arrive, the governor crept into his office. Soon after that Gensard, General Lunn and his men came up from the wharfs. The prince and general joined Ethreday and Donella.

Ethreday welcomed Prince Gensard, nearly falling into his arms with glee, but dropping his open arms at the prince's scowl. "You did the impossible! You saved us!" Ethreday seemed to content himself with clapping his hands.

Donella hid a grin at the prince's fastidious expression as he backed away from the bureaucrat.

"Did you see the enemy ship sink in the harbor?" Gensard's eyes gleamed with satisfaction. "My ship was far enough away that we were in no danger of getting pulled under, too."

Donella shuddered at the thought.

"I d—didn't watch the b—battle." Ethreday turned white, but Prince Gensard seemed not to notice.

"I did," Donella chimed in.

General Lunn bared his teeth in a grin which Donella thought scary rather than reassuring. "My men defeated another ship. We threw the dead overboard and raised the Laketown flag. In a bold move, our ships both rammed the last enemy ship, leaving it to sink into the sea beyond the harbor."

Ethreday kneaded his hands. "Are you sure they are truly gone? Will they come back?" He pulled a handkerchief out and wiped moisture from his brow.

"No, they won't be back. They might have started this," Gensard puffed out his chest, "but I finished it."

"You have the whole city's thanks." Ethreday pulled a bottle from the cabinet behind his desk and offered the first shot glass of liquor to the prince, then the general.

Gensard grinned, his expression radiating satisfaction. He swigged the drink and placed the glass on the desk. "I wish to clean up."

As he passed her, Donella registered the cloying smell of blood and sweat lingering on his clothes.

An hour later, Ethreday still examined Lauressa's agreements. Glancing out his office's window, Donella observed a blur of black on Laketown wharf against the setting sun. Idly watching its fast progress through town, she realized with a start that a horse raced toward the mansion.

Sensing trouble, she stepped onto the balcony and focused the spyglass on it.

Could it be Seeker? The rider seems too small.

Wait! Was that Jimzy in the saddle? That boy! What did he think he was doing?

Donella's heart plummeted. Only one thing made sense. *The palace was in trouble!*

"Excuse me!" Donella called to Ethreday as she left.

Once out of the office, she ran down the stairs, through the mansion, and into the courtyard. She gulped in air, her heart racing with foreboding.

Seeker's hooves made sparks as he galloped along the cobblestone streets, as he approached the open courtyard gate. Donella lost her footing on the cobblestones, tripped, and fell in front of the horse. Seeker came to an abrupt halt, lifting his forefeet off the ground. On her knees, Donella flung her arm across her face.

The tableau seemed to freeze for a long moment. Then Jimzy, for it was him, came tumbling off.

Donella's heart stuttered. Had her reckless move killed him?

"Jimzy!" Donella pushed herself up and crossed over to him. "Are you hurt?" She knelt beside him and felt for broken bones.

"No thanks to you!" Jimzy sat up. "What a fool thing to do! We might have run you over." He clambered to his feet without her assistance and brushed himself off.

Relief gushed through Donella. Standing, she put her hands on her hips. "And just what are you doing here? I thought we talked about helping the Reina by watching her back."

"The palace is under attack!" Jimzy's eyes filled up, and he quickly brushed them with the back of his hand. "I came to find you! I stole the horse to come as quick as I could."

"What?!" Donella grabbed his hand and pulled him toward the mansion. "Come on! We'll find Prince Gensard."

He resisted. "What about Seeker? Someone could steal him."

In her haste, Donella had forgotten about Seeker standing beside them.

"Watch my horse," Donella shouted at the gate guards as she dragged Jimzy away.

"Quick! Tell me what happened."

Jimzy tried to match her strides. "I heard clashing and shouting outside the stable. I had given Seeker a carrot to munch on." His voice pitched higher. "I didn't mean no harm."

"It's alright. Go on!"

They entered the main hall and Donella asked the nearest guard for directions to the prince's room. He told her its location, and they headed up the stairs.

"What happened next?" Donella fought her impatience.

"Peeking outside, I spied dozens of scary men come out of that foggy door thing. All in black with drawn swords. I knew the Reina was in danger. But I couldn't warn her! They was between me and the door." Jimzy trembled beneath her fingers.

"So I remembered how you said the horse could go through the mist and find you."

Donella squeezed his hand. "You did the right thing."

Ahead, she spotted Prince Gensard leaving his room.

Catching sight of her, his gaze went to the boy. Gensard frowned. "This is no place for children."

She spoke over him. "The page comes from Reina Lauressa. The palace is under siege!"

Gensard threw back his head. "What?" His nostrils flared. "Get me to her! Now!"

Donella led them back to the horse.

Gensard grabbed Seeker's bridle and mounted. He reached down his hand imperiously to Donella, who took it. He pulled her up behind him.

"We can't leave the boy," Donella protested.

"And we can't waste any more time!" But Gensard held out his hand to the boy. "Up," Gensard commanded Jimzy, standing small and lost.

Holding the child before him, Gensard kicked the horse into a gallop. Citizens moved out of their way as they raced headlong to the wharf.

When they got to the waypost, Donella slipped off Seeker and helped Jimzy down. "Do you want to ride the horse through the portal?" she asked the prince.

"No, he will only slow me down."

Gensard dismounted. He fastened his shield to his left arm and drew his wickedly curved scimitar. "Now."

Donella's heart thumped uncontrollably, her breathing ragged, her hands sweaty. She slowed her breathing to calm herself. Touching her ring to the waypost, she focused on the palace.

When it appeared, Gensard stepped through the mist, and the portal closed behind him.

Let him be in time, she prayed fervently to the One Who Fashioned All. She knew she didn't pray enough, but hoped He would not hold it against her, but answer her.

Suddenly, a strong presence pulled at her from the portal. It reminded her of the day she found Guy.

"Dulee firth," reverberated through her mind.

Guy was in trouble!

Donella pulled her dagger from its hiding place. "I'm going to help Guy. Stay here with Seeker," she instructed the lad.

Jimzy reached up and grabbed her hand. "Take me along. Please! I don't know where to go! I never been away from Mintala." A desperate plea shone in his eyes. "I won't be no trouble."

Donella relented. The boy would only get into mischief if she left him. "Very well."

Relief crossed his face.

She hefted him back on Seeker and gave him a stern look. "But you had better mind me. This is not a game, Jimzy. I don't know what we are going into."

When Jimzy gave his solemn promise, Donella again faced the waypost. She reached out and concentrated on Guy's presence, which was like a river current pulling her in. She grabbed the horse's bridle and stepped through the swirling mist.

Immediately, soldiers carrying torches, crossbows, and swords surrounded them.

"I come in peace, in the name of Reina Lauressa." She held her hand out, prominently displaying her ring. "See the courier's token?"

One of the men inspected it. He glanced at Jimzy and rummaged through Seeker's saddlebag. "They're clear."

At the signal, the soldiers stepped back. Only then did she see bodies strewn around the waypost. *A battle must have raged here!*

Anxiety escalating, she scanned the area for Guy, but didn't see him. Yet his presence echoed from the portal.

"What happened?"

"One of your kind was injured holding the gate," a soldier told her.

"Where is he? Is he bad?" Fear clenched her stomach.

The soldier pointed to a man bending over a body, with a young man in attendance beside a campfire. Jimzy slid to the ground, joining her, and they ran to where Guy lay. He was unconscious, his chest bare.

Donella sucked in her breath at the sight of two bloody wounds. She assumed the thin man in a gray robe was a healer. He had a basin of bloody water on the ground beside him. He smeared a paste on the wound on Guy's side, which was sewn closed. He removed a strip of clean cloth from the bag at his side and unrolled it. The smell of herbs mingled with the metallic smell of blood.

Donella knelt beside Guy, Jimzy hovering over her shoulder. "Is he going to be alright?" Her heart stuttered.

The healer looked up from his work. "The dagger missed the main artery, fortunately. He is young and strong. He'll survive."

With the young man's help, the healer first wrapped Guy around the middle. Then they bandaged his shoulder.

Donella sighed with relief. She met the other boy's gaze.

"I'm Guy's friend, Hiram. We was imprisoned together on the pirate ship."

"I've heard Guy talk about you. I'm Donella, another courier. And this is Jimzy, royal page to Reina Lauressa."

Hiram's Adam's apple bobbed. "You never seen anything like what Guy did today. He rushed over to the post when the invaders started going through it. Two of them stabbed him, but he closed the way to them. I ran for help. I feared I came too late."

Guy moaned and opened his eyes. He winced when he tried to move. His gaze fell on Donella. "You came! I wasn't sure you would hear me."

The healer helped Guy sit up and ordered a soldier to help them get Guy to a bed. When they got him settled in Usher's tent, they propped Guy up. The healer instructed Donella and Hiram, "Make him rest. Don't let him open the wounds. I'll check on him later."

Hiram held a waterskin up to Guy's lips. Guy sipped.

"I thought you was a goner!" Hiram put the waterskin down when Guy had enough. "You were so brave. I couldn't have stood up to those raiders as you did, not without a weapon!"

"You took a terrible risk!" Donella burst out. She knew she shouldn't scold Guy, but she couldn't help it.

Guy jolted upright and tried to gain his feet. "The Reina! She is in danger!" Guy gasped, his face twisting in pain. "We must alert Prince Alloryn!" He looked from Hiram to Donella.

She put a hand on his good shoulder and kept him from rising. "Shh, I know. Jimzy came to warn me."

"I rode Seeker, Guy! Boy, is he fast! I was so scared, but I had to find Donella."

Donella brushed a stray lock from Guy's forehead, which was

hot to her touch. "I sent Prince Gensard to her rescue. He will not let anything happen to her. You know how capable he is. Even if he only battles for the glory of it." She tried to make Guy smile. "He will save her, if only to crow of it to his rival, Prince Alloryn."

Guy gave a weak grin. "I sensed you opening it," he mumbled, feverishly. Then he grasped her hand and spoke forcefully, "I need to find Prince Alloryn and let him know."

"It's late. Someone can go in the morning."

Holding Donella's glance, Guy demanded, "No. That's too long. Help me onto Seeker."

"You are in no position to ride." Donella shook her head. "I'll go."

Hiram rummaged around, gathered up some of Usher's store of dry food and he offered it to her for her journey. He handed her a full waterskin, which she took gratefully. She might have a long ride ahead of her, depending how far away Alloryn was.

Donella thanked him and left the tent. She grabbed Seeker's bridle and climbed on his back.

Guy followed, leaning on Hiram.

"Which way?"

Guy gave a sigh, of frustration or pain, she didn't know which. "West of here. The prince led most of his men to meet up with Odem's force along the coastline."

As she turned Seeker in the right direction he called after her, "Donella, be careful!"

"Always!" she shouted back. Then she kicked Seeker into a gallop, heading out of the camp in the moonlight.

Seeker's hooves pounded on the beaten gravel road. *Hurry, hurry,* they seemed to say in Donella's mind.

The image of Reina Lauressa rose before her eyes: the chestnut hair, the intelligent eyes, and the smile just below the surface. Prince Alloryn would want to be by his pregnant wife's side. She leaned lower over Seeker's back and spurred him on to greater speed.

I did the right thing. Gensard, for all his faults, seems to care for Lauressa. He would do his best to protect her. Donella might make fun of his arrogant ways, but she did not doubt his abilities.

The miles flew by.

Several times over the next hours, Donella slowed Seeker down to a canter. She didn't want to tax him too greatly.

She dismounted at dawn when they reached a stream. As Seeker drank and nibbled grass, Donella let the fresh water dribble down her chin as she took a soothing drink from her cupped hands. Cool drops refreshed her face as she splashed the fresh water on it. She refilled the waterskin.

She ate a handful of nuts and dried fruits that Hiram gave her. Then it was time to remount Seeker.

A few hours later, as Donella reached the summit of a small hill. A ship floating in the bay below. Hope flared in her chest as she recognized the royal blue palace livery.

Seeker didn't need much urging to put on a burst of speed toward them.

Bodies from both sides lay strewn about. Donella rode, circumventing them, searching for Prince Alloryn.

Seeing a figure commanding the men, Donella slid off Seeker and headed that way, averting her eyes from the carnage. The stout soldier stopped speaking when he spotted her.

"I have an important message for Prince Alloryn!" Donella showed her ring. "Do you know where I can find him."

"Aye. He left a contingent here to fight the enemy as they landed, but he headed further west."

Donella sighed. She thought she'd caught up with the prince. She and Seeker would just have to carry on.

Chapter 26

Gensard's gut wrenched as he exited the portal. He fought down the rising bile in his throat. Blinking, he took stock of his surroundings.

The courtyard between the palace and the guard's barracks stood empty, which was unusual.

A movement caught his eyes. Torches flickered in the second-floor palace windows, as if someone ran down the hall, causing the light to flare from one window embrasure to the next.

Gensard ran to the palace entrance. Stepping inside, he listened intently. He thought he heard a faint sound as of blades clashing. Torches flickered in the empty halls. Orienting himself, he headed away from the possible skirmish and toward the Reina's private rooms.

He wasn't here to help the house guards defend the palace. He was here to save Lauressa, even at the cost of his life.

Running down the corridor, he met no one. Taking the steps two at a time up the grand staircase, he saw blood on the stairs. Yelling and weapons clashing came from the hall on the left, so Gensard ran that way.

An injured house guard held the corridor against two men in black hoods and black capes, their backs to Gensard. The palace guard's right arm hung limp, bloody gash showing. His left-handed sword blocks looked awkward, but the guard pressed on, notwithstanding.

Gensard grabbed the nearest torch.

He slashed the back of the man nearest to him with his scimitar. The blow, which should've severed his spine, cut into leather. With a cry, the man spun toward him, weapon at the ready. But his wound didn't give him full range of motion. Gensard easily blocked the swing and countered with an overhand slash. The man's body and head toppled separately to the floor.

The second hooded man disregarded his victim and attacked Gensard. Gensard caught the blow with his wickedly curved blade and slid past the sword. The scimitar connected with the man's sternum, but the leather vest the man wore took most of the blow. Gensard thrust the lit torch in the man's face. Dropping his sword, the invader put both hands up to his burnt face, screaming. Gensard's blade sliced through the attacker's throat. He fell beside his comrade.

"My thanks, noble prince!" The palace guard held his injured arm against his chest.

"Where is the Reina? Is she safe?" Gensard desired to find Lauressa without delay.

"In her chambers. I was heading that way when the alarm sounded."

"Point me in the right direction. Then see to that injury." Gensard replaced the torch, then removed a dagger strapped to his leg.

"I'd rather defend my princess against these pagans." The stalwart guard gritted his teeth with determination.

Gensard admired the man's courage. "Lead on."

The two charged ahead up more stairs, encountering and slaying several Canteor invaders. Gensard dispatched most of them, but the injured man fought passionately, making up for his awkwardness.

At last, they came to the Reina's private apartment on the top floor. Eight guards fought desperately against three times that number. Equal amounts of black-hooded assassins lay dead on the floor with those in the royal uniform.

Gensard took on two men, slicing the back of one's leg, effectively taking him out of the fight, hamstrung. The second went down with a gut thrust.

Three men cried out as their comrades fell and tried to corner Gensard. He threw his dagger into the neck of one, fell to his knees to avoid being sliced by the second, while his curved blade opened the man's abdomen.

The third man struck while Gensard was distracted, but the blow bounced off his mail shirt. It broke through some of the links, and warmness dripped down Gensard's left arm.

Snagging his dagger embedded in the dead man, Gensard gained his feet. He circled and attacked. A chop to the sword-arm shoulder, then a dagger to the interloper's left side. The man fell, blood gurgling from his lips.

Whether the house guards recognized him or were heartened by the reduction in numbers of enemies, they redoubled their efforts. Senses heightened, Gensard settled into battle-mode. The skirmish continued until he and the guards overcame the Canteorans.

Surveying the carnage, Gensard wiped his brow. He recognized Captain Rodrek, the unit's commander.

Rodrek directed his few remaining men, seemingly oblivious as his blood trickled from a head wound. "Sergeant, get the wounded to the infirmary. Lieutenant Cedron, search the palace for any more assassins." Rodrek saluted Gensard. "Many thanks for your help. We were in a tight corner before you came."

"Your men fought well." Gensard gave a nod to the captain and banged on the Reina's door. "Lauressa, it's Gensard. Are you alright?" He heard steps approach the door. "It's safe now."

The bolts slid back, the door opened, and Lauressa peeked out. Her hair was tousled, her eyes had blue smudges under them. In her right hand she held a bejeweled dagger, which, in spite of its fanciness, looked lethal. She sighed on beholding her rescuers.

Her pale fragility twisted Gensard's insides.

"You came! Thank the One Who Fashioned All!" The dagger disappeared into the folds of her maroon gown. Lauressa invited Gensard and Rodrek into her parlor, where several ladies-in-waiting huddled together, fear evident on their faces.

"What is the immediate situation, Captain?"

"I estimate at least thirty invaders. We dispatched most of them outside this room. Prince Gensard turned the tide when we were at our lowest. We lost at least five men. Many more are wounded. I sent Lieutenant Cedron and the uninjured to find and capture any remaining assassins."

"How did they enter the palace?" Lauressa spoke calmly, but she clenched her trembling fingers together.

"They overwhelmed the guard at the waypost, Your Majesty." Rodrek ran a hand through his hair, "But not before he sounded the alarm. Which reminds me—" Rodrek's gaze landed on an older page, whom he motioned over. "Find my Sergeant in the infirmary. Help him with the wounded. Then tell him to have all the invaders searched, living or dead. Remove all their rings."

Lauressa nodded in agreement. "Tell them to send the rings to the archivist Libran. He will know what to do with them, Bane."

Lauressa faced Gensard with a puzzled expression. "Donella said Laketown was besieged. What news have you for me? And how did you know we were under attack?"

"I took charge of the Laketown forces and ships. We sunk the sea raiders' fleet. As to your second question, your page rode a horse through the portal to alert us." Gensard paced to the window, scrutinizing the courtyard and fortifications for enemies.

Satisfied, he turned around to face Lauressa, hand on hilt. "Alloryn should have provided for you better."

Lauressa's expression stiffened at the not-so-subtle jibe at her husband. Anger sparked in Captain Rodrek's eyes.

"No insult intended, Captain. You and your men acquitted yourselves well today." Gensard's brow wrinkled. "But I think Alloryn should have sent Lauressa into hiding." Gensard's scowl deepened as he gazed at her. "You are an obvious target."

"I should have anticipated an attack. Especially since this is not the first time Canteor used the portal to gain access to the palace."

Gensard gritted his teeth as she defended her husband. But her safety was more important than his jealousy. "It is not too late to go into hiding. I know a place where you will be safe."

Unexpectedly, Captain Rodrek agreed with him. "Your safety is paramount, Your Majesty. Please, listen to him."

"Very well. But only on the condition that you both get yourself attended to by the healer in the infirmary first." The set expression on her face brooked no argument.

Donella followed the road along the coastline, tasting the tangy salt on her lips. The miles blurred together into one endless ribbon of weariness. She hoped to meet the prince soon. Seeker pounded bravely on, but she knew he was as tired as she.

Midday came, then late afternoon.

When they came upon a stream, she dismounted. Saddle sore, she stretched her muscles. Squatting down she dipped her hand in and tested the water to make sure the tide hadn't pushed salt water upstream. Finding it fresh, she let the stallion drink. Cupping her hands, she slaked her burning thirst.

She wished she had time to wash off the stink of sweat and dust.

She heard voices. Senses tingling, she scanned the inlet for a sight of ships, knowing sound carries over water. Nothing. Standing, she turned in a circle, looking for any movement.

She spotted several horsemen heading her way. Her pulse spiked. Seeing no cover on the empty shore, she mounted Seeker and prepared to ride back the way she had come.

"Halt!" The words floated in the air, as hooves pounded closer.

She kicked Seeker to gallop, but he was spent and only spurt a short way before the others overtook them.

The group of horsemen surrounded her. "In the Reina's name, state your business."

Donella sighed with relief at the Reina's crest on their surcoats.

"I have a message for Prince Alloryn. The palace is under attack! Reina Lauressa is in grave danger!" Donella faced them, pleading, "Help me get the word to him!" She thrust out her ring hand.

A soldier with a bushy red beard peered at it. Seemingly satisfied, he commanded, "Surrender your weapons and I will lead you to him." He put out his hand.

Donella paused fractionally, hoping they weren't disguised Canteorans. With no choice, she pulled her dagger from her belt and passed it over.

The soldier led her back the way he had come, while the others continued on their way. Nearly forty-five minutes later, they met up with the tail end of Prince Alloryn's company. Passing oxen pulling wheeled cannons, soldiers on foot, and cavalry, Donella's escort led her to the front of the cavalcade. The royal pennant snapped in the breeze.

Settling his horse in formation beside the mail-clad prince and his generals, the red-bearded warrior saluted. "Your Highness, this girl claims the palace is under attack."

Alloryn and his entourage guided their horses to the side of the road and halted, swiveling in their saddles as Donella pulled Seeker to a stop beside them.

"A page sought me out with the awful news! I sent Prince Gensard to Reina Lauressa as soon as I heard. Invaders used the waypost at Tulken Harbor to access the palace. Guy was injured closing the portal on them. But he stopped some of the enemies from passing through!" The words tumbled out of Donella.

Prince Alloryn's expression became grim as she spoke. "You have done well, Donella." His posture tensed, causing his horse to side-step. "Tell me, which waypost is closest to us?"

Donella concentrated on her tokens at Tulken Harbor, Laketown, and the southern garrison. "Odem at the garrison ahead."

The prince motioned to one of the riders beside him. "General Rishidan, see that this young lady is fed and rested. You have charge of the men. Continue in pursuit of the enemy until you arrive at the southern garrison. Commander Odem will return you to the palace from there."

Prince Alloryn gestured to his companions. "You heard her. The palace is under siege. Talud, and the rest of you, follow me!" He spurred his horse forward.

As her need for urgency faded, Donella drooped in the saddle. The hours of riding left her drained. She wasn't even hungry anymore. But when the general's men brought her bread and cheese, she forced herself to eat.

Afterward, she gratefully crawled into a wagon as it rumbled west. Seeker was tied to the back, also having eaten. She prayed for Lauressa's safety and Guy's recovery. She drifted off as soon as she curled up.

Several days later, the Reina's formal dining room overflowed with guests. Lit with myriad candles, adding to the heat, the tables held the remains of a large supper. Guy, Donella, Brodyn, Hiram, Commander Odem, Captain Rodrek, Prince Gensard, Prince Talud, Usher, and Evodia drank celebratory wine. Reina Lauressa sat at the head of the table with her husband, and, on a stool at her feet, sat Jimzy.

Guy's arm hung in a sling. His shoulder didn't hurt him unless he moved it around too much. Same with his ribs.

He didn't dwell on his stab wounds but felt relief at the outcome of events. His biggest fear, up till now, was not living up to everyone's expectations. Freezing up instead of acting. But when the Canteor invaders used the portal to reach the Reina, his only thought had been to stop them. No matter the cost to himself.

Donella had, of course, jumped right into the fray. Riding to find Prince Alloryn, *she* never considered the danger, as far as Guy could tell. *Didn't she fear running across the enemy as she searched for the prince? Seemingly not.*

She sat on a stool beside him, occasionally sharing a glance with him, as they listened to the others tell their part in repulsing the invaders.

"Talud's ships defeated the Canteorans in two sea battles. One ship eventually limped away." Alloryn stroked Trekker's head on his lap as the wolfhound leaned against him.

"In Laketown, we sank all the ships, after dispatching most of the pirates in hand-to-hand combat," Gensard boasted, his lips sneering. He wore a princely outfit of a purple silk tunic with a gold-embroidered dragon emblazoned on it. The dragon's sinuous form wrapped from front to back, as if it embraced the prince in its grip. His black leggings barely showed between his tunic and high polished boots.

As if Gensard hadn't spoken, Alloryn continued, "That ship will carry back word to Prince Pashmi, Potentate of Canteor, to beware Valdeor's wrath."

Gensard scowled fiercely and grunted. He drank deeply, reached across the table, and refilled his wine glass. Guy figured he didn't like his rival putting him down.

Lauressa broke the unspoken tension. "And you, Gyfar, what happened to you?" She quizzed him, curiosity in her gaze.

He hadn't shared the details of his experience with anyone, spending his days in the infirmary. Guy folded his hands on the table.

"Hiram and I appeared in the middle of a skirmish between the prince's camp and a group of archers. I couldn't understand why the archers fought with no backup. What was the purpose? If I planned it, I would've used a distraction to pull men away from the waypost. Then, while troops were engaged elsewhere, I would use the portal to attack a strategic target. So, I acted on that."

Guy gestured toward his friend. "Hiram figured out you were the likely target, Your Majesty."

Hiram blushed.

Guy continued, "When we got there, the assassins poured through the portal. I could only think of stopping them. I redirected the portal to a massive sea storm battering a coast."

Guy paused at the memory. Bone-chilling cold invaded his body. Swirling winds surrounded him.

"I sent the invaders there." Guy's voice was low with the horror of what he'd done. He stared at his folded hands. "Then I wrested the portal closed to anyone but me."

"I wonder what happened to those men?" Donella said softly, so only Guy heard.

Guy shrugged and she shivered.

"Very hard to do." Usher nodded. "A battle of wills."

Hiram took up the tale. "I brought the remaining soldiers at the camp to Guy's aid. He was bleeding from stab wounds. I told the healer I thought Guy was a goner for sure. I'm so glad I was wrong." He grinned at Guy.

"I heard what the leader said to his men before he disappeared." Hiram's gaze sought Lauressa. "I knew you was in mortal danger. But then a horse came riding through the mist, carrying her," he pointed to Donella, "and the little fella."

"I sent Prince Gensard to your aid before answering Guy's call." Donella leaned forward. "I knew the prince would do his best to defend you."

"Of course. My scimitar is ever at your service." Gensard bowed from his seat. Lifting his eyes, he earnestly stared at Lauressa.

"And my sword." Captain Rodrek gave a gentle nod, his head bandaged.

"You both have my everlasting gratitude." Prince Alloryn toasted them. "And to Donella, who rode a night and a day to find me." He lifted his glass to her and Donella blushed.

Reina Lauressa touched her medallion. She hadn't spoken as the group fitted together the puzzle pieces of the events. "Fortunately, Rodrek and Gensard protected me. Rodrek, for your service, we will knight you."

Captain Rodrek gasped, then beamed.

"They insisted I hide until the crisis was over," she placed a hand on her stomach, "for the baby's sake."

Exclamations of good wishes and discussions broke out around the table.

When the gaiety died down, Odem's somber voice interrupted their conversations. "My intelligence reports say we've routed them. For now." Odem's expression remained stern as they all turned their eyes toward him. He pushed his wine glass away. His gaze connected with each in turn. "Prince Pashmi is very ambitious, from the accounts I've heard. And Donella's spy claims Pashmi wishes to spread his false religion beyond Canteor's shores."

Guy clarified, "The spy, Harban, insisted his god would

conquer Valdeor. It's a holy maxim in their beliefs to subdue unbelievers." He suddenly recalled the Guardian's warning of a pagan invasion. But he kept it to himself for now.

Lauressa spoke, a distant expression on her face. "I'd forgotten their creed."

Odem nodded. "What I need is a reliable source in Canteor, preferably in the palace itself."

"What you mean is we have won the battle," Prince Alloryn's eyes narrowed, "but still face a war."

"A battle won is still something to celebrate." Usher, who had been unusually quiet, spoke into the silence following the prince's statement. "We defeated Prince Pashmi's fleet, when, to my knowledge, Valdeor had no fleet a month ago. Do not forget that! It will take time for Pashmi to build another. And we have that time, as well, to prepare for what comes next. So cheer up!"

"He is right," Prince Talud remarked. "Morale building is very important. Lauressa, you should send word of our victory to all the villages and cities. Ask for new recruits for your army and navy. Meanwhile, we plan for the future." Talud raised his glass in a salute. "To victory in the name of the One Who Fashioned All!"

"The All-seeing God!"

"Valdeor!"

"Long may the Reina live!"

Donella clinked her glass with Guy's, eyes smiling at him above the rim.

Evodia whispered, "Well done, my dears." She patted Guy's good arm and winked at Donella.

Guy drained his glass of mild wine with the rest of them. He hadn't shared his visions with anyone but Donella and Usher, when his mentor visited him in the infirmary.

His destiny still awaited him.

But, for now, he was satisfied to be with friends. And glad to have done his part defending Valdeor with courage.

Acknowledgments

This book couldn't have happened without the following: my editors Ann Westermann and Margie Cichoke; formatter Michelle M. Bruhn; cover designer Emily Hickman; my sister Sue Peek and her suggestions; and my husband Tom who told me to keep writing as long as I have stories to tell.

And thanks to my readers who asked for more stories about Lauressa and Alloryn.

Author Bio

Sandra Hanley spent her childhood making up stories and illustrating them. An avid reader, she has devoured about 3000 books. She taught elementary school for eight years, and middle school for five. Her students knew her as Miss Millovitsch. She has traveled to Europe and New Zealand, as well as through most of our beautiful states. Her other hobbies, besides writing and dreaming up imaginary worlds, are painting, reading, and crocheting.

Be sure to sign up for her newsletter at www.sandralenahanley.com to receive notice about Guy and Donella's further adventures as they search for the Isle of Origin in *Pilgrims of Valdeor*.